ALSO BY JOEL A. SUTHERLAND

House of Ash and Bone

The Whisperings

JOEL A. SUTHERLAND

tundra

Text copyright © 2025 by Joel A. Sutherland
Cover art copyright © 2025 by Jorge Mascarenhas

Tundra Books, an imprint of Tundra Book Group, a division of
Penguin Random House Canada Ltd., 320 Front Street West,
Suite 1400, Toronto, Ontario, M5V 3B6, Canada
penguinrandomhouse.ca

Published simultaneously in the United States of America by Tundra Books of
Northern New York, an imprint of Tundra Book Group, a division of Penguin
Random House Canada Ltd., P.O. Box 2040, Plattsburgh, NY 12901, USA

Tundra with colophon is a registered trademark of Penguin Random House Canada Ltd.

All rights reserved. No part of this book may be reproduced, scanned, transmitted, or
distributed in any form or by any electronic or mechanical means, including information
storage and retrieval systems, without permission in writing from the publisher, except
by a reviewer, who may quote brief passages in a review. No part of this book may
be used or reproduced in any manner for the purpose of training artificial intelligence
technologies or systems.

The authorized representative in the EU for product safety and compliance is Penguin
Random House Ireland, Morrison Chambers, 32 Nassau Street, Dublin D02 YH68,
Ireland, https://eu-contact.penguin.ie

*Publisher's note: This book is a work of fiction. Names, characters, places and incidents either are
the product of the author's imagination or are used fictitiously, and any resemblance to actual persons
living or dead, events, or locales is entirely coincidental.*

Library and Archives Canada Cataloguing in Publication
Title: The whisperings / Joel A. Sutherland.
Names: Sutherland, Joel A., 1980- author
Identifiers: Canadiana (print) 20240469127 | Canadiana (ebook) 20240469135 |
 ISBN 9781774881019 (hardcover) | ISBN 9781774881026 (EPUB)
Subjects: LCGFT: Horror fiction. | LCGFT: Novels.
Classification: LCC PS8637.U845 W55 2025 | DDC jC813/.6—dc23

Library of Congress Control Number: 2024945759

The author wishes to thank the Ontario Arts Council for its support.

Edited by Peter Phillips
Designed by Emma Dolan
Image credit: (beetle) Михаил Н / Adobe Stock
Typeset by Erin Cooper
The text was set in Bembo MT Pro.

Printed in Canada

1 2 3 4 5   29 28 27 26 25

In loving memory of my mom. I still hear your voice, soft and quiet, like a whisper on the wind.

Chapter One

MY HEART BEATS IN time with the music filling my head. *Ta-tump. Ta-tump. Ta-tump.* I check the classical music playlist I downloaded ages ago on my old iPod to see what I'm listening to. Something called "Der Freischütz." It's dark, creepy, ominous, but it's also soothing in an odd way. It drowns out the memories—memories I wish I could forget—that fill my head whenever things get too quiet.

"Joana?" my dad, Jack, says, his voice muffled.

I pluck the earbud out of my left ear. The music still playing in my right ear blends with the thrum of our car's engine. "Yeah?"

"I'm bushed. You hungry yet?" The bags under Dad's eyes are puffy and dark, making him look ten years older than he is. That's what happens when you flee town in the middle of the night. It's a far-too-common look for him. For us.

I shrug. "I could eat."

Dad glances at my brother's reflection in the rearview mirror. "How about you, Petey?"

Peter doesn't answer. The sun has just risen, an orange so bright that the sky looks like it's on fire, but he's not asleep.

He's staring through the window, his forehead pressed against the glass, silent.

"Petey?" Dad says.

"My name's not Petey."

"Since when?"

"Since forever."

Well, since he turned thirteen and decided he'd outgrown the nickname. That was about three months ago. The fact that Dad has already forgotten speaks volumes.

"Since forever?" Dad says quietly, as if he's asking himself the question. "I've called you Petey since forever."

"The only constant is change," Peter mutters under his breath, quiet enough to give the impression he doesn't want us to hear him but loud enough to ensure we do.

Dad sighs.

The only constant is change is one of Dad's expressions, repeated so often that it's become one of our family's clichés. But clichés are clichés because they're at least a little true. And this one couldn't be truer. I forgot what stability feels like years ago.

I pause the music and remove my right earbud, resting the cord around the back of my neck. It's time to turn things around and stop the three of us from plunging down a dark hole we might not be able to crawl out of all day. I look over my shoulder at my brother in the back. "Hey, I hear Burlington's the blueberry pancake capital of the world," I say. It's Peter's favorite breakfast.

"Really?" he asks, perking up a little.

"No, not really," I say with a laugh. "But I'm sure I can find a place with decent reviews."

Dad shoots me a quick, concerned look. "Nothing too—"

"I know, I know, nothing too expensive." I pick his phone up out of the cup holder and type and scroll, type and scroll, until I find the perfect place. "Here we are. Darcy's Diner. Pancakes look thick, and it's listed as one of the best values in all of Burlington."

"Is it nearby?" Dad asks as he brings our car, Victor—a Crown Vic older than me that looks like a cop car from an eighties action movie—to a stop. The traffic light bathes my dad's face in a red glow.

I check the phone. "It's located in some place called the Church Street Marketplace."

Dad frowns and rubs his stubble the way he does when he's trying to concentrate. "Don't remember a place in the Marketplace called Darcy's Diner."

Now it's my turn to frown. "You spend much time in Burlington?"

Dad abruptly stops rubbing his jaw and grips the steering wheel tightly in both hands. "Oh, you know, just work. Odd jobs here and there."

"Okay," I say casually, masking the curiosity coursing through me. Dad has never mentioned working in Burlington before. Just about every other city and town throughout Vermont, sure, most of which we've lived in for brief periods of time. But never Burlington. Which is a little odd, with it being the largest city in the state. But that's far from the oddest aspect of our lives.

Time to change the subject. "So, breakfast?"

"What do you say, Pe—Peter?" Dad asks my brother, catching himself before calling him "Petey."

"Can I see the pancakes?" he asks me.

I hold the phone out for him to see. "Check 'em out. Three on a plate and big enough for us to split."

Peter opens his mouth to protest but I cut him off with a wink and a knowing look. He closes his mouth and nods, catching my meaning. We've spent so much time together that we've developed our own language—a language without words.

"You're right, Joana," he says with a hint of put-upon disappointment. "Definitely big enough to split."

"All I need is coffee," Dad says, parking Victor on a side street and killing the engine. "And coffee is the same in any diner across the country, so Darcy's it is."

It feels good to get out and stretch in the early morning sunlight. We've only been on the road for about an hour, but I'm tired and sore. Broken, disturbed sleep is my norm. A breeze that's bitter enough to raise goosebumps on my forearms and send a shiver up my spine howls down the street. I tie my knit scarf tightly around my neck, hating how cold it already is. It's only Labor Day, and I'm not yet ready to admit that autumn is lurking around the corner. I'm good with autumn but not with autumn's buddy—winter—who always follows close behind. The wind grows stronger and I shiver again, this time from the base of my skull to the small of my back, like someone unseen has brushed the icy tips of their fingers down my spine.

"Someone is walking over your grave," Dad says with a half-smile. Another one of his expressions.

"Can you tell them to knock it off?" I say with a laugh I hope doesn't sound too forced. Because I don't feel like joking around. That shiver felt . . . *different*.

Something grabs my shoulder and I flinch.

It's Peter, giving me a friendly pat that's not even hard. Why am I suddenly so tense?

"Don't worry, sis," Peter says as he walks past me. "I got your back. After you die, I'll keep an eye on your grave." He hunches his back and squints his eyes. "Get off the grass, you little punks!" he says in a terrible imitation of an old man's voice.

I laugh again, but it's genuine this time. If Peter's mood has improved enough to goof around, I'm happy. "You're going to spend your retirement sitting in a cemetery?" I say as I shoulder my backpack and close the car door.

"Nah, I'll bury you in my front lawn."

I pick up a pinecone and aim for the back of his head but miss by a country mile. I'm a fast runner but have never played any sports. We've never lived in one place long enough for me to join a team.

Dad leads us along a quaint street lined by tall trees. The houses are old and big, a little run-down but charming. Wraparound porches, red brick walls, and windows watching the street like large eyes. I unzip my backpack, grab Peter's Polaroid camera, and hand it to him.

"Thanks," he says with a knowing smile. He looks for a good angle and then snaps a shot of the street. The camera spits the picture out slowly. He pinches it between his fingers, careful not to touch the developing picture, and fans it in the air. Dad told him to do that years ago when he gave Peter the camera for Christmas, and my brother's done it ever since.

We cross a couple of streets and pass a sign that reads *Welcome to the Historic Church Street Marketplace.*

I love it immediately. It's basically one long street with no traffic. There's a scattering of people walking, chatting, laughing, and popping in and out of several cafés. The road is made of brick, trees provide shade and refuge for chirping birds, and a church steeple stands tall at the far end of the street.

"I can definitely see us living here," I say, but the moment the words pass my lips my excitement falters. We won't live here long. We've moved so many times I've lost count. The longest we've ever stayed anywhere was six months, maybe eight.

It's always the same. We move somewhere. A few months—sometimes only weeks—of relative peace and quiet follow. And then, without warning, we flee in the middle of the night. It's a routine that has become as certain and as apathetic as death. Dad never says why, but I know.

He hears things. Things only he can hear.

Click! Peter snaps a pic of the church.

"Don't forget how much each picture costs, Peter," Dad says kindly.

Polaroids are basically Peter's one and only self-indulgent splurge, so he ignores Dad and we carry on.

"Here we are," Dad says, nodding at Darcy's Diner. He stops in front and looks the restaurant up and down, rubbing his jaw. *Scritch-scritch-scritch.*

The rich smells of coffee, bacon, and pancakes waft out of Darcy's in waves, making my mouth water. I pass Dad and open the door, bumping into a girl my age as she exits in a rush.

We both yell in surprise and jump apart. She manages to keep a grip on a coffee in a take-out cup but drops a small paper bag to the ground. It misses a puddle by half an inch.

"Sorry!" I say, bending to pick up the bag for her.

"Leave it!" she snaps. "I was right there. What are you, blind? Or just stupid?"

"Well, I . . ." *I wasn't the only one walking through the doorway,* I think, but the words die on my lips. I'm stunned by how she went from zero to nuclear so quickly.

"There's no need to talk like that," Dad says.

She ignores him and bends to pick up her bag. Her purse slips off her shoulder, spilling some of its contents on the street. She groans in frustration and hurriedly collects her belongings, shoving everything back in her purse. It's a Michael Kors, I notice, and possibly worth more money than Victor (even with a full tank of gas).

Peter approaches but the girl tells him not to bother, thanks, she's got it, and springs back to her feet. The sum of her parts—her expensive yoga clothes, her subtle makeup, her straight jet-black hair, her body that must be the result of disciplined diet and exercise—equals *pretty*, but the way she's reacted to a simple accident cancels all that out. She turns and leaves without another word.

Good riddance, I think as I watch her walk away like the street is her own personal runway. "You shouldn't have gone to help her," I say to Peter, hating how petty I sound but too frustrated to stop myself. "She's clearly perfectly capable of helping herself."

"I wasn't helping her," he says.

I frown. He smiles, then looks down and lifts his shoe. I follow his gaze and spot the twenty-dollar bill pinned beneath his foot.

"Did that . . . ?"

"Fall out of her purse?" Peter asks, his voice thick with innocence. "Who can say? All I know is"—he picks up the money and puts it in his pocket—"we don't have to split breakfast anymore."

I laugh, then notice Dad eyeing us, his expression unreadable. The girl turns a corner and disappears. Dad's probably going to make me chase her down to return—

"Karma," he says, opening the door and holding it for us. "If you're an ass, the world makes you pay for other people's pancakes."

Peter and I laugh as we pass Dad and enter the diner.

A sign tells us to *Please Seat Yourself* so we find a cozy booth, one of the last available, and slide into it. It's nice and warm inside, but I keep my scarf on for the comfort it gives me—it was my mom's. Dad takes three menus from a metal holder at the edge of the table and hands one to each of us. It's a big menu filled with the standard fare—eggs any way you want them, omelets, French toast, oatmeal. I already know what I'm going to order, so I close my menu and scope the place out. It's quaint and kitschy, with signs like *Coffee Spelled Backward Is Eeffoc* and *Until I've Had My Coffee I Don't Give Eeffoc About Anything Else* covering nearly every inch of available wall space. As good as it smelled outside, it smells about one hundred times better inside, and I catch sight of the daily specials board: *Eggs Benedict, Tropical Fruit Salad (No Cantaloupe—We Promise!), Pumpkin Spice Latte.*

It seems a little early in the year for pumpkin spice, but who am I to judge? Then I notice that the place is decked out for Halloween, with ghost and witch decorations blending in with all the knickknacks and signage.

There's a boy behind the counter, matching customers' orders on paper slips with plates coming out from the kitchen in the back. Tall, nice features, curly hair. He's cute. Would it be weird if I used Peter's camera to take his picture? Of course it would be weird. *Super* weird. He catches me staring at him—*oh god, be cool*—and smiles.

"Welcome! Be there in a sec," he calls out to us over the din.

I smile and nod and quickly look away, my cheeks burning. Luckily, neither Peter nor Dad seems to notice. My brother is studying the menu like he's cramming for the most important test in his academic life, even though we all know what he's going to order, and Dad is reading the newspaper he brought with him.

The boy tops up the coffee mugs of two customers seated in the booth beside ours—an old man and woman who are short, hunched, wrinkled, and white all over, and who haven't said more than two words to each other since we sat down—then approaches us.

"Good morning, happy family," he says with a wave. "Coffee?"

"I don't give eeffoc," I say, immediately wishing I hadn't.

"Huh?" the boy says, mildly taken aback.

My cheeks burn and I quickly look away, pointing at the sign near the door. "Coffee spelled backward."

"Oh, yeah. Right," he says with a generous smile—generous because my attempt at humor wasn't deserving of his kindness.

"I'll have some, please," Dad says. He flips one of the clean mugs on the table right side up and places it on his newspaper. As the boy fills the mug, Dad squints at his name tag. "Thanks, William."

Dad always, *always* does that. He reads people's name tags in restaurants and stores and drive-thru windows and then talks to them like he knows them personally. It's super embarrassing, and this time it's worse since he got the boy's name wrong.

"Uh, it's pronounced, um, *Willem*." He glances at Peter before his eyes—hazel with flecks of green—settle on me. "How about you two? Coffee? Juice?"

"Actually, I was thinking of getting a pumpkin spice latte." Since it was Peter who grabbed the twenty, I probably should have asked him first—my brother and I usually just ask for tap water—but I can't ask my little brother for permission to splurge in front of Willem. "Nice to find a place making it so early in the year."

Willem looks over his shoulder at the daily menu board, then back at me. "Yeah, right. If you want the truth, that's actually a bit of false advertising. The food specials change daily, but we've served pumpkin spice lattes every day since I started working here a year ago. The place has a bit of a reputation for the macabre. The owner keeps a few Halloween decorations up year-round and goes all out in October."

"Oh?" I say, my curiosity piqued. "Why?"

"Years ago, this place used to be a bar called the Witches' Brew."

Dad clears his throat and says, "Can I get some cream?"

"Sure thing," Willem says. "One pumpkin spice latte, some cream, and—" He points at Peter.

"Orange juice, please," Peter says.

"And one OJ, coming up." Willem makes his way back to the counter, topping up coffee mugs as he goes. I try not to stare.

Dad sips his coffee. He never drinks it black. He must be on cruise control, lost in thought. The lines on his forehead match the bags under his eyes, deeper and angrier than usual. I'm not surprised. This life we lead . . . how could it not take a toll? Constantly moving, never settling, working odd jobs, looking after Peter and me alone, carrying memories heavier than the few meager possessions we own.

I hear him every few months . . . muttering in his sleep, talking to himself. And I know what that means. Every time he starts up with that, we move. He began talking last night. All alone, in his room, in the middle of the night, and I knew. I knew I'd better try to get some sleep, because he'd be waking my brother and me in a few hours, before sunup, telling us to pack our things (I stopped unpacking years ago) because it was time to go. And that's exactly what happened. That's why we're here, eating breakfast in Darcy's Diner and starting over in Burlington.

I hear him often, but I saw him once. Years ago. Talking to himself. But I couldn't shake this feeling . . . a feeling that, although he was sitting alone at the kitchen table in the run-down apartment we were living in at the time—just one more run-down apartment in a long line of run-down apartments—that he *wasn't* talking to himself. That he was talking to someone. Or *something*.

I shake my head, but the memory sticks. It's always there, hiding in some dark crevice of my brain, waiting to pounce. Forcing me to face a reality I'm perpetually running away from.

A while ago, I found a folded piece of paper in Dad's jeans when I was doing the laundry. It was a letter he'd written to my mom after she was . . . well, after she died. In it, Dad told her that he didn't know how much longer he could keep running from the Whisperings—that's what he called the voices in his head, always written with a capital *W*, as if he was referring to a specific person. I got about halfway through the letter before I regretted reading it. It was deeply personal and clearly not intended for my eyes. I folded it quickly, stuck it back in his pants pocket, and started the wash, hoping the letter wouldn't survive. Wishing I could erase the words from my memory as easily.

Other than that one time I wondered if Dad was talking to someone I couldn't see, the reality I've long suspected but never told anyone is that Dad is crazy. That the Whisperings aren't real. That he doesn't talk to people no one else can see. He talks to himself, plain and simple. And the voices in his head—*his voice*—tell him to move. And so, we move. Ever since I was four years old and Peter was a newborn baby. For most of my life, I didn't question our lifestyle. If your parents told you the sky was green and the grass was blue from the day you were born, you would believe it. You would accept it. It would be your reality, and always moving is *my* reality, but one of these days he's going to move . . . and I won't.

The only thing stopping me is Peter. I need to keep him safe. It's what gets me out of bed in the morning, what keeps me going, what keeps me vigilant even when things seem to be okay.

Because as much as I love Dad, and as much as I trust him—he's never hurt or threatened us in any way—sometimes I'm a little scared of him.

He's never harmed a hair on our heads, but I'm painfully aware of the violence he's capable of inflicting on others.

"Beware!" Willem says loudly, knocking me out of my own head. I blink and shiver, unsure how long I've been lost in thought and realizing I've been twisting my ring obsessively. I quickly place my hands flat on the table, one on top of the other. Willem places a latte in front of me. "This drink is very hot, and you wouldn't want to scald your pretty lips on your first pumpkin spice latte of the season, would you?" Is he flirting? If he is, he's not very good at it. Which is kind of sweet, in a dorky way.

"Thank you," I say, telling myself he's probably just being friendly and hoping for a bigger tip.

Willem hands Peter his juice and Dad a bowl of creamers. "Sorry about the wait, but it looks like you made do without. Top up?"

Dad's mug is empty. "Yes, please, William."

"I'll get the pot," Willem says. "And it's Willem."

After he leaves, I wonder how rude it would be if I changed booths and sat on my own.

Dad sets his mug aside and picks up the newspaper. "Huh," he says pointedly.

"What?" Peter asks.

"Will you look at that?" Dad hands us the newspaper he's been studying. It's the classifieds section of the *Burlington Free Press*. Dad's mug has made a perfect brown circle of coffee runoff around one of the listings. Dad taps it.

BASEMENT FOR RENT
IN BEAUTIFUL
DOWNTOWN BURLINGTON

> Three bedrooms, kitchen, separate entrance, laundry shared with owner on ground floor. Walking distance to Church Street Marketplace, shops, restaurants, schools, and parks. Monthly

rent negotiable; may be reduced for handyman willing to help renovate historic house. Appointments only; thrill-seekers and looky-loos not welcome.

"Three bedrooms," Dad says. "Walking distance to schools, not to mention the Marketplace. And reduced rent for a handyman. Sounds pretty good, right?"

"Thrill-seekers and looky-loos not welcome?" Peter asks, reading my mind—that's the part that sticks out to me too. "What does that mean?"

Dad shrugs as Willem returns and refills his mug. "Says it's a historic house. People love any opportunity to get into places like that and nose around a bit. The owner is probably sick of the unwanted attention and doesn't want to waste their time with people who aren't actually interested in renting. Hey! Careful—that's hot!"

Willem snaps out of a daze and looks mortified when he sees Dad's overflowing mug. "Sorry!" he says, hurriedly placing the coffee pot on the table and producing a rag to wipe up the spill he's made.

Dad uses a couple of napkins to wipe coffee off his hands, then dabs at the soaked newspaper.

"I am so, so sorry," Willem says again. "Let me make it up to you. Your drinks are on the house."

Dad grunts and waves his hand dismissively. "It's okay, it's okay. What distracted you, William?"

I want to crawl into a dark pit and die. I want the booth to turn into a black hole and swallow me into nothingness. I want to cease existing altogether.

Willem doesn't correct my dad's pronunciation of his name. He takes another sideways glance at the newspaper—do I detect a hint of confusion, or a trace of fear in his eyes?—and asks us if we know what we want to eat.

DAD MADE THE CALL and the owner, a woman named Mrs. Cracknell, picked up after the first ring. For some reason I still can't explain, I wish she hadn't. But she did, and she asked my dad a few questions. She seemed happy with his answers because she told us to come over as soon as we could.

And that's how we came to be standing on the weedy and cracked sidewalk in front of one of the creepiest houses I've ever seen.

But despite it looking like something out of an eldritch horror story, and although we haven't set foot inside yet, I know the house is something else too. Something more.

Home.

Chapter Two

"HOW LONG DO YOU give this place?" I whisper in Peter's ear, careful to ensure Dad doesn't overhear. "Three months? Two?"

He gives the house a once-over and purses his lips in thought. "One," he says with finality.

That's not a bet I want to take. You can tell the house used to be stunning, but it's fallen into such a state of disrepair that it's hard to imagine us living here for long, even if there is something about it that makes it instantly feel like home to me. It's a three-story Victorian mansion with gray slab steps leading from the sidewalk to the front door, a triangular roof, a red brick facade, and a round tower coated in vines that have crept up its sides to dangle from the roof like thin tentacles blowing in the wind. Perched on the peak of a slight incline, the house looms over the street. The paint is peeling from each of the nine window frames facing the street, and the lawn is a jungle of weeds and dead bushes.

The house is dying a slow death, I think, and although I have no personal connection to it, seeing it this way makes me feel a little sad.

My breath catches in my throat. There's an old woman sitting on the porch, so perfectly still and pale—her shoulders draped in a gray shawl—that she blends in with the house. She's staring at us.

"She's got good bones," Dad says, and it takes me a moment to realize he's talking about the house, not the woman.

"I should hope so," the woman says, her voice scratchy but surprisingly loud. "She's got a number of years under her belt, and she might be past her prime by a hair, but I'll be damned if this isn't the finest house in all of Burlington."

She doesn't get up from her seat or invite us to join her. For an awkward moment, the three of us stand on the sidewalk, no one speaking, before Dad walks to the porch. Peter and I follow.

"Good morning," Dad says. "I'm Jack Guest. You must be Mrs. Cracknell." He holds his hand out to shake, but she just stares back at him inquisitively. "We spoke earlier on the phone. My kids and I are here to see about renting the basement."

A line of ants march between Mrs. Cracknell's feet, under her seat, and up the wall of the house. If she knows they're there, they don't seem to bother her. Her eyes dart to Peter, then me, then at Victor parked on the street. "That your car?"

"Yes, ma'am," Dad says. He begins to lower his outstretched hand, but she reaches out and shakes it. She even manages a slight smile.

"Where are my manners?" she says, letting her guard down and looking a touch ashamed. "It's nice to meet you Jack . . . Guest, did you say? Interesting surname. My, my, what a firm grip you have."

Dad laughs awkwardly and pulls his hand out of her grasp, then slips his hands into his pockets. "Thank you. I work with my hands a lot. That's what drew me to your ad in the paper. I'm a handyman."

"Any electrical or plumbing experience?"

"Check and check."

Mrs. Cracknell's expression warms a few degrees more. She eyes me and Peter, not unkindly. "These two fine specimens must be your children."

"That's right—my daughter Joana, and my son Peter," Dad says, waving a hand at each of us in turn.

"Let me guess," she says. "Thirteen and seventeen?"

"That's right," I say.

A bit of a breeze whistles through the trees, rustling leaves and making branches sway. Mrs. Cracknell's face falls. "It would have been better if you didn't have children," she tells Dad.

Dad frowns, caught off guard by her odd comment. "Well, I do, and they're good kids. Quiet, well-behaved, and respectful. You won't even notice them half the time they're home—they're practically ghosts to me." He laughs uncomfortably, three sharp barks meant to convey an easygoing and reassuring tone that miss the mark. He's nervous.

"That's not what I meant," Mrs. Cracknell says. She glances at her house, then back to me and Peter. With a shake of her head, she adds, "Never mind all that. I'm simply not having a good day and am afraid I'm mucking things up. How about you three come in and let me fix you a cold beverage. Do you like lemonade?"

"Who doesn't?" I say.

Peter nods agreement.

"Splendid," she says, taking me gently by the hand and leading me to the front door. She releases my hand and grips the handle but doesn't open it. She seems to be hesitating. Without turning to face us, she says, "The pipes are old and cranky, a little like me. They rattle sometimes, and groan. If you think you hear anything odd, that's probably it."

Peter and I share a look that says *What. A. Weirdo.*

"I'll be happy to take a look at the pipes." Dad says. "If, you know, we end up moving in."

"That would be lovely, Jack," Mrs. Cracknell says. The door opens with a shrill creak that pierces my ears.

"I'll be happy to take care of that too," Dad says. "A little WD-40 and you won't be able to hear anyone coming or going."

"If you say so." Mrs. Cracknell says, leading us slowly through the front hall. It divides the house in two, with large rooms on the left and right and a staircase leading to the second floor. I spy antique furniture in a sitting room on the left and a dining room on the right. I get the sense Mrs. Cracknell has lived here a long time on her own, another thought that carries a tinge of sadness on its back.

I trip on the edge of an antique rug with tassels but manage to quickly regain my footing.

"Watch it!" Mrs. Cracknell shouts in concern.

"I'm okay," I say, wondering if she was more concerned for me or for her rug.

We pass a mirror on the left as tall as my dad and I'm a little relieved to see Mrs. Cracknell's reflection in it.

Phew, not a vampire.

Be nice, I chide myself.

"This leads to the basement," she says, pointing to a door on the right. "There is also a side entrance from outside for direct access to the apartment, but you can come up through here when you need to do laundry. But never after dark. I'm a light sleeper. The laundry room is through there." She points down a short hall to our left that intersects with the one we're in. She continues down the center hall to the back of the house. "And here's my kitchen. The heart of my home. Don't mind saying I'm a good cook and an excellent baker. I can fix you anything but stupid. Cookie?"

She offers us a plate of cookies and I instinctively take one before having second thoughts. I just met this woman and she's more than a little odd. Dad notices me hesitate and nods encouragingly, not wanting me to be rude. I don't want to be rude either, but I also don't want to be dead. What if she's a psycho? What if the cookie is poisoned? What if—?

Peter's loud crunch jostles me out of my thoughts. "Mmm!" he says enthusiastically.

If Peter dies, I don't want to live, so what the hell. Death by cookie—not a horrible way to go. I take a bite. It's delicious. Buttery, but not greasy. Sweet, but not sickly.

"Thank you," I say.

"You're welcome, dear," Mrs. Cracknell says. She pours three tall lemonades and hands one to each of us. Ice cubes clatter and clank as beads of condensation drip down the sides of the glasses. "How about you bring your drinks on the tour? I'm sure you're eager to see the basement."

Dad nods. "Feel free to point out what needs the most urgent attention down there."

"No!" Mrs. Cracknell says sharply with a shake of her head. She takes a deep breath and her expression softens. She even manages to smile weakly. "No, that won't be necessary. There's so much that needs attention up here. Outside too. If you decide to move in, you'll need to promise me you won't make any changes to the basement."

"Oh, okay," Dad says. I can tell by his tone that he won't be able to keep that promise. He never sits still for long, and once he sees a job that needs doing, he'll do it. It's not only how we afford rent and food—it's in his nature.

"Right," Mrs. Cracknell says. "Well, follow me." She leads us out of the kitchen, back into the hall, and to the basement door. She pauses before opening it. "I like you three," she says over her shoulder without facing us. "I have excellent intuition, and I can tell you're good people. The basement isn't much, but I hope this works out. I think you moving in could be good for me. Good for the house."

Good for the house? What does she mean by that? An image fills my head of the house slowly consuming us, breaking us down and absorbing our nutrients as if we're three little fish that have unknowingly swum into the belly of a whale.

The oddity of what she said seems to dawn on Mrs. Cracknell, and she quickly adds to Dad, "I mean to say, you'll be good for the house if you're as skilled a handyman as you claim to be." She opens the door and slips down into the darkness.

I follow her with Peter and Dad close behind. It's so dark that I keep my hand on the wall as a guide. The staircase has open risers, with an empty space between each step. I've always hated that—I can't help but picture something lurking in the shadows beneath me, ready to reach through one of the openings to grab my ankle as I pass. One of the steps close to the bottom sags under my foot with an angry groan, throwing me slightly off balance.

"I can fix that,' Dad says. "Oh, wait. No repairs in the basement."

"That's right," Mrs. Cracknell says, her voice disembodied in the pitch black. "I step over that one every time I need to come down here, and I'm sure you'll soon remember to do the same." She flips a switch at the bottom of the stairs—an odd feature that there's a switch at the bottom but not the top—and suddenly we can see.

Most basement apartments we've rented over the years have been open concept, with only one or two closed rooms. This basement is nothing like any I've ever seen, and I've seen a lot. It has a long hall running the width of the house, with—I do a quick count—seven closed doors and no windows. No wonder it was so dark before the light was turned on. The bottom half of the walls is made of light-tan wood while the top half appears to be drywall painted mint green. It's cold and sterile and makes me feel like I'm in a hillbilly hospital. At the far end of the hall is another set of stairs mirroring the one we just came down, which must be the side entrance Mrs. Cracknell mentioned. The hallway makes me feel claustrophobic and anxious.

"It doesn't make a grand statement when you first enter," she says, "but the rooms are a decent size and serviceable enough."

I open the first door on the left. Much to my surprise, the bedroom is bright and cheery, with a streak of sunlight cutting through a window near the ceiling. The room is fully furnished, with a large, old-fashioned bed, a chest of drawers, and a writing table and chair. Mrs. Cracknell and I clearly have different interpretations of "decent size." The bedroom is larger than any I've ever slept in, but there's also something slightly off about it. Something I can't quite put my finger on. A housefly buzzes around my head and lands momentarily on my neck. I brush it away.

"Let's move along," Mrs. Cracknell says, closing the door and trapping the fly within.

The rest of the rooms are equally large and cozy. There are two more bedrooms, a bathroom, a family room, a kitchen, and a seventh room that is sealed by a padlock.

"Nothing of interest in there," Mrs. Cracknell says in a tone that strikes me as being too well-rehearsed to sound casual. "Just the furnace, water heater, and some shelves filled with odds and ends."

When our tour ends back at the stairs, Mrs. Cracknell asks what we think. Dad looks at me and Peter questioningly. Before replying, I look at Peter in much the same fashion, wanting to gauge his reaction before committing to my own.

He smiles at me, then at Dad, and says he likes it.

A feeling of warmth fills me. If Peter's happy here, I'll be happy here. Maybe Dad will be happy here too. Happy enough that, maybe, he won't hear the Whisperings and we'll be able to stay for more than a few months.

I tell myself to slow down. One step at a time.

"I like it too," I say.

Dad smiles and nods.

Mrs. Cracknell smiles in kind, and for a moment everything seems better than it has in ages. But then she glances at me and her smile vanishes. She's quick to return it, but when her expression changed—which lasted no longer than a heartbeat—a completely different emotion had weathered her face.

Grave concern.

"I'll help you move in," she says.

MOVING IN TAKES ALL of five minutes and there's no need for Mrs. Cracknell to help. I toss my bag on the bed in the first room we saw on the tour, lay my scarf gently over the back of a chair, and I'm done.

The rest of the day passes slowly. Peter disappears for a bit to explore the neighborhood, Polaroid camera in hand. In the kitchen, Dad hangs up the wall-mounted wooden key holder—in the shape of a giant key, naturally—that I made for him in sixth-grade shop class and he hangs his keychain on one of the hooks. I waste away the time listening to music on my iPod, watching TV, reading outside in the sun, scrolling on Dad's phone, and registering to attend Burlington High School. The new school year starts tomorrow, Tuesday. I'm no stranger to all the bullshit that comes with being the new kid in class, so I'm not exactly jumping for joy, but at least it's easier when you're not transferring schools mid-year once everyone has formed their pathetic little cliques and can't possibly make room for you to sit at their table in the cafeteria. I've lived through that particular slice of hell more times than I'd like to count.

After dinner my mind won't settle, so I change and go for a jog. It works. The thrum of my heartbeat and the burn of my lungs pulling in cool, nighttime air clears my head. I make my way west through the Church Street Marketplace since it's the only place in the city I know, and stop for a moment across the street from Darcy's Diner to catch my breath. The sign in the door has been flipped to *Closed*, the lights are turned off, and the chairs have all been stacked on the tables. It's empty.

What were you hoping for, to catch a glimpse of Willem as he mopped the floors?

Okay, so maybe familiarity wasn't the *only* thing that had propelled me in this direction. I carry on.

The marketplace was charming in the day, but it's stunning at night. The shops and restaurants cast yellow light on the trees that line Church Street, and while some of the stores are closed, others are full of life. Couples walk arm in arm with content smiles, friends talk and laugh on patios, and I'm far from the only jogger navigating the streets. There's an undeniable energy—a buzz—in the air. Not for the first time, I could see myself living here on a more permanent basis, but I remind myself to not get too attached. That can only lead to disappointment and heartbreak.

I take a right on Main and then head south on Pine Street, and the excitement of the marketplace fades away behind me. I jog along a path beside the road as cars drive past, with homes and apartments on my left and dense woods to my right. Every so often I catch a glimpse of Lake Champlain through the trees. As I cross a street called Flynn Avenue, I see something that appears to be a skinny, forty-foot tower, but it's starting to get dark, so I continue without pausing. I've been jogging for more than twenty minutes, am beginning to get tired, and the dark is rapidly descending, so I'm about to turn back when I see a sign for Red Rocks Park and decide on a whim to check it out.

The dirt path twists and turns through tall trees full of green leaves with hints of red and orange. There are benches and picnic tables but few other people, making the woods feel quiet and solemn. The ground rises as I jog toward the lake, and it's dark enough that I nearly step off the edge of a cliff as soon as I exit the treeline. I come to a hard stop and swear, kicking dirt and rocks over the edge, my arms pinwheeling to maintain my balance.

Once my pounding heart settles a little, I peer over the ledge. It's a good twenty or thirty feet down to the lake below. Water crashes against jagged rocks jutting through the surface.

I nearly died. And no one knows where I am. They might never have found my body.

I take a deep breath, wipe a line of sweat from my forehead, step away from the cliff, and jog back the way I came. There's no point in dwelling on what might have been, especially when "what might have been" is a premature death and a watery grave. One foot pounds the pavement after the other, and by the time I've returned to Mrs. Cracknell's house, my brush with death is a distant memory.

The side door creaks loudly, announcing my return, and I head down into the basement. I grab a bottle of water out of the kitchen fridge on my way to the bathroom. Dad is already asleep—I can hear him snoring behind his closed door—and Peter is watching some nature show about the world's deadliest predators.

"Hey, Jo," he says as I pass by the family room. He doesn't take his eyes off the screen. "Good jog?"

I hadn't told him what I was doing when I left. "Yeah. How did you know?"

"I can smell you from here." He glances my way and smiles.

"Jerk," I say in good humor, twisting the cap off my bottle and spraying him with a shot of water. It splashes on the couch too.

"Hey!" Peter says, jumping up and raising his hands protectively. He's still smiling and laughing. "Cut it out! If Mrs. Cracknell finds out, she'll kill you!"

I raise the bottle threateningly. "Promise me you won't tell her, and I promise I won't spray you again!"

"I promise, I promise—you win!"

I smirk and turn with an extra spring in my step. "You should know by now that I always win." I leave Peter to his show and slip into a hot shower. The heat soothes my muscles and works the knots out of my back. I take my time, using the mismatched, nearly empty bottles of shampoo and conditioner on the edge of the tub. A spider crawling up the tiles comes eye level to me and I splash it with cupped handfuls of water—the little bugger puts up a good fight, but eventually I'm victorious and it washes down the drain. By the time I turn off the water, I feel like a new person. I'm still not jumping for joy at the prospect of going to yet another new school, but I'm ready to face whatever the day has in store for me. I slide open the curtain, grab my towel, and pause.

There are wet footprints on the tile floor, leading from the edge of the tub to the closed door—leading *under* the closed door.

"Peter?" I call, wrapping the towel around my body but not yet stepping out of the shower.

"Yeah?" he answers.

"Did you take a shower before me?"

"No," he says. "You the hygiene police now?"

It must have been Dad. I don't bother asking Peter to confirm this because it's the only plausible answer. But there's something bothering me, something that's not quite right.

The footprints. They're small. Like a ten-year-old child left them.

I get out of the shower slowly, careful to avoid the water on the floor. I cross the bathroom, leaving my own wet trail, and grip the handle, hesitating for a moment. After a deep breath, I swing the door open. My entire body is tense and I'm grinding my teeth, but the hallway is empty. I exhale slowly and force myself to relax, then look at the floor. The footprints continue down the hall. They lead to my bedroom . . . and my door is open a crack.

Was it open before? Or closed? I can't recall.

"Peter, if you're messing around with me, I swear to god I'm going to make you eat so much shit."

"What the hell are you talking about?" he says, appearing in the hall.

"The footprints," I say, pointing at the ground, unable to look at them any longer. "The wet fucking footprints."

Peter looks down the length of the hall and then back at me. He's frowning. He didn't know. He didn't have anything to do with this.

"Did you . . . ?" he asks, the question unfinished, the unsaid words drifting in the air like smoke.

I shake my head and grip the towel a little tighter.

"Should I get Dad?" he asks.

"Let's not wake him," I say, while a voice in the back of my head screams *We should definitely wake him!* But I'm probably overreacting. There must be a reasonable explanation. And I'm going to feel like a fool once I figure it out.

"Maybe Mrs. Cracknell has a visiting grandchild," I say.

"Or a great-*great*-grandchild," Peter adds.

"And her shower upstairs is broken," I continue, "so she let him come down here and use ours."

"And I didn't see or hear him. Because of the TV."

"Yeah," I say, painfully aware of how many bus-sized holes there are in our story.

"How long are we going to stand out here?" Peter asks. "Let's just find out who's in your room."

But he doesn't move. Not that I would let him take the lead—he's my baby brother, and I'm not going to let some little great-great-shithead with wet feet and no sense of boundaries freak me out. I nod and take the first step, pausing at the door to peer through the open crack. I don't see anyone or anything unusual. I don't hear anything unusual, either. Peter and I share a look, and then I push the door open.

The footprints lead under my bed.

"You've got to be kidding me," I say. I've seen this movie countless times, and I'm not about to become a victim. I'm certainly not about to become the scared damsel in distress. "All right, listen up, whoever's hiding under my bed! You have exactly three seconds to get the hell out of my room before I go full-on batshit crazy, grab the heaviest thing I can find, and start swinging!"

Peter looks at me like I've lost my mind. I shrug, not knowing what else to do.

For a few beats, nothing happens. It's long enough for me to think Peter and I might be sharing a hallucination. But then I hear shuffling sounds, soft and low. Something moving under the bed. Coming out.

But nothing surfaces. At least, nothing we can see.

I hear footsteps, so quiet they're almost imperceptible. They pitter-patter across my room to the closet. Then, silence . . .

"Jo?" Peter says, his voice cracking. "What's happening?"

"I don't know," I whisper.

I steel my nerves yet again, get down on my hands and knees, and peer under the bed. My own face stares back at me, reflected in a small wet puddle, and I see fear in my eyes.

"Is this place . . . ?" he says, unable to complete the question.

My stomach feels like a wet towel wrung out to dry. I hate not having answers for my brother. No *good* answers, anyway.

"If you want to sleep in my room tonight," Peter says, eyeing my room warily, "that would be okay with me."

As childish as that seems, I can't fathom sleeping in this room. Not tonight, at least. I nod and say, "I'll get in my pajamas and be right there."

Once he's gone, I change as quickly as possible and step into the hall.

Rattle rattle.

I freeze on the spot, my throat constricting so tight it hurts to breathe. The rattling sounded like a door handle, and it came from the direction of my closet. I turn slowly. The closet door is still closed. I watch the handle, expecting to see it tremble and turn. But that doesn't happen. I count to three. Nothing happens. I leave before something *does*.

Then I slip and nearly fall. It's hard to believe I managed to forget about the wet footprints, but they're still there. I toss my towel on the ground, step on it with one foot, and slide it along the hall, mopping up the water. When I reach the bathroom, I toss the towel through the doorway to the edge of the tub, telling myself I'll hang it up in the morning.

"Roll over," I tell Peter as I enter his room. "And don't you dare pull the blankets off me in the middle of the night."

He smiles and rolls over, and I feel okay. Okay enough to sleep, and that feels like a small miracle.

But sleep doesn't come easily. For hours, it doesn't come at all. I toss and turn and twist my ring as the minutes tick slowly by and the moonlit shadows stretch from one side of the room to the other. Finally, everything begins to shut down—I don't exactly *fall* asleep but tumble into it fitfully. Images, dark and depraved, flash across my closed eyes. Sounds, otherworldly and unsettling, fill my ears. For a split second, I register blackness—a small slice of sleep—before waking with a jolt.

I sit up, blinking. Something's not right. I rub my eyes, trying to make sense of the nonsensical, and then it hits me. Peter is gone.

No, no, no, that's not quite right. Peter isn't gone—I am. Gone from him. Gone from his room. Gone from his bed.

I'm alone. Back in *my* room. Back in *my* bed.

Something's under the bed, I think. *Something wet. Something—*

Rattle rattle.

It's the closet handle again. But this time I didn't just hear it. This time I *saw* it.

Chapter Three

NOT TONIGHT, I THINK to myself. *I'm not having this tonight.* It's an internal show of bravery, and I'm painfully aware that it's not one hundred percent genuine. Truth be told, I'm scared to death and the last thing I want to deal with is a ghost in my bedroom closet, in the basement of a real-life Scooby-Doo haunted mansion. All I want to do is pull the covers over my head like I'm four years old again and ride out the night until the sun comes up, but there's one thing stopping me from doing that—the same thing that has always stopped me from running away from my fears.

Peter. He's young for his age, sometimes shy and often nervous. If I hide, if I don't deal with whatever the hell is going on, what might happen to him?

Not tonight.

I slip out of bed and walk with determination, fists clenched and feet stomping on the floor. I want whatever I'm sharing a room with to hear me coming. I want the ghost in my closet to fucking fear *me*.

"Who's there?" I demand as I swing the closet door open with force.

Other than an insect that quickly scurries out of sight and a few bent clothes hangers clinging to a metal bar, the closet is empty. But I know it's not *really* empty.

"If you're in here," I say into the dark void, "show yourself!"

Nothing happens, and my boiling temper begins to cool.

With a sigh, I realize how frightened I am beneath the surface. Like, full-on, knees-shaking, pulse-pounding, light-headed terror. Whenever I'm truly afraid, like I am now, I typically respond by swearing and yelling and standing my ground—I'm a fighter, not a flighter. But deep down inside, the fear always lurks.

"I'm not going anywhere," I say, more to myself than anyone—or anything—else. The declaration surprises me. We just arrived here. It hasn't even been a day yet. Why have I dug my heels in so deeply? Why not ask Dad to find a different apartment? There must be hundreds of options in a city the size of Burlington.

Because I'm a fighter, I remind myself.

But if Peter wants to leave, that will be different. If he doesn't want to stay, I'll think of a way to convince Dad to move. I don't think that would be too difficult—it's probably only a matter of time before he hears the Whisperings and makes us leave anyway.

I'm about to close the door and return to bed when I notice something in the back of the closet. The walls are covered in old-fashioned wallpaper, a dark pattern of black leaves and flowers on a cream-colored background. It's ripped and peeling in a few spots. The side walls appear to be made of rust-red brick. But on the back wall, where the wallpaper is peeling in the bottom corner, I spy a wooden board.

I knock on the side walls. My knuckle makes a dull *tap-tap-tap*. Solid.

I knock on the back wall. This time, my knuckle makes a *thud-thud-thud*. Hollow.

I take a step back, a heavy feeling in my gut.

There's something hidden back there.

"Fuck no," I say, shaking my head. I close the door and slip back into bed. I'm not taking flight—I just don't want to know what's on the other side of the back wall of my closet. Not yet. Because I'm bone-tired, and I don't have the bandwidth to deal with whatever is hiding there.

Not tonight, I think for a third time.

I close my eyes, twist my ring, and shut out the world. Before long, my breathing settles into a rhythmic pattern. I'm subtly aware that sleep is just around the corner, but then I hear something new.

Ta-tump, ta-tump, ta-tump.

It's a heartbeat. Irregular. Three quick beats followed by a long pause. Faint, and I think it's coming from the walls.

I'm about to head back to Peter's room when the heartbeat stops. I listen and wait. The room is quiet and still, so I decide to stay, but just in case, I grab my earbuds out of my bag and set one in each ear. I turn on my iPod, notice it's a little past 3 a.m., and play some soft classical music. Soon, I'm drifting off.

The next thing I know, my eyes blink open. Early morning sunlight fills my room. I sit up and rub my face, then look around. There aren't any wet footprints on the floor, nothing has been moved, and the closet door is still closed—everything is exactly as it was when I fell asleep.

I tie my hair back in a ponytail and shuffle along the hall to the kitchen. Peter is sitting at the small table, eating a bowl of Cheerios he found in the cupboard. I grab a bowl and join him. The cereal is stale, but I've eaten worse. We don't say much—his eyes are baggy and he barely acknowledges my existence. Finally, I can't take the silence any longer and have to say what's been infesting my mind.

"So, about last night."

He drops his spoon into the bowl and a small splatter of milk splashes across the table.

When he doesn't say anything, I add, "We can talk to Dad about moving, if you want."

He shakes his head. "I don't know. Maybe it was just in our minds, you know? Like, maybe there's some sort of logical explanation for what we saw."

I nod and force a smile. "Yeah, sure. Maybe." But I know there's no way it wasn't real. "Hopefully tonight will be better. I barely slept at all."

Dad enters the kitchen. There's an awkward pause during which the three of us look at one another in turn before Dad breaks the silence. "What kept you up?"

"Nothing," Peter says quickly. A little too quickly. He's never been a good liar, so I help him out.

"We think Mrs. Cracknell fell asleep with the TV on upstairs."

Dad nods but looks unconvinced. I'm not sure he bought the lie, but he lets it go. He opens a kitchen cupboard and the door hinge squeaks and sags. "Gonna have to fix that," he says, taking out a bowl and joining us at the table.

"She said not to touch anything down here," I say.

"Yeah, well, we'll see about that," Dad says.

TEENS GREET EACH OTHER excitedly, hugging and fist-bumping as I slip between them, silent and unseen like a ghost. They catch up on their summer vacations and compare class agendas while I keep my head down and walk quickly through the school halls. My eyes are dry and a wisp of a headache is threatening to explode at any moment. If I can just get through the day, I can take a nap as soon as I get home. Five and a half hours. No problem.

After homeroom, I check my agenda and find my first classroom, English. I'm one of the first to arrive so most of the desks are up for grabs. I head straight for the back corner, toss my backpack on the floor, tuck my scarf into it, and slump down in the seat. My eyelids droop involuntarily and I struggle to stay awake as I stare out the window, propping my head up with my hand. I want to rest my head on my desk but if I did that it would be game over, lights out. As other students filter into the classroom, they catch sight of me, run a quick mental search to confirm they don't know or recognize me, and pick a seat as far away as possible. I try not to take it personally. I try to make it seem like I don't notice, but after a few minutes, the only two empty seats are to my right and in front of me.

The teacher, Mr. Culliver, keeps glancing from the wall clock to an attendance sheet on his desk to the two empty chairs. It's 9:03, and he seems to be debating whether or not to launch into whatever brilliant opening speech he has planned for us or wait for the final stragglers to arrive. He opens his mouth to speak the moment the door opens, and in walks someone I recognize.

At least this time, I'm not in the doorway to bump into her.

It's the girl from Darcy's Diner, the one who was a real bitch. But she also paid for my pancakes—even if she didn't know it—so she's got that going for her. Of all the girls in class, she's by far the most well-dressed and put together, just like yesterday, and I wonder who she's so desperate to impress. From the way everyone looks at her and sits up straighter, it's clear she's well-known, well-liked, or well-feared. Probably all three equally.

She scans the class, looking for a place to sit, and that's when her gaze settles on me. She frowns for a moment, probably trying to remember how she knows me, and then her face falls. She's quick to regain her composure, but she doesn't move.

"Nice of you to join us, Triss," Mr. Culliver says. Maybe it's his British accent, but something in the way he says it sounds like he's not her number one fan, and my appreciation for him goes up a notch. "Please take a seat."

A girl seated beside the empty desk in front of me shoots her hand in the air and beckons Triss over. "Triss! I saved you a spot."

Triss smiles and weaves between the tables and chairs. She's like a gazelle, tall and lean and graceful, but more predator than prey.

"Hey, Alicia," Triss says. She then turns her attention to me. A half-smile tugs one side of her mouth upward as she asks me, "You okay?"

I stutter a little and look around the class, caught off guard by her question. Why is she speaking to me? And what does she mean by that?

Before I answer, she tucks a strand of her perfectly straight and shiny black hair behind her ear, nods, and says, "Cool." She turns her back on me and sits down.

Alicia looks from Triss to me and back to Triss, sensing the tension between us. And since she assumes Triss just somehow got the better of me, she laughs.

I see how it's going to be. Triss wants to start the school year off on the wrong foot with me, and she wants her fan club to be witness.

Fine. If she wants a fight, she's got one. My imagination immediately kicks into high gear, picturing all the ways I can retaliate, when the door opens and in walks the only other person in Burlington I recognize.

"Willem," Mr. Culliver says. "Last to arrive. The summer break hasn't improved your punctuality, I see."

"Sorry, Mr. Culliver, I just, um, had trouble finding the classroom."

"I somehow doubt that, seeing as I taught you eleventh-grade English in this very room last year. Please sit. There's one spot remaining in the back."

Willem sees the empty desk, but not me. At least, I don't think he sees me. And even if he did, he probably wouldn't remember me—he must have served dozens of people yesterday, and hundreds throughout the week, and—

"Hey there, Pumpkin Spice," he says with a laugh as he nears my desk.

I suck in a small breath, surprised. Not only does he remember me, he remembers my order.

Triss remains statuesque as he passes her table, and says, "Hi, Will."

"Hi, Triss," Willem replies. There's not a lot of warmth in his words. Do they know each other?

Of course they know each other. Not only do they go to

the same school, but yesterday she was leaving the diner where he works. Had that been a coincidence, or had she gone there to see him?

"Hey," I say as he sits down beside me.

"Twice in two days," Willem says with a smile. "Must be fate."

Alicia glances back at us, not bothering to hide the shock and curiosity lighting up her face. Triss doesn't move a muscle and continues to stare dead ahead, which seems to speak volumes.

"I don't know," I say, trying to nail the right mix of amusement and apathy to make it clear that I'm interested but not *too* interested—not an easy balance to strike. "This isn't a very big city." I smile. "Maybe you're stalking me."

"Hey, you came into my diner, remember? Not the other way around."

I shrug. "Maybe I'm stalking *you*." My cheeks immediately flush. *Maybe I'm stalking you?* Since when do I flirt so openly? That's not my style—I move towns too frequently to put down roots.

He pulls a small notepad and a pen out of his shirt pocket, shakes them for emphasis, then sets them down on his desk. "First day of school and I've already got a scoop on a stalker on the loose."

I give him a quizzical look, not sure I catch his meaning.

"When I'm not serving pumpkin spice lattes to pretty girls, I write for the school paper," he says. "Willem Toth, reporter for the *BHS Register*, at your service."

My heart begins to race and I find myself at a loss for words, which is extremely awkward but also probably for the best. *Do not engage, Joana,* I tell myself. *Be friendly, sure, but romance? Forget it.*

It's the smartest play. How can I find the time for dating when I need to deal with whatever the hell is going on in my new apartment?

But the shot of adrenaline now coursing through my veins, a by-product of the mere *thought* of having a boyfriend, is a welcome diversion. I ride the high straight through to the afternoon.

MY GYM TEACHER, MRS. Howerton, is in no mood to sit idle or waste time.

"Rugby," she says loudly, walking before us with a determined look in her eye and a rugby ball clutched tightly in her left hand, "is a game for barbarians, played by gentlemen."

The thirteen girls sitting on the grass—myself included—stare silently at her, curious to know where she's going and wondering why she made the boys stay in the gym, but not daring to speak.

Mrs. Howerton makes a show of scanning her audience. "But since you appear to be neither barbarians nor gentlemen, I will need to train you into something else. Something more fearsome."

There's a moment of quiet anticipation before a girl to my left raises her hand. "Mrs. Howerton? This is just, like, gym class, right?"

"Very astute, Laney," Mrs. Howerton says. "This is 'just' gym class, but tryouts for the school team start later this week and I plan on getting a head start on our competitors. Who can tell me how many years it's been since we won regionals?"

"Twelve years," Triss says. She's sitting beside Alicia and another one of her suck-ups—I mean, *friends*—a girl named Summer. They're as far from me as possible, with the entire class between us. I'm surprised Triss knows the answer to Mrs. Howerton's question. Does Burlington High send their cheerleaders to rugby matches?

"That's right, twelve years," Mrs. Howerton says. "And I'll be damned if that streak extends to thirteen. This is the year we bring home the trophy, ladies, and I'm looking for some fresh blood to help us achieve that."

Without warning, Mrs. Howerton throws the ball at Laney. Laney tries her best to catch it but fumbles and drops the ball to the ground.

"I'll keep looking," Mrs. Howerton says. "All right, everyone, line up along the side of the pitch. Let's run some drills and see what you've got! No contact for now—let's start with the basics."

I couldn't care less about the school rugby team, but I can't help but feel butterflies fluttering in my stomach as I take my place and start running and throwing and catching, following Mrs. Howerton's orders. This gym class is the closest I've ever come to trying out for a team sport. I'm so distracted by the anxiety coursing through my veins that I forget all about the wet footprints I saw and the heartbeat I heard in the walls last night. I don't even think to keep an eye on Triss . . . not until I catch an awkward pass from Laney, begin to sprint toward the opposite end of the field (what Mrs. Howerton called the "pitch"), and see Triss chasing me with a look in her eye that can only be described as "murderous." Does she want to tackle me or kill me?

She's fast too. Really fast. But not as fast as me.

I cradle the ball in one hooked arm and pick up my pace. High knees, fist pumps, sharp breaths, and grim determination. My eyes are on the end zone, or whatever it's called in rugby. My heartbeat thunders in my ears—*ta-tump, ta-TUMP, TA-TUMP*—and I spare a quick glance over my shoulder.

Holy shit. Triss isn't too far behind. She's more athletic than I would've guessed.

But I cross the line and slow down to a trot, smiling, victorious. It feels good to run, but it feels better to beat Triss.

WHAM!

The next thing I know, I'm on the ground looking up, my head pounding and my side aching. Triss is lying beside me, her arms wrapped around my torso. She uses me as a prop to push herself up and says, "Sorry, but it doesn't count until you touch the ball to the ground. You lose."

I get to my knees, then my feet. I feel a little unsteady, but I try not to show it—I don't want to give Triss the satisfaction.

"Mrs. Howerton said no contact," I say, keeping my tone calm and even. The insult Triss paid me yesterday outside the diner springs to mind and I smile, tasting a hint of copper in my mouth and wiping a drop of blood from my lips. "What are you, deaf? Or just stupid?"

Triss takes a few threatening steps toward me. We're face-to-face, her stare sharp enough to cut glass.

"Rugby's not for the weak," she says. "You better toughen up."

I'm plenty tough, I think, and I'm about to say it when Mrs. Howerton appears.

"Triss," she says firmly. She points at the track surrounding the pitch. "Five laps. Go."

Triss smiles at me. "Worth it," she says under her breath. She turns and begins jogging, her ponytail swaying side to side. Alicia and Summer share a laugh.

"Make it ten!" Mrs. Howerton calls out to Triss before turning her attention to me. "And you. Where did you learn to run like that?"

"I don't know," I say with a shrug. "I just like to run, I guess?"

"Well, Miss I-Don't-Know, I've got news for you: you're on the team."

"But I—"

Mrs. Howerton holds up a finger and cuts me off. "I don't want to hear it. You're on the team."

"But—"

She turns and walks away. "Practice begins next week. I'll see you there, because you're on the team."

I sigh and spread my arms apart, then drop them, giving up. "I'm on the team," I say to no one.

"WHAT DO YOU MEAN, you're on the team?"

Dad is sanding the chipped paint off one of Mrs. Cracknell's window frames, but he stops working to talk with me.

"Exactly what I said: I'm on the team. The, uh, rugby team."

"I didn't know you were going to try out."

"Neither did I."

"You don't know the first thing about rugby . . . do you?"

"I didn't, but I do now."

"All right," Dad says with a bemused laugh. "Tell me everything you know about the sport."

"Um . . ." I think back to what Triss said after she tackled me. "It doesn't count until you touch the ball to the ground."

"What doesn't count?"

"I don't know!" I throw my arms in the air in exasperation. "Points. A touchdown. Whatever. I'm fast, so I made the team. You should be happy for me."

Dad puts his sandpaper down, removes his work gloves, and wipes the sweat off his forehead. He takes a few steps toward me and places his rough hands on my arms, giving my biceps a gentle, loving squeeze. "I am very happy for you. Truly. I'm just a little surprised. I had hoped this move would be good for us, and I thought maybe, in time, we'd settle in nicely. This is a lot quicker than I had expected, that's all." His gaze is pulled past me and he waves to someone on the street. It's Peter. "What's next? A job? Boyfriend? Girlfriend?"

I cringe—why do parents always have to say such embarrassing shit? "Who knows?" I say noncommittally, but my thoughts are pushed to Willem.

"Hey, Petey," Dad says, and my brother cringes too. "Your sister here made a sports team."

"Bullshit," Peter says immediately.

"Ouch," I say.

"Language," Dad says. "But it's true. Rugby. Right, Jo?"

I nod. "Didn't even need to try out."

"Let me guess," Peter says. "The coach saw how fast you are and recruited you on the spot. Am I right?"

"Yeah, pretty much."

"Fire," he says, impressed. "I'll come watch your first game."

If we're still here by that time. "How was your day?" I ask him.

"Not too bad. Pretty good, actually. I sat next to this kid named Ash. He seems cool."

"A good day for the Guests," Dad says with a wide grin. He doesn't look nearly as tired and anxious as usual, so he must not have heard the Whisperings last night, or the 3 a.m. heartbeat that kept me up.

What if the heartbeat wasn't real? I suddenly think. *What if it was only in your head? What if it was just like the Whisperings?*

No, the heartbeat was real. And if I hear it again, I'm not going to ignore it. I'll find it. And then I'll—

"Are you having a party on my lawn without me?" Mrs. Cracknell calls out as she walks through the front door, carrying a tray full of glasses. "My invitation must have been lost in the mail."

"The kids were just filling me in on their first day of school," Dad says jovially. He waves a hand at the house, showcasing his work. "I'm just about done sanding the ground-level window frames. I'll need a ladder for the ones up there. Do you have one?"

She nods. "In the garage, but I can't say for certain how steady it is. It's as old as Methuselah."

"Is that old?" Peter whispers to me.

Not knowing who or what Methuselah is, I can only shrug.

"Thank you." Dad says. "I'm sure it'll be fine."

"Well, don't just stand there looking like a rangale of deer in a beam of headlights," Mrs. Cracknell says. "Come on up here and help yourselves to a cold drink."

With thanks, we each grab a glass and take a seat on the front steps. The conversation is a little awkward and stilted, but Mrs. Cracknell means well and the lemonade is just as delicious as the day before. She soon excuses herself and Dad, Peter, and I head down to our apartment. Dad brings a pot of water to boil and cooks a box of Kraft Dinner. I elevate the culinary experience by microwaving a hot dog, cutting it into bite-sized bits, and stirring it in with the powdered cheese and milk.

"Magnifique," Dad says after his first bite.

Peter nods. "It's good," he says with a smile.

"Nothing but the best for us," I say, intending it as a light-hearted joke but hating the way it sounds a little sad.

We eat the rest of the meal in silence.

After dinner, I go for another jog to Red Rocks Park and back, and by the time I return I'm basically asleep on my feet. After a quick shower, I pull back the curtain hesitantly and breathe a sigh of relief. There are no wet footprints on the floor. As I brush my teeth, I stare at my reflection. The skin around my eyes is dark and puffy—I stretch it out with my fingertips and it springs back when I let go. I sigh, turn off the bathroom light, walk to my room, and slip into bed.

With my head on the pillow and the sheets pulled up close under my chin, I stare at the ceiling. There's a brown water stain directly above my head. The more I stare at it, the more it begins to look like a heart—not like on a Valentine's card but a real, beating heart, covered in arteries and veins and valves.

Ta-tump, ta-tump, ta-tump.

The heartbeat. It's faint, but unmistakable. Is it coming from the ceiling? Could the stain actually be . . . ?

I stare at the stain intensely for a minute, as long as it takes to reassure myself that it's not beating. It doesn't even look that much like a heart, to be honest. I feel a little silly to have thought so, but the heartbeat continues.

The sound seems to be coming from all directions at once. Maybe that's why I couldn't pinpoint its source the night before. I get out of bed and walk around the room, listening intently and feeling the walls with my fingers. A slight vibration tickles my fingertips with every beat. I'm on the right path.

The sound gets slightly louder as I approach the closet. My feet carry me toward the beat, even though a voice in the back of my head is telling me to turn around and return to the safety of bed.

I nearly laugh. Safety of bed? Nowhere in this room is safe. I continue inching forward. Getting warmer, metaphorically speaking. The air is actually chillier the closer I get to the closet. I grip the doorknob, take a steadying breath, and exhale. My breath comes out as a misty cloud that dances for a moment before disappearing. I open the closet. Empty. But the heartbeat is louder. Am I losing my mind? I place my palms on the side walls, then close my eyes, steady my breathing, clear my mind, and focus all of my attention on the present moment.

TA-TUMP, TA-TUMP, TA-TUMP!

My hands recoil and my eyes flash open, half expecting to see a monster standing directly before me. The heartbeat is louder than ever. And I think it's coming from the hole in the wallpaper in the bottom corner of the back wall.

I crouch down and reach a trembling hand out, hesitating. I notice a small hole in the wood. Do I actually want to do what I'm thinking of doing? But if I don't do something, I'm going to go mad. I close my eyes, slide a finger in the hole, and poke and prod in the dark to see if I feel anything.

The heartbeat stops.

But I don't. I feel wet wood, mushy with rot. It crumbles at my touch and tumbles out in damp chunks, covering my feet and widening the hole. I shake it off and keep searching, able to insert a second finger, then a third, then my entire hand, but I still don't feel anything unusual. I'm about to give up when something moves. Something skittish. It tickles the back of my hand, raising the hairs on my forearm and making me feel like I'm going to be sick. I retch and yank my hand free. The *something* is still there, its teeth or claws digging through my skin, deep into my flesh. It's brown and hairy and—

It's some sort of beetle. Not hairy, but with a dark pattern that makes it look like a spider. I shake my hand and send the insect to the ground. It scurries back to the hole in the wall and perches on the ledge. I shiver and wipe the back of my hand on my pajama pants.

The beetle taps its head on the wall three times. *Ta-tump, ta-tump, ta-tump!*

That tiny little beetle has been making the heartbeat noise all this time?

It's times like this I really wish I had my own phone, or a computer—any way to google stuff like a normal person. But we don't have the money for two phones, and I don't want to sneak into Dad's room to use his.

I need a job, I think—not for the first time—as I crawl back into bed.

And that's when it hits me. There was a *Help Wanted* sign posted at Darcy's Diner. I'd make a good server. And it would be a bonus to already know one of my coworkers.

I imagine Willem and me joking around and telling stories while on break.

He laughs at something I say. Our hands touch.

Our eyes lock in that knowing way. He leans in.

We kiss, our lips lingering, tingling. My breath catches in my throat and my heart drums in my chest, mimicking the sound the beetle made.

Ta-tump, ta-tump, ta-tump.

We're all alone. Willem leads me to the back. I follow.

"NO!"

I sit up straight in bed so quickly I bite my tongue and taste blood.

"Don't you dare hurt her!"

It's Dad. He's screaming in his bedroom. Screaming at someone.

The Whisperings, I think as I feel all the blood drain from my head, making me dizzy. *He already hears the Whisperings.*

Chapter Four

MY SPIRITS SINK AS goosebumps prickle my skin. I'm simultaneously creeped out by whatever is happening in Dad's room and depressed by the knowledge that we'll be gone by sunrise. I wanted to stay here in Burlington. Was it too much to think that this could have been the beginning of something a little more permanent, something normal?

"No!" Dad moans in anguish, the word stretched out and pained.

I turn on the light and rush down the hall. His door is open a crack. I'm about to open it all the way when I pause.

What if he's not alone?

In a way, crazy as it sounds, it might be a bit of a relief if there's someone else in there. It would mean he's not talking to himself again.

I lean in and call his name. He doesn't answer. The door creaks as I push it all the way open. The hallway light illuminates the room.

Dad isn't in bed. He's standing, facing the corner of the

room. It's impossible to tell what he's looking at, other than the wallpaper.

"I can't, I can't," he mumbles. "Kill her."

"Dad?" I say, hearing a quiver in my voice. He's scaring me. The way he's talking takes me back to the night Mom died. The night she was *murdered*.

"Kill her. Kill her kill her kill her kill her—"

"Dad!" I take a step toward him, pretty sure there's nothing there but needing to know for certain.

He starts to suck in small gasps of air, a sad, woeful sound that makes me pause. "You killed her," he says softly. Then, he screams. "You killed her! You killed her! YOU KILLED HER!"

His mania breaks me, shattering me from the inside out. A shiver shakes me from my core straight through to the tips of my limbs. I leap forward, grab hold of Dad's shoulder, and spin him around to face me.

His eyes look at me, but he doesn't see me. He looks straight through me, his eyes darting left and right, his brow furrowed and his mouth agape. "What?" he says in confusion. "What happened?" His eyes land on me and he blinks rapidly, then rubs a hand over his face. "Isabelle?"

My mother's name.

A tear slips down my cheek. "No, it's Joana," I say, taking his hand and guiding him back to his bed. I sit on the edge beside him. "Who were you talking to?"

He doesn't answer, so I repeat the question. "You woke me up. Probably woke Peter too, and maybe even Mrs. Cracknell. I wouldn't be surprised if you woke half the street."

"I was talking to . . ." He frowns as his words trail off. "I don't remember."

I've never told him I've heard him talking to himself before, never told him I know what he calls the voices in his head, but I need to kick-start his memory. If there's any hope we might be able to stay here, even just a little longer than we've stayed anywhere else, it's time to tackle this directly.

"Were you talking to the Whisperings?"

He sits up straight, his mouth snaps shut, and he stares at me intently. If I were able to hear his thoughts, I'm sure they'd be racing a million miles per second, trying to process what I just said. "No, it was just a dream, but . . . I've never told anyone about . . . how do you know?"

I break free from his intense stare and look down at my lap. "I read a letter you wrote to Mom, years after she died." I pick at a piece of skin around my thumbnail. A spot of blood wells up and runs over my knuckle. I put my thumb to my lips until the bleeding stops. I hate what I'm going to ask, but I need to ask it anyway. "Are they real? The voices? Or . . . ?"

"Or am I crazy?" Dad sighs, but he doesn't sound exasperated or upset. It's the sigh of someone releasing a lungful of breath they've been holding for days, weeks, months, years. "I often ask myself that same question. And I'll admit I used to think—maybe hope is a better word—that I *was* crazy, and that the voices I heard were only in my head. But I gave up on that thought, that hope, a long, long time ago."

Finally speaking openly and honestly about this with Dad feels like the best drink of water after the longest drought, despite the water tasting tainted. "Why? If you can't see who's speaking, how can you be sure it's not . . . ?" I tap the side of my head.

"I just know. The same way I know that I love you and

your brother, despite not being able to see my love." He points to his chest. "I feel it. In here."

That makes sense, so I nod. "Then who is it? And why do they speak to you?"

Dad shakes his head. "I have no idea. It started after your mother's death. The voices have haunted me ever since."

"Is it . . . her?"

"No. Would that I could speak with her again, even if only one final time. No, the voices are sometimes different, sometimes the same. They whisper in my ear in the middle of the night as I sleep. They murmur, mumble, and mutter, often nothing more than a stream of indecipherable nonsense. Clear words sometimes jump out of the noise, like fish flying from the water, and sometimes the voices yell. But they all want, and need and demand."

"Want and need and demand what?"

"Life. They all make demands of my life, and they're jealous of us, Jo. They're jealous of the living. And I'm afraid, so goddamn afraid, that they'll take what they want if I let them. That they'll take my life, or worse, yours, or your brother's. I know this sounds crazy—see? I told you. But you must believe me, I wouldn't move us so often if it wasn't absolutely necessary. I know the voices, the Whisperings, are real. And I know they'll hurt us, maybe kill us, if given the chance. They follow me, everywhere we go. Each move buys me a little time, but they follow. As relentless as waves crashing on the shore, they follow." He drops his face into his hands and moans, a sad, quiet sound.

My soul feels the same way—sad and quiet. I place a hand on his back and take a deep breath. "We're going to get through this,

Dad. We're going to figure this out. But we can't keep running. You've tried that for thirteen years, most of my life, and it hasn't worked. It's time to try something new. It's time to stay."

"But what if they come?" His voice is quiet, feeble. It's the voice of someone spent, drained. "What if they do something terrible to us, something terrible to you?"

I'm pretty sure ghosts can't kill people. But I have no way of knowing that for certain. There's not exactly a user's manual for this. "We'll figure it out. We'll stop them."

He raises his head and looks at me, his expression unreadable, and I'm concerned he won't agree, that he's lived with his fear of the Whisperings for so long that he can't imagine doing anything differently, but then his face softens and his eyes water, and he nods his head.

"Okay," he says. "Sometimes I forget you're not a little kid anymore. I've been so busy trying to protect you, you grew up in a flash and I feel like I missed it."

"I'm still your kid, Dad, but I can help you too. You can't keep facing all this alone. You should speak to someone again, like you used to."

"You're right. I'm going to find a new support group to join. It's been a couple towns since I've gone to therapy, so I'm overdue. Plus, I kind of miss the watered-down coffee and stale cookies." He laughs. "It feels good telling you some of this. Trust me, I've wanted to, I just didn't know how."

"You need to tell Peter too."

Dad nods. "Yeah, you're right. 'Petey, I need to tell you something. I hear ghosts. I call them the Whisperings. And I'm afraid they might try to harm us. That's why I've moved us from town to town, but they keep following. But now, we're going to stay right here and, well, I have no idea what we're going to do. Thought you should know.'"

He looks up at the ceiling and then back at me. "I wonder how he'll take that?"

"It's a lot to process," I admit. "Just make sure you don't call him Petey."

"THOUGHT YOU SHOULD KNOW, Peter," Dad says, bringing his recap to a close. It's early morning and we're sitting in the kitchen, three bowls of soggy Cheerios forgotten on the table.

Peter looks from Dad to me and back to Dad again. "Okay," he says, then scoops a spoonful of milky mush into his mouth.

He took the news remarkably well.

"Are you . . ." Dad says, pausing to look at me then back at Peter, "okay?"

Peter fills his mouth with another spoonful of cereal. "Sure. Actually, if this means we don't need to keep moving every few months, I'm better than okay." He sits and thinks for a moment, then adds, "But I'm sorry you've been dealing with this on your own for so long, Dad. At least, now that we know, Joana and I can help you . . . however we can."

Dad smiles wide enough to wrinkle his face, looking like he's holding back tears. He exhales loudly. "I can't tell you how good it feels to have shared all that with you." He takes his bowl to the sink and turns on the tap. The bowl acts like a water slide, shooting water out of the sink and onto the floor. Dad turns off the tap, too happy to care about the mess. "Like a great weight has been lifted off my shoulders."

I'm happy too, maybe happier than I've been in years. But then Dad steps in the puddle on the floor and leaves wet tracks behind him as he goes to get a dish towel. I stare at my reflection in one of his footprints, remembering that the Whisperings aren't my only concern.

I need to go to school, but afterward I need to get answers for some questions I have about this house. I need to have a conversation with Mrs. Cracknell.

WHEN I GET HOME from school and rugby tryouts—I made sure to purposefully call it rugby *practice* in front of Triss since I've already made the team, before Coach Howerton has made any other decisions—I find Dad doing repairs outside. He tells me Peter has gone over to his new friend Ash's house, presenting me with the perfect opportunity to get to know our new landlord a little better.

I knock on the front door, but no one answers. After a moment, I knock again, thinking of another expression Dad is fond of saying: madness is doing the same thing twice and expecting a different result. But on the other hand, Mrs. Cracknell is really old, and, sure enough, after another minute or so, I finally hear the sound of feet shuffling through the hall inside.

"If you're selling something," Mrs. Cracknell says through the closed door, "I'll save you some time and send you next door, where you might have better luck finding a fool to be easily parted with their money."

A laugh escapes my lips. "It's me, Mrs. Cracknell. Joana."

A series of metallic clicks and clanks fill the air as Mrs. Cracknell unlocks several bolts and then opens the door.

"Hello, dear," she says with a smile. "Everything okay?"

"Not exactly. I think you're going to need to call in an exterminator."

Her face falls, but she doesn't look surprised. Resigned, maybe, or regretful. "Ah. I see. I knew it would be a matter of time before I had to have this talk with one of you. Thought it would be with your father, but no matter. Come on in. Lemonade?"

She steps back and holds the door for me. I nod as I walk inside. She points to a sitting room to my left. "You make yourself comfortable and I'll be back before you can say knife."

"Knife?" I ask, perplexed.

"It's just an expression," Mrs. Cracknell says over her shoulder as she turns and shuffles away.

That's when I notice something odd. There appears to be a red stain on the wooden floorboards near the rug, peeking out from between a couple of tassels. Is it . . . is it blood?

"Knives are sharp and to the point," Mrs. Cracknell continues from the kitchen, speaking loudly.

She and Dad share a love of expressions, but most of hers are from a different era. Speaking of a different era, I enter the sitting room and drop myself down on one of the old-fashioned wingback chairs. A plume of dust rises around me, the tiny particles dancing in a shaft of sunlight. The chair is patterned with faded tree branches, autumn leaves, and small brown birds. It's surprisingly comfortable, so I place my backpack on the floor by my feet and settle in. I'm enjoying the view of the street through one of the room's large windows when Mrs. Cracknell returns and hands me a glass of lemonade.

"You don't want one?" I ask.

She holds up a hand and sits in a matching chair. "Diabetes. I always make my own lemonade, and I don't skimp on the sugar, so I haven't been able to drink it in years. Now, what was it you saw in the basement?"

Wet footprints, something hiding in my closet, a rattling doorknob. The answers come fast but they're not the answers I want to give, not yet. Best to start with the bug.

"I saw an unusual insect. It came out of a hole in my closet's wall. I googled it today in my school library." I take a piece of paper out of my backpack, unfold it, smooth it on my thigh, and hand it to Mrs. Cracknell. It's a printout from Wikipedia. "A deathwatch beetle. I heard it the past two nights, tapping away in the walls. Sounded just like a heartbeat at first." I laugh at how silly that sounds now, in the light of day. "Turns out that's a common mistake to make."

Mrs. Cracknell studies the paper a moment longer, then hands it back to me. She doesn't say anything, and her expression is hard to read.

"You're not concerned?" I ask. "Like I said, it was *in* the walls. There are probably more—"

She holds up a hand and waits for me to fall silent before speaking. "When I moved here, so many years ago I no longer recall the date, I heard the same sound in the middle of the night. And like you, I also thought it was a heartbeat before I spotted one of the beetles. I called an exterminator, they fumigated the house, laid down traps, and guaranteed that would wipe out anything living under this roof. But the very next night?" She raps a knuckle on the coffee table, mimicking the beetle's sound. *Ta-tump, ta-tump, ta-tump.* "The exterminator returned, repeated the process and the same guarantee, but then . . . ?" *Ta-tump, ta-tump, ta-tump.* "Seven times I had the house fumigated, and seven times the beetles didn't die. The exterminator couldn't understand it, and he eventually stopped returning my calls. It took some time, but I eventually grew accustomed to the sound. I even came to appreciate it. A little white noise can do wonders for your sleep. I also changed my perspective. The beetles had been here long before me. They'll probably be here long *after* me too. Did you know that some people consider the rattling of deathwatch beetles to be a bad omen . . . a warning of impending death? I've listened to it for decades now, and I'm still kicking. It's actually the way they attract mates, nothing more."

"Yeah, I read that on Wikipedia."

"I don't know what that is," she says.

"It's a website that . . . never mind. You're not concerned about the beetles damaging the house?"

"I was at first, but like me, she's still standing."

I appreciate the way Mrs. Cracknell refers to her house as "she," no doubt a result of having lived in one place for so long. A completely foreign concept to me.

"You said the beetles were here a long time before you," I say. "How do you know?"

She sighs and sits back in her chair, looking at me like she's upset with herself. I get the feeling she let something slip she hadn't meant to. "The house sat empty for years before I bought it. It was chock-full of dust and cobwebs and garbage when I moved in. I even found a family of possums in the attic. Took a good deal of work to whip her into shape. I suppose all manner of insects would have had their run in here during that time."

"A house this large and beautiful, so close to the marketplace? Why did it sit vacant for so long?"

Mrs. Cracknell eyes me with another sigh. "You're as persistent as a mosquito, aren't you?"

I shrug innocently and keep my mouth shut. If given enough silence, people have a habit of filling it with talk, even if they'd rather not. And Mrs. Cracknell is a talker.

"All right, I'll tell you." She casts a nervous glance around the room, as if she thinks there might be someone listening in. "The family that lived here long before me, well, they all . . . died."

The way she said it makes me certain they didn't just *die*, but I don't say that. The seconds tick by and I settle into them, wondering what else Mrs. Cracknell might say if given the time.

After a few moments, she slumps in her seat with a scowl. "Fine. That's not painfully accurate." She laughs bitterly. "Speaking of pain, they were murdered. By the man of the house, right here in their home. After that, no one wanted to move in, not while the memories were so fresh. People said the house must be haunted after what had happened. But I didn't believe in any of that, and I've never been one to pass on a steal of a deal. The city's superstition was my personal gain."

Of course a man killed his family here, in the house I've just moved into, the house I don't want to leave. *Of course*.

"What was their name?" I ask, my mouth dry. "The, um, murdered family?"

Mrs. Cracknell thinks for a beat, then says, "Their name was Keil. The press called this place the Burlington Kill House—instead of the Keil House, get it? I doubt many know the details today, but back then, the story was the talk of the town. The husband, he was a professor at the university. Entomology."

"Entomology?"

Mrs. Cracknell nods. "The study of insects. Maybe that's where the deathwatch beetles came from."

"Not just from the years no one lived here?" I ask with a casual tone.

"No," Mrs. Cracknell admits. "And now, my dear, you know every single sordid secret I can share about my house. Do you regret moving here?"

I take a sip of lemonade to wet my throat. "Not at all," I say. I'm starting to grow attached to the old girl, and I'm not going to let anything change my mind. Not wet footprints, or beetles tapping in the night, or anything else.

IF I HAD A phone, I'd immediately start digging up dirt on the Keils, but that will have to wait. Instead, I decide I might as well begin planting some roots. If we're going to stay, it's best we start acting like it.

The late afternoon sun bathes the street in a golden glow that warms my skin and lifts my spirits. It pushes me forward with optimism as I cut through the neighborhood and enter the Church Street Marketplace. The walkways are alive with people and noise and energy. I reach Darcy's Diner and enter without crashing into anyone, which is nice for a change.

"Pumpkin Spice!" Willem calls out from behind the counter, and at first, I think he's announcing that someone's drink is ready, but he's looking directly at me and smiling widely.

"How long are you going to keep calling me that?" I ask as I walk to him.

"That depends. How long are you planning on living?"

"Oh, I dunno," I say with a dramatic shrug. "Until I die, I guess."

Willem points a finger at me and makes a fake shooting sound, then says, "That long, then. I could call you P.S. for short if you'd prefer."

"Nah, Pumpkin Spice is fine. P.S. sounds too much like an afterthought."

"You're right, and you're far too special to be that."

My heartbeat picks up speed. *Ta-tump-ta-tump-ta-tump.* Flirting with Willem is turning into one of my favorite things to do in Burlington, and another reason I want to stay so badly.

"So," he continues, "what brings you into Darcy's Diner on this fine day? The usual? Pumpkin spice latte and a stack of pancakes?"

"Actually, I'm here because of that." I point at the *Help Wanted* sign on the wall.

"You want to work here?" He sounds surprised, maybe a little dubious.

"Sure. You don't think I'm qualified?"

A half-smile tugs at one of his cheeks, creating a cute dimple. "No, I just don't know how I'd get anything done with you here all the time."

"That's not my problem, and also, you can't not hire someone because of that." I make a show of looking around the diner. "I don't exactly see a lineup of applicants. So, do I have the job?"

"Whoa, whoa, whoa! Slow down. First, I don't do the

hiring." He looks me up and down. Is he checking me out? "And second, it doesn't look like you brought a résumé."

"Well, no," I admit, slightly deflated. "But I'm really good on my feet and can answer any questions your boss might have. That's a good quality in a prospective new hire, isn't it?"

"Yeah, but the owner isn't here right now—it's just me and Chaz, the cook in the back, and—"

"So, phone him," I say, interrupting Willem.

"The patriarchy is alive and well, I see."

"What?"

"Phone *her*—the owner's a woman."

"Don't be a dick," I say with a laugh, knowing he's teasing me and not minding at all.

"All right, sure, this is me not being a dick." He picks up the phone and dials, muttering to himself loudly enough for me to hear. "Just call up the owner, tell her someone who couldn't be bothered to bring a résumé is demanding to be interviewed right now, but don't worry, she's good on her—hey, Meera, how's it, uh, how's it going? No, no, everything's fine. There's someone here who wants to apply for a job, and . . . I don't know, sixteen?" He looks at me questioningly.

I point my finger up in the air, indicating to raise my age by a year.

"Seventeen years old, and . . . Qualifications? She likes lattes . . . Hobbies? She plays rugby . . . Sure, here she is." He covers the phone's microphone with his hand. "That would have been much easier if you'd brought a résumé."

"You did great," I tell him with just the right amount of sarcasm. I take the phone and chat with Meera for a moment, then hang up.

"Well?" Willem says.

"Well, what?" I reply coyly, enjoying drawing the moment out a little.

"Don't bury the lede! What did she say?"

I walk slowly to the *Help Wanted* sign and pull it off the wall. "You got the gig."

"I got the gig," I say, allowing myself to smile genuinely. It's not every day you get your first job. "She also managed to drop three f-bombs into two sentences."

"She doesn't even censor herself in front of customers." Willem returns the smile. "Well, there goes my productivity. When do you start?"

"Right now. You're training me. Can I make a call?"

He waves at the phone, then the diner. "Mi casa es su casa."

I call Dad to tell him I'll be home late, then Willem starts walking me through some of the basics. Two or three times he remarks that I wasn't kidding when I said I'm quick on my feet, but it's not exactly rocket science. The coffee grind goes in the filter, the baked goods go in the glass cabinet, you write the people's food orders down on a piece of paper so Chaz knows what to cook, and the money all goes in the cash register. Easy peasy, lemon squeezy.

"Not a bad first shift," Willem says after the last customer has left and we've tidied up the joint.

"I learned from the best," I say.

Willem straightens his collar and says, "That's why they pay me the big minimum-wage bucks, plus tips. Speaking of which." He takes the cash out of the tip jar and divides it in half, giving me the extra penny. "For your troubles."

I do a rough count of the money before I stuff it in my pocket. It looks to be about forty or fifty bucks—more spare cash than I've ever had in my life. And I earned it. I'm so proud I feel like I might spontaneously combust.

We turn out the lights, flip the *Open* sign over to *Closed*, and lock the door. It's dark outside and the marketplace is much quieter now. Chaz waves goodbye—nice guy, big and hairy—leaving me and Willem alone.

"Which way do you live?" he asks.

"That way," I say, pointing southeast.

"Me too. I'll walk you home. If you want."

I nod. "Thank you." I've been out jogging twice, but I still don't know where you shouldn't walk alone after dark. Although we walk casually, we only have time to trade a few jokes before we've reached Mrs. Cracknell's house.

"Well, this is me," I say.

He looks at the house, then me, then smiles, then laughs, and suddenly his face falls flat, like someone just told him his dog died. "Wait. You're not joking? You actually live here?"

"For a whole three days," I say.

"I saw the rental listing in the paper your dad was reading the other day, but I didn't think you'd actually move in."

My cheeks redden and I try to keep my voice from rising. "Yeah, well, the rent is low. It's not like my family and I had a lot of options, okay?"

Willem looks at the house suspiciously, as if he still can't believe I live there, then smiles and nods. "Of course, yeah, of course. I get it I live in a small, run-down row house not too far away. This place is a palace compared to that! Sorry if I, you know, made you feel bad."

"It's okay," I say, still a little self-conscious. "What do you know about it?"

"Honestly, not a lot. Kids in the neighborhood have always said it's haunted. We used to dare each other to knock on the front door. I got up the nerve to do it once, back when I was eight or nine. An old lady opened the door and I took off like lightning." He laughs at the memory.

"That would've been Mrs. Cracknell. She's nice. Makes a mean lemonade. You could come over sometime after school or work."

"For a drink with a ghost? I don't think so."

"She's not dead!" I say, giving his arm a swat. We laugh. "For a drink with *me*."

"Yeah, I'd like that. And with so much character, I'm sure the house has seen some history. Maybe I could write an article about it—you know, for the school paper."

"Yeah, maybe," I say, not loving the idea of him writing an article for others to read, but thinking he might be able to help me research the place. I leave him standing on the sidewalk and head toward the side entrance. Halfway there, I turn around. "Good night, Willem."

He hasn't moved an inch, watching me as I walk away. "Good night, Pumpkin Spice."

THE DAY HAS FULLY caught up with me by the time my head hits the pillow. My back aches, I'm exhausted, and I feel completely drained mentally and physically, like a water balloon with a hole in it. But instead of sleeping, the night replays on an endless loop in my head—everything Willem said, everything I said, every time I caught him looking at me when

I looked at him, but more than anything, the mind-blowing thought that I have a job. I'd pinch myself if I wasn't certain I was still awake.

"Ow!" I say, pulling my right arm close to my body and rubbing the back of my bicep.

Something grabbed me. Something *pinched* me.

It's dark, but there's no one else in the room. I peer over the edge of the bed, just in case. There's nothing there.

It was your imagination, I try to convince myself. *You thought of pinching your arm, and your mind tricked you into feeling it.* Maybe, but how does that explain the small scratch I can feel on the surface of my skin?

The temperature drops sharply and a breeze flows over me. With a shiver I sit up, then flip the switch on the bedside lamp. The light doesn't turn on. I slide to the other side of the bed and try the second lamp, but it's not working either.

"Seriously?" I ask the darkness, my breath frosty. The power must be out, causing the furnace to stop working. I rub my arms and sigh.

I can't leave it. *I want* to, but I can't. I have to go check. I slip out of bed and test the switch by the door, just to be sure.

Flick. Flick. Flick-flick-flick-flick-flick.

The overhead light doesn't turn on.

I peer out into the hall. It's empty. As I pass Peter and Dad's rooms, I pause for a beat and listen. Silence from both, other than some soft snoring. No Whisperings, at least, which is a relief. I'm nearly at the furnace room before I remember it's locked. All I want is to go back to bed, but I'm already up, so I'll need to wake Mrs. Cracknell and ask her for the key.

Only . . . the door is open a sliver. The padlock is on the floor.

The cold probably woke Mrs. Cracknell too, and she's already in there taking care of things. That's got to be it.

I push the door open. The room is pitch black.

"Hello?" I whisper.

No answer.

My vision slowly adjusts to the dark. Shadows begin to materialize. The furnace is an antique, the type that burns wood or coal or something. It has a big iron grate that reminds me of a mouth. This old piece of crap can't seriously still be operational, can it?

I lift the furnace's latch and open the grate.

A small face peers out at me from within.

"Oh my god," I say as I fall backward.

It's a baby. There's a burnt baby in the furnace.

I look again—it's just a small pile of charcoal. The smell tingles my nostrils. There's another odor mixed in with the sharp, smoky smell of the ash, something like . . . burnt hair, maybe? I look up and spot a more modern-looking furnace behind the old one, and can't help but laugh, feeling a little silly for having thought a house as big as this one was still heated by the antique furnace.

The newer furnace isn't running, confirming what I assumed was causing the cold. All I need to do is find the breaker box, flip a switch, and I can go back to bed as the basement warms up.

I scan the small room and spot the breaker box on the wall to my left. I open the metal panel and run my fingers over the switches. All of them are positioned to the right, except for one that is flipped to the left. The furnace doesn't turn back on when I flip the switch, but a light somewhere in the basement comes on. I poke my head through the doorway. The light is coming from my bedroom.

That explains why the lights didn't turn on in my room, but what about the furnace?

The light from down the hall is faint, but it helps me see a little better. I spot a wooden drop pole with a light switch near the modern furnace. I don't know who would've turned it off, but it's worth a shot. I reach for the switch but am a little too short. The original furnace is in the way. I step up on the edge of its mouth, my toes dipping in ash, and raise myself up. For a moment I lose my balance and grab the pole, afraid of falling. I manage to regain my footing and hold myself up, but my ring catches on the edge of the light switch box and slides off my finger. It falls, ricochets off the furnace's open grate, and lands with a dull thud in the bed of ashes.

"Shit," I say, turning my attention back to the light switch. I flip it and, miraculously, the new furnace turns on and begins to hum.

It's the first thing that's gone right since I woke up.

I hop back to the ground, crouch, and peer into the furnace. I can't see my ring, but it's the only piece of jewelry I own so I'm not giving up that easily. I reach my hand into the ash and root around blindly. I'm relieved when my fingers touch something solid and small. I pull it out.

It's not my ring.

It's a tooth.

I drop it in disgust. It skitters across the ground like a cockroach retreating from the light and disappears down a floor drain.

I examine the gray dust on my fingertips. Against my better judgment, I hold my hand close to my nose and inhale. It's faint, but I think I detect a metallic odor.

It smells a little like . . .

I shudder.

C'mon, Jo, just admit it. It smells a little like blood. Burnt *blood.*

Just get your ring and get back to bed, I think. With a coil in my gut, I reach my hand out, pause, then force it back into the furnace before I chicken out. I root around in the ash until I find what I'm looking for. Before putting the ring back on my finger, I take it to the bathroom, clean it, and then hurry back to my room.

As I rush toward my bed, the closet door opens a crack.

I freeze, feeling as if my heart might explode.

The bedroom door slams shut behind me, making me jump and swear.

The room is empty.

"Who's there?" I ask.

No one answers.

I march to the closet, throw the door open, and look inside. It's empty too.

Ta-tump, ta-tump, ta-tump.

It's the goddamn deathwatch beetle again, hammering its goddamn head against the goddamn wall.

"Enough!" I say, knowing how crazy I sound. The beetle didn't open the closet door or slam the bedroom door shut, but it's going to bear the brunt of my anger and fear me all the same. Overcome by misplaced rage, I rush into the closet, grip the edge of the hole in the wall, and pull with all my strength. A chunk of soft wood breaks free and years of dust swirls in the air. There's no sign of the beetle—it must have scurried deeper—so I rip off another chunk of rotten wood, then a third. There's still no sign of the insect, so I stop and listen.

Silence. Then—

Ta-tump, ta-tump, ta-tump.

"Screw you!" I yell, surrendering completely to my delirium. No longer driving the bus, I'm merely a backseat passenger, along for the ride whether I like where I'm headed or not. I lean back, brace my hands on the floor behind me, pull my legs in tight to my body, and then kick as hard as I can. The soles of my feet turn into a battering ram and slam into the closet wall, punching a hole wide enough to crawl through.

At the same moment my feet bust through the wall, an overhead light turns on. Not in the closet, or in the bedroom behind me, but from somewhere in front of me.

"What the hell?" I say, brushing my hair out of my face.

There's a secret room that had been hidden by the closet wall. A small, empty room painted a deep, dark burgundy.

I remain on the floor, my head pounding, my mind racing, unable to move. The air feels heavier, charged, alive.

And I know—with unshakeable certainty—that I've uncovered something truly evil.

Chapter Five

MY SENSES, MY GUT, my brain—*everything*—screams at me to leave the red room alone. But I stay, rooted to the ground, unable to run, unable to look away.

The brightly painted walls can't conceal how oppressively dark the room feels. The air is oddly humid, pulsating out in wafts that feel sticky and moist.

Before I know what I'm doing, I step through the hole.

Entering the room is a little like walking through a wall of water. It's hard to breathe, my lungs never feeling quite full. My ears fill with pressure, making it hard to hear and amplifying the sound of my own heartbeat. *Ta-tump, ta-tump, ta-tump.*

I look around slowly. The space is about the size of a storage room but completely barren. The concrete floor—also painted dark red—has a drain in the center. *What happened in here?* I wonder. *Why was it boarded up, and by whom? Were they trying to hide something, keep someone out?*

Mr. Keil did something here, I think with assurance. *Something sinister.*

Not that there's much to see, but I've seen enough. It feels like I've been in the room for an eternity. I turn to leave but freeze.

There's a small bed, a cot, against the wall.

How can that be? The room was completely empty a heartbeat before. I close my eyes and rub my face, expecting the bed to have vanished when I look again, but it's still there.

A small, round face peers up at me from the darkness beneath it.

I gasp, taking a step backward. My heart feels like it's going to explode.

It's a young girl, three or four years old. She's shaking, her eyes wide with fear. She holds a trembling finger to her lips—*shh*—then points behind me to the hole I punched through the wall.

Slowly, I turn and look, my blood turning to ice.

I don't see anyone, but that doesn't mean someone isn't there.

I feel it in my bones. I sense someone. Someone sinister.

The girl pats the ground three times rapidly to get my attention. She waves at me frantically, telling me to join her under the bed.

I feel paralyzed, uncertain what to do and scared beyond belief. And then I hear footsteps coming from the bedroom.

A shadow steps through the hole. Enters the red room. Looks from the girl to me. Stares at me with an intensity I've never felt before, as if not looking at me but *inside* me.

The ground tilts under my feet as if the world has spun off its axis. Maybe it has. Nothing makes sense anymore. Nothing is real. Welcome to my nightmare, risen before my very eyes.

Standing before me—the shadow that entered the room—is my mother. In the flesh, back from the dead.

"Mom?" I say, my voice hoarse. A tear streaks down my cheek.

"Get under the bed. Now!"

Without hesitation, I do what she says. I drop to my hands and knees and slide like a snake beneath the bedsprings, pressing up tight against the little girl. I'm so scared that I'm afraid my soul might flee my body, leaving behind a hollow pile of skin and bones, but lying beside the girl gives me a small shred of comfort. It's better being with someone than no one.

Mom scans the room, but the bed is too small to conceal all three of us beneath it and there's nowhere else to hide.

A deep, gruff voice calls out, distant and close at the same time. "Ready or not, here I come."

Then more footsteps in the bedroom. These ones are heavy, slow, and taunting.

Ta-tump.

Ta-tump.

Ta-tump.

Mom stops searching for a hiding place. She closes her eyes, squeezes her hands into fists, takes a deep breath, then looks at us. Two helpless little girls hiding under the bed, terrified beyond all rational thought. And that's when it hits me like a blow across the back of the head.

Ta-tump.

I've seen all this before.

Ta-tump.

I've lived it.

Ta-tump.

The girl beside me *is* me.

"Slide as far back into the shadows as you can," Mom says. She sounds resigned. Her face is resolute, as if carved from stone. "Stay hidden, stay safe. Close your eyes, cover your ears, and whatever you do, don't come out."

We do as she says, pushing ourselves backward, leaving twin trails of scattered teardrops in our wake. I wipe them up with my sleeve, just in case. Because *he's* coming, and whatever happens, he can't find us.

I wish I could wipe my sleeve over my mom and make her disappear too, but there's nothing I can do to help her.

That's not true, I think, the voice in my head sounding vindictive and poisoned, a twisted version of my own. *You can help her. You can save her. You can do something, anything, instead of hiding under the bed like a big fucking baby, like a worthless excuse for a daughter, like a—*

"Little pig, little pig, let me cave your skull in," the man—my uncle Roman—says. He puts a hand on the edge of the hole and leans inside the red room. He smiles widely, but there's no warmth in it. His skin is wet and waxy, and his eyes are like a pair of glass marbles shoved tightly into too-small sockets, devoid of life. "Found you," he says, ducking low as he steps into the room with his right foot, dragging his left foot behind him with a limp and propping himself up with the long-handled tool he's carrying. *Ta-tump.*

I wish I could slide back farther, but all I can do is hope I'm back far enough to be hidden from his sight.

You coward, the hateful voice in my head says, and I try my best to ignore it.

"You don't need to do this, Roman," Mom says.

Uncle Roman nods and takes another step. *Ta-tump.* "But I do."

"We haven't done anything to you," she says.

Ta-tump. "But you have."

Mom shakes her head. Her face is ashen. "I can't fight you. I can't protect myself. But please, do what you're going to do to me and then leave. Go. Don't hurt Jack and the kids."

Ta-tump. He's in her face now, mere inches separating them. "I'm afraid I can't do that." He raises the heavy tool he's been using as a makeshift crutch and grips it tightly in both hands. It's a splitting maul, with a sledgehammer on one side and an axe on the other. "Me and my block buster here have work to do, and I'm going to see the job through to its end."

"Why?" Mom asks. The emotional dam she had been trying to maintain finally bursts and she sobs. "Why? This is madness. You fucking brute, this is goddamn *monstrous.*"

"You took everything from me," Uncle Roman says. "My leg." He taps the handle of his splitting maul, his block buster, against his left pantleg, and the prosthetic leg concealed within rings metallically. "My inheritance. And you."

Mom shakes her head. "Your leg was an accident. You can't blame us for your parents' will. And I was never yours to take. I'm *no one's* to take. I never loved you. I love your brother."

With a deep grunt, Uncle Roman hefts the splitting maul up in the air and raises it above his head, sledgehammer-side facing Mom's head.

I let out a whimper. Not *me* me, but the younger version of me. The little girl living through this unspeakably tragic event for the first time. I'm not sure whether to pity or resent her. Is it better to know what comes next? Or to have another twenty or thirty seconds of ignorance?

Uncle Roman lowers the splitting maul. Mom's eyes flick to the bed and back to her brother-in-law. It's a momentary mistake, the slightest motion, but it's enough for my uncle to notice, and he looks our way. He gets down on one knee, lifts the sheet hanging over the edge of the bed, and peers into the darkness.

"Found you, Joana," he says as happily as if playing a game. In his mind, I suppose he is.

Young me keeps her eyes shut tight and her hands on her ears, just like Mom instructed, but I can't help but look.

"Come on out, girl," Uncle Roman says.

Young me shakes her head and starts to cry.

"Come," he says, holding out a hand.

"Leave her alone!" Mom screams.

Uncle Roman ignores her. "Tell you what. I've had a change of heart, Joana. If you come out, nothing bad will happen to you. You and your mom can go free, unharmed. We'll pretend none of this ever happened."

Young me cries harder, louder.

"But if you make me drag you out, kicking and screaming, well, no one's going to walk out of this room but me and my block buster, trailing your blood behind."

Young me doesn't say anything, but I know exactly what's going through her head. It's the same awful thought that has haunted my nightmares for thirteen years.

Whatever you do, don't come out. Don't come out, don't come out, don't come out, don't—

What have I done to deserve living through the worst moment of my life twice? Hasn't the memory, burned into my brain, been punishment enough?

You didn't do anything to save her, the voice in my head answers. *You could have come out—he said you could both leave—but look at you, cowering under the bed, doing nothing to help yourself, nothing to help your mom. You're responsible for her death. Her blood is on your hands.*

What happens next happens in a blur, and I'm powerless to look away. Young me opens her eyes too and the images imprint on her mind, never to fade away.

"Leave her alone!" Mom screams as she jumps on Uncle Roman's back, wrapping her arms around his thick neck.

He stands up and lunges backward with a roar. He slams his back against the wall, crushing Mom with his weight. The back of her head hits the wall with a crack and she falls limply to the floor. From under the bed, I can only see her waist and legs, not her upper body and head—a small mercy.

Uncle Roman raises the splitting maul and swings it down in one fluid, devastating motion.

The wet, meaty sound that follows fills my ears and turns my entire being inside out. I'm overwhelmed by the most excruciating pain, like a thousand tiny razors slicing through me from the inside. My younger self and I lie side by side, disbelieving eyes wide and wet, hands held over our mouths, unable to fully process what we're witnessing.

Uncle Roman raises the splitting maul again and rotates it in his palms, axe-side now facing out, and brings it down with a crack, then again, and again, and again. Blood splatters the walls and a slow red stream flows beside Mom's legs. He raises the tool again—

But Dad grabs the handle from behind and yanks the splitting maul free from his brother's hands. With a primal yell, he chops the axe into the base of my uncle's neck. The blade slices through his shoulder and imbeds itself deep in his chest. A stream of blood squirts out of the wound in time with his final heartbeats as Roman turns and looks at Dad with an equal measure of annoyance and confusion. He takes a few staggering steps forward—*ta-tump ta-tump ta-tump*—and then collapses beside Mom.

Dad drops the splitting maul to the ground and squats low to look at me.

"Jo," he says heavily, his voice bearing the weight of what just happened, a weight that he'll try to get off his shoulders in a countless number of community therapy groups in a countless number of towns across the state for years to come, probably the rest of his life. He holds his hands out for me, and I reach for him before realizing he's stretching for the young me, not *me* me. He pulls her out and wraps her in his arms and buries her face in his chest so she can't see anything else and gets out of the bedroom as quickly as his feet will carry him.

And I'm left alone with the bodies.

But I blink and the bodies are gone. So is the bed and the splitting maul and the blood. It's just me, lying on the floor of the red room in Mrs. Cracknell's basement. It's deathly quiet, the silence amplifying the voice in my head.

Once again, you did nothing. You're not a fighter, you're a flighter. You should lie there on the ground all night and think about what you've done—what you didn't do.

"No," I answer, wanting to say more but leaving it at that. I don't need to explain myself to the voice. I get shakily to my feet, feeling like I've been through a war, and leave. I'm no more aware of what unspeakable acts Mr. Keil did in the red room than when I first entered, but I'm also no longer quite as afraid of not knowing. Mrs. Cracknell's house might be haunted, but the ghosts in the basement can't be as disturbing as the ones I carry with me everywhere I go—the ghosts of my past. The ghosts haunting not a house but my head.

Chapter Six

I WAKE THURSDAY MORNING with a headache and the certainty that what happened the night before wasn't a dream—it was real. It doesn't make sense, not in any traditional sense that I can wrap my mind around, but I felt the younger version of me trembling as we hid under the bed. You can't feel something that's not there.

The red room. It must have been the red room, somehow making the impossible real.

I get out of bed and step inside the closet. Sure enough, the hole I kicked in the wall is still there, and the room behind it is empty. Seeing the red room brings back the memory of blood flowing past my mom's legs, so I pick up the largest pieces of drywall and prop them in the hole, trying to block it from view. It's pointless—the pieces keep sliding and falling—so I toss them to the ground in frustration. If I tell Dad I found the closet wall like this and ask him to patch it up, he'll grab his toolbox before I finish speaking. Mrs. Cracknell doesn't need to know.

On second thought, as awful as the room is, it might be best to leave it open. Covering it won't make it go away, and as long as it remains open, nothing will be able to hide in there.

I ignore the suspicion that there's no shortage of things hidden in plain sight in this basement and head to the kitchen in search of food. I'll feel better after I eat, I hope.

Dad's drinking a coffee and Peter's eating a bowl of the stale cereal. Hard to believe it's only been a few days—feels like I've lived a lifetime or two since moving in. I join them at the table and pour myself a bowl. They don't ask if I heard any loud noises in the middle of the night, so I don't bring up what happened. The cereal isn't exactly the feel-good miracle cure I was hoping for, so I only eat half and wash the rest down the drain, then rush off to school.

I find myself in the same kitchen chair the next morning, and Saturday morning too, eating half a bowl of the same stale cereal out of the same bowl, rinsing the rest down the same drain, the same silence stretching thin between me, Dad, and Peter, and the same headache fogging my head from the same tapping of the same deathwatch beetle. But I've stayed out of the red room, and at least I haven't seen anything like I saw two nights ago.

Maybe a little air will help clear my head.

"I think I'm going to go for a hike," I say.

"Can I come too?" Peter asks.

"Yeah, sure," I say. "I could use the company. Do you need to work today, Dad?"

He takes a sip of coffee and sets his mug down. "There's nothing that needs doing that won't be waiting for me later. A hike with my kids sounds like the perfect way to pass a Saturday morning."

"Cool," I say. "On my jogs I've come across a place not too far away called Red Rocks Park. It has some great trails."

"Nice spot," Dad says with a faraway look in his eyes. "Very scenic."

"I'll bring my camera," Peter says.

We walk outside but don't get far before heading back to get bundled up. It's sunny, but the wind is cold and sharp enough to bite. I put on my coat, a hat, gloves, and Mom's scarf. I look at myself in the mirror by the door. For a split second I see Mom's face, covered in blood, where my own should be. I hurry outside, rejoining Dad and Peter on the sidewalk.

"Lead the way," Dad tells me.

We walk south, the familiar route I've jogged. The houses look less foreboding, the trees healthier, and what I had previously thought was an odd, skinny tower along the way is actually the world's tallest filing cabinet. It's covered in stickers, graffiti, and rust, so of course Peter insists we take a selfie standing in front of it. He angles his Polaroid camera up from beneath our faces—a terribly unflattering angle—and still can't get the top of the cabinet in the frame.

"Burlington's so weird," he says, fanning his developing photo.

"Just like us," I say with a laugh, feeling ten times better already—well enough to tell Dad and Peter what happened Wednesday night as we carry on. They should know.

I skip over what happened in the furnace room—if Dad knew I found a tooth I'm certain he'd make us leave—but otherwise I spare no details. Once I'm done, after a moment of stilted silence, Peter asks in a quiet voice, "Has anything like that happened to you before?"

I shake my head. "Not like that. I've had nightmares, more than I can count, but they've never been so real. I felt the younger version of me shaking, and Mom looked at me." I point to my chest to emphasize I mean *me* me, not young me. "She spoke to me. And I know I wasn't sleeping."

Dad is grimacing as if in physical pain. "You don't think . . . it wasn't the Whisperings, was it?"

At first, that thought had concerned me, but I quickly decided what I experienced wasn't the same as what Dad has been dealing with since Mom died. "No, I didn't just hear Mom and Uncle Roman but saw them too. Plus, it was a scene from my childhood, not a random voice from an unknown spirit."

"Were you hallucinating?" Peter asks.

I shake my head again. He's closer than Dad, but not quite right. "I don't think so. I think it was real—crazy as that sounds. Like a memory come to life."

"How?"

"The red room," I say with as much certainty as is possible in a conversation like this. But I've been thinking about it a lot—I've hardly thought about anything else the past two days—and it's the only part that makes any sense, in its own twisted way.

"I'll patch the wall as soon as we get back," Dad says.

"Sealing the room won't make it disappear," I say. "It'll still be there."

Dad looks tense, his eyes squinted and his mouth drawn tight. "No, I don't like it. The room was hidden for a reason, and the sooner we hide it again, the better."

"What if I promise to not go in it again?" I ask, knowing I can't promise any such thing.

Dad sighs, a long, drawn-out sound filled with anguish and discontent. "Fine. But I want to check it out thoroughly, and if I find anything—anything at all—I'm sealing it up. And if I ever catch you in there again, I'm sealing it up. And if at any time I change my mind—"

"You're sealing it up," I say. "Thanks, Dad." I give him a hug, touched by his concern.

"I'm sorry you've had nightmares for so long," he says. "I wish I'd known."

I shrug, trying to cover how awful my dreams have been and how heavy they've weighed on my soul. "It's okay. There's nothing you would have been able to do, and I've learned to cope. Whatever doesn't kill you . . ."

"Makes you stronger," he finishes with a sad smile that wilts shortly after it appears.

Luckily, Red Rocks Park is just ahead, breaking up what's turned into a thoroughly depressing conversation. I inhale deeply, savoring the crisp smells of pine needles and woodsmoke. Thin shafts of sunlight cut through the canopy of branches above. The trail is alive with the sound of leaves rustling in the breeze, birds chirping to one another, and squirrels scurrying across the forest floor. I instantly feel lighter, cleaner, at peace. I needed this.

Parents with small children, couples young and old, people walking dogs, and Saturday morning joggers pass by, everyone enjoying the serenity of the woods. A boy about Peter's age approaches and, when he catches sight of us, smiles.

"Petey!" he calls.

"Hey, Ash!" Peter says. He turns to me and Dad and says, "My friend from school."

"*He* can call you Petey?" Dad says.

"He just kind of did it," Peter says with a shrug. "And then some other kids at school started doing it, and now all my friends call me Petey."

"Ouch," Dad says jokingly.

"What's up?" Ash asks as he approaches.

"Not much. Just going for a walk with my dad and sister."

"Hey," I say with a wave.

"Are you here by yourself?" Peter asks Ash.

"Nah, I'm with my sister. She's too busy texting her friends to keep up. I got tired of waiting."

Ahead, a girl turns a corner and walks toward us. She's glued to her phone and doesn't see us, which buys me a few seconds of peace before the inevitable war begins.

"Your sister is Triss?" I ask Ash.

He nods. "I can tell by your tone that you've met."

"Yeah," I say with a sigh. "We've met."

"Ugh, you stupid bitch," Triss says, and for a split second I think she's speaking to me. I'm about to fly off the handle when I realize she was speaking to her phone while texting. She glances up and the look of shock on her face when she sees me is priceless. She recovers quickly, and in the space of two or three seconds she replaces her surprised look with her regular look of disdain, followed by a smile so forced it couldn't possibly be confused with the real deal. "Oh, hello, *teammate*."

"We're not teammates yet," I say, trying my best to keep an even tone. "Coach hasn't made final cuts yet."

"You seriously think there's any chance I won't make the team?"

"No, of course not. I've never been so lucky."

Sensing the tension between us, Peter and Ash walk off a bit and Dad follows them. I wish I could join them, but I don't want to give Triss the satisfaction of leaving.

She ignores the dig and changes the subject, smiling even more haughtily than before. "I heard you started working at Darcy's Diner. Serving people greasy food for minimum wage and penny tips. How noble of you."

"Where did you hear that?" I only started a few nights ago. How does she already know?

"A little birdie told me," she says.

"Who?" It must have been Willem.

Triss leans in close and whispers in my ear. "A little birdie I've slept with."

All the blood rushes out of my head, making me feel dizzy. I try to think of something to say, but nothing comes.

"Oh, you didn't know?" Triss says, twirling a strand of hair between her fingers. "Willem and I dated for two years. We broke up this summer, but he's still got a thing for me. Calls and texts me every day. It's actually a little pathetic. Like an unwanted dog who won't leave my doorstep."

"Okay," I say, finally finding my voice even though I have nothing worthwhile to say. "Whatever."

Triss stops playing with her hair and places a hand flat against her chest. "Do I detect a hint of jealousy?"

"Of you?" I laugh. "Fuck no."

She smiles, this time genuinely. "Don't lie to me. You like him! You want him the way I've had him. Well, have fun with that. Just so you know, he was nothing special." She takes a half-step back and looks me up and down. "You two will make a perfect couple."

I'm speechless, a feeling I'm not accustomed to and one I absolutely detest. I hate her. I hate her so much. I ball my fists and feel the blood rush back to my head, my cheeks burning and my eardrums pounding with my heartbeat. *Ta-tump, ta-tump, ta-tump.*

"Well, see you around." Triss flashes another quick smile as she steps around me. "Ash, let's go."

Ash says goodbye to my brother and catches up with his sister.

"I didn't know Triss was Ash's sister," Peter says. "He's *nothing* like her."

"I see her disposition hasn't improved since Monday," Dad says.

"Let's just go," I say, quickly resuming our walk. I try to steady my breathing and focus on the beauty of the forest, but I can't diffuse the anger boiling inside of me, or the images filling my head. Images of Willem and Triss kissing, peeling off each other's clothes, lying down . . .

"Don't let her get to you," Peter says, startling me out of my thoughts. "She's not worth it."

"You're right," I say. "But that's easier said than done."

The path takes us into a clearing and along a cliff, revealing a stunning view of the lake. The water, far below, sparkles in the sunlight.

Dad stops to admire the sight. Peter and I walk a little ahead.

"If we live here longer than usual," Peter says, "you were bound to make an enemy or two eventually. So, at least you've already got that out of the way." He smiles optimistically.

"I feel better already." I wrap an arm around his shoulder and pull him close to my side. "I'm the one who should be looking after you, not the other way around."

He laughs. "You've looked after me all my life. I'm old enough now to help you when I can."

"Given all the crazy shit that's happened, I won't turn that down."

"Let's take a selfie to mark the occasion," Peter says.

We stand with our backs to the lake, our heels a few inches from the edge of the cliff, and smile. Peter raises his camera in the air and takes a pic.

"This is going to be a good one," he says, looking out at the water as he waves the developing picture in the air.

A strong breeze picks up and blows the picture out of Peter's hand. It flies over the edge of the cliff and then plummets sharply, catching in the branches of a scraggly bush jutting out of the rock.

"Oh, no!" Peter says, taking a step forward.

I raise my arm and hold him back. "I'll get it."

"But *I* dropped it."

"You've already done something nice for me today, so now I can repay the favor. Plus, I've got a longer reach."

He nods and watches as I get as close to the edge of the cliff as possible. I brace my feet in a rock crevice and hold onto the branch of a small tree, look down at the photo in the bush . . . and then all the way down to the water below. My head spins, I feel dizzy, and my stomach does a quick flip. I'm about sixty or seventy feet up. It's not just the height that freaks me out, but the rocks jutting out of the water near the base of the cliff. If I fell . . .

I rip my gaze away from the lake and focus on the bush. *Just get the picture*, I tell myself.

"Joana!" my dad yells from far behind. "What the hell do you think you're doing?"

I reach a little farther. Almost there . . .

"Get back up here right now!"

"One second," I say through gritted teeth. I inch my grip along the tree, adding the distance I need to pinch the picture. "Got it!" My arm is burning from the strain, but I push past that and pull myself back up toward solid ground. I'm almost there when I'm tugged back toward the cliff's edge.

I look down, panic-stricken, and see that my scarf—Mom's scarf—has become tangled in the bush. I pull myself up, but the bush yanks my neck back down.

"Shit," I say, my heart beginning to beat harder.

Ta-tump! Ta-tump! Ta-tump!

Everything speeds up—not just my heartbeat but my mind, time, the entire world. Everything is happening all at once and I'm powerless to control any of it.

Desperate, I pull harder.

The scarf tightens around my neck, cutting off oxygen.

One of the bush's thicker branches has pierced the scarf's wool, and it's not budging.

My fingers slip a little off the tree branch.

Ta-tump! Ta-tump! Ta-tump!

I'm hanging on by my fingertips and they're screaming from the strain.

If I let go, I'll fall.

To your death the voice in my head says casually.

Ta-tump! Ta-tump! Ta-tump!

I try using my free hand to untie the scarf from around my neck, but the photo gets in the way.

Drop the picture, I tell myself, but for some reason, my hand doesn't comply.

My fingers slip a little farther along the branch, burning my skin.

If they slip any farther, I'll fall.

To your death! the voice in my head, now gleeful, reminds me.

I suppress a mad, panicked laugh.

Ta-tump! Ta-tump! Ta-tump!

"Jo!" Peter yells desperately.

I think he's been yelling this whole time, but my brain hasn't been able to process his voice.

I look up.

He's standing there, looking terrified, frozen with fear.

I want to tell him everything's going to be okay, but I can't.

I can't bring myself to lie to him.

Ta-tump! Ta-tump! Ta-tump!

"Joana!" Dad says, running toward me with wide eyes and a terror-stricken look.

Ta-tump! Ta-tump! Ta-tump!

He tries to slow down but he's moving too fast.

Ta-tump! Ta-tump! Ta-tump!

His feet slide to a stop, spraying me in the face with tiny rocks and dirt.

Ta-tump! Ta-tump! Ta-tump!

He reaches out a hand to grab my fingers—the fingers that are a second or two from slipping free.

Ta-tump! Ta-tump! Ta-tump!

In his haste, he miscalculates and slams his hand against the tree branch, and my hand is knocked free.

Ta-tump—

I fall, and with my last clear thought, I kick off hard away from the cliff.

—*ta-tump*—

I somersault backward and my head hits something hard.

—*ta-tump!*

The world fades to black.

Chapter Seven

WAKE UP . . .

Wake up . . .

Wake up!

It's not until I open my eyes that I realize I'd been asleep, but I hadn't dreamt. No mother, no uncle, no hiding under my bed, no murder, no nothing. Just blackness. Lights out.

My body is all-over sore, my head is pounding, my mouth is dry, and my eyes feel blinded by the light.

Where the hell am I?

I'm in a bed, covered by a threadbare blue-and-white striped sheet. A plastic mask covers my mouth and nose. An IV is inserted in the back of my hand. Machines beep and whir beside the bed, monitoring my vitals.

I'm in a hospital.

You fell, I remember. *You watched the world flip upside down and you hit your head and your dad and brother screamed and their faces shrank above you as the lake rushed up to greet you.*

"Dad!" Peter says. He sits up straight in a chair against the wall and whacks Dad's arm with the back of his hand.

Dad wakes up—he'd been dozing in his chair—and looks from Peter to me. "Whassat? Oh my god, Jo—you're awake! Nurse! Nurse!" He gets up, hurries to the door, and calls out into the hall. "Nurse! It's my daughter! It's Joana! She's awake!"

I try to tell him that I'm okay, but my throat is raw and I'm not sure if I should remove the mask covering my mouth. Not to mention that I feel like I've been hit by a bus.

Not a bus, I remind myself. *A lake.*

Dad returns to my bedside and Peter stands across from him. Both are looking down on me like the dwarves at the end of *Snow White*, crying over her dead body in the glass casket before the prince shows up to kiss her, break the curse, and save the day. A fairy-tale ending. If only happily-ever-afters happened in real life.

I want to stand up. Failing that, I want to sit up. At the very least, I want to say something, but for the time being, all I can do is stare helplessly at them.

"Thank god you're awake, Jo," Dad says. "The doctors didn't know how long you'd be unconscious. I was afraid you'd be in a coma for, well, a long time."

Coma? How long have I been asleep? I shift in bed. My legs and back scream at me, forcing me to lay still. I touch my fingertips tentatively against the back of my head and feel the tiny pinpricks of stitches. At least the scar will be hidden by my hair.

"I was able to get this for you," Peter says, laying Mom's scarf on the bed beside me.

I pick up the scarf and clutch it tightly against my chest, still unable to speak and thank my brother. But he picks up on how I'm feeling and nods.

A nurse enters the room and looks at me with a smile. "Well, hello there, Joana. It's good to see you awake." She's about to say more, but Dad interrupts her.

"This is Faith. She's one of the RNs that have been looking after you while you've been here."

He's clearly done that thing he does where he reads someone's name tag and then acts like they're old friends. At least he got Faith's name right, unlike Willem's.

"That's right," Faith says, giving Dad a pacifying smile before turning back to me. "You just relax while I check your vitals. What a lovely scarf that is."

It nearly killed me, I think. *No, I nearly killed me. I never should have tried to grab Peter's picture.*

Faith picks up a clipboard from the foot of my bed and scribbles on it as she checks the monitor beside me, takes my blood pressure, and performs an examination.

"How is she?" Dad asks, his voice taut with nerves.

"She is . . ." Faith scans her clipboard. "Doing well. Remarkably well, given what she's been through. You're a tough cookie," she tells me with a smile. "I called the doctor currently on duty, Dr. Sivika, and she'll be here as soon as she can. For the time being, the morphine will help with the pain."

Faith's voice grows distant, even though she's standing right beside me. It's like I'm on a conveyor belt, being whisked away.

Help me, a voice whispers in my ear. *Help me, help me, help me . . .*

I am being helped, I think, my head suddenly feeling light and airy. *I'm in the hospital and I'm doing well. Remarkably well. Faith said I'm a tough cookie.*

Help me, the voice whispers one more time, but now the

voice isn't coming from where I thought—inside my head—but from the room.

There's a girl, roughly my age. Peeking out from behind Dad. No one seems to notice her, but I do. How could I not?

Her skull is cracked wide open. The left side of her face is covered in wet blood and a flap of flesh folded over from her head wound. I can see the insides of her skull: fractured bone and spongy brain.

"*Haaa . . . maaa,*" she groans.

I try to speak, but I can't. I try to point her out to the others, but I can't. I try to fight off the feeling of drowsiness that is flowing through my veins and forcing my eyes to grow heavy, but I can't even do that.

My body feels like it's floating above the bed, and I drift back into a deep, troubled, drug-induced sleep filled with dreams of falling, falling, falling . . .

I SIT ON THE couch between Dad and Peter, staring at our TV without trying to follow the show they're watching. My mind is elsewhere, distracted and troubled.

The timeline of events is still hazy in my mind, but I was unconscious for a little less than a day and was discharged from the UVM Medical Center two days after I woke up. Fortunately, they offered free care because of our financial situation—we don't have insurance and there would have been no way we'd have been able to afford it. I'm off school for at least a week to recover. Doctor's orders. Seven days in this house, in this basement. After what I've already seen down here, I'm afraid I'm going to lose my mind long before I'm feeling better physically.

I can't be on my feet for more than fifteen or twenty minutes, so I had to call Meera, my new boss, and tell her I wouldn't be able to work for a bit. Not exactly the first impression I wanted to make, but she was remarkably cool about it and told me to take as much time as I needed. *Health and family come first*, she said. *Everything else—work included—comes a distant fuckin' second.* But without school and work, I won't get to hang out with Willem. Then again, after what Triss told me in Red Rocks Park, maybe a bit of time on my own won't be the worst thing.

No jogging for the time being, Dr. Sivika said, which sucks. What am I supposed to do? Sit inside and stare at the walls—the *insect-infested* walls? No thank you.

Rugby is right out, obviously, until I've been cleared to play again. The doctor was surprised with how well I've already recovered from my head injury. I only had a mild concussion, and I was lucky I didn't hit my head more than once as I plummeted to the lake.

Lucky. That word was repeated over and over while I was in the hospital. Lucky I only hit my head once. Lucky I hit water, not rocks. Lucky the impact didn't do worse damage. Lucky Dad isn't afraid of heights, is a strong swimmer, and didn't hesitate to jump as soon as I fell. Lucky he was able to pull me to shore. Lucky he knows CPR and was able to keep me breathing and my heart beating while waiting for the paramedics to arrive from a call placed by a Good Samaritan out for a walk with her stepkids.

I'm afraid I've spent a lifetime's supply of luck. From here on out, the only type of luck I'll have is bad.

"Thanks again, Dad," I say. "If it weren't for you—"

He interrupts me. "You might not have fallen. I hit the branch you were hanging onto."

"I was a second or two from slipping free. I was going to fall no matter what, and you jumped into the water and pulled me out. If it weren't for you—" Dad opens his mouth to interrupt me once more, so I raise my voice and speak over him. "*If it weren't for you, I* would have died. So again, thank you."

With a nod, Dad says, "You don't need to keep thanking me, but you're welcome."

"Get used to it," I say. I could thank him a million more times and it wouldn't be enough.

He nods. "I should thank *you* for encouraging me to look into therapy again. I found a free community support group that meets every Thursday evening in the First Baptist Church, so I'm going to go this week."

"That's great, Dad. I'm happy for you."

He opens his mouth to say something more, then closes it and smiles—a mostly happy smile, but there's an undercurrent of sadness hidden beneath the surface—and turns his attention back to his show.

I fall back into my own head, which is the last place I want to be. Other than thinking about all the things I'm not going to be able to do for the next week or so, the other thought that has dominated my mind is the dead girl.

That's all she was, just a thought, I try to reassure myself. *A figment of your imagination. A painkiller-induced hallucination. She wasn't real.*

But she *sounded* real. *Wake up,* she said. *Help me,* she pleaded. "*Haaa . . . maaa,*" she moaned.

And she *looked* real. Her blood, her skull, her brain. It all looked so terribly real.

Dad laughs at something on TV, something I heard but didn't *hear*, and I wish I could peer into his head. Crack his skull open, poke and prod around, and find the answers to so many things I wish I knew. In addition to the voices he's heard since Mom died, has he ever seen anyone—anyone who wasn't there? Because that's what I think that was—the dead girl in the hospital.

I don't truly think she was a figment of my imagination. And she wasn't anything like what I saw the other night in the red room. I think she was a bona fide ghost.

My pulse quickens and I practically have to bite my lips together to stop from blurting that out. But if I admitted that I not only heard but *saw* a Whispering myself, I'm certain Dad would make us move on the spot. For me and Peter, he was willing to stay and deal with the Whisperings himself, but would he stay knowing I have to deal with them too? Not a chance.

So as much as it pains me, I have to keep Dead Girl a secret. From Peter too, so I don't need to worry about him slipping up and telling Dad.

"I'm going to bed," I say, standing up too quickly, which causes my head to spin. I place my hand on the back of the couch for balance.

Dad stands beside me and puts an arm around my waist. "I'll help you to your room."

"I'm fine," I say. "Don't worry about me. Stay and watch your show."

"Nonsense," he says.

There's no arguing with him, so I lean into him and let him help me down the hall and to the side of my bed. I sit on the edge, trying to keep my eyes off the closet, but he goes straight to it and opens the door.

"You really did a number on this wall," he says. "Remind me never to pick a fight with you."

I laugh. "Yeah, you better not get on my bad side."

"It's going to take *all* my willpower to not fix this." He cranes his head through the opening, into the red room, and looks around without setting foot inside. After a minute he grunts, exits the closet, and closes the door. He doesn't say anything about the red room—how it made him feel, whether or not he heard or saw anything inside it—and once again I wish I could look inside his mind.

"Well, good night," he says. "Call me if you need anything."

"I will," I say with a nod.

He turns out the light and closes the bedroom door.

And everything is silent.

Shadows from the trees outside my window sway on the wallpaper. The wind whistles and shrieks, dampened by the house's—the old girl's—walls. I think about grabbing my iPod but I'm too tired. My eyelids grow heavy. I feel my breathing slow. The bed begins to swallow me as sleep drags me down.

Crrreeeaaakk . . .

My heart leaps into my throat as I sit up.

The closet door is open a crack. Didn't Dad close it? I think back, my pulse quickening, but don't remember. *Think, think, think . . .*

A voice, singing, drifts out from within the closet, as soft and sweet as spun sugar. "*Too-ra-loo-ra-loo-ral. Too-ra-loo-ra-li.*"

A hand emerges from the darkness. It grips the edge of the closet door, then guides the door open.

"*Too-ra-loo-ra-loo-ral. Hush now, don't you cry.*"

It's a woman.

Oh my god.

It's Mom.

"*Too-ra-loo-ra-loo-ral. Too-ra-loo-ra-li,*" she continues singing.

I must be dreaming, but I know I'm not. This is happening. It's the same version of my mom I saw in the red room a few nights ago, only not a memory. She's here, she's now.

"*Too-ra-loo-ra-loo-ral. That's an Irish lullaby.*"

She steps out of the closet, smelling strongly of lavender. Her gaze falls on me and her eyes smile.

"Jo," she says. Just that—just my name. She clasps her hands together and walks toward my bed.

I wipe away a thick tear, smearing wetness across my face.

"How is this possible?" I ask.

Mom shakes her head with a smile. "That's not important," she says as she gently wipes the rest of my tear away with her thumb.

A tiny jolt of electricity shoots through me. I've wanted to feel Mom's touch ever since she was killed, but something about it feels . . . off.

"What *is* important," Mom continues, "is that you come with me."

"What?" I don't understand, so I search Mom's face for a clue to her meaning. Something passes over her features, like a shadow or a shimmer. I blink and it's gone. "What do you mean? Why?"

She leans in close, the smell of lavender overpowering, and whispers urgently in my ear. "You're not safe here."

"Why not?" I ask, knowing the reason. The wet footprints, the tooth in the furnace, the red room, the things Mrs. Cracknell told me. "It's the Keils, isn't it? It's Mr. Keil. They haven't moved on, they're still here, and he's dangerous."

Mom nods slowly. "What a clever daughter you are." The shadow flickers across her face once more, and this time I catch a glimpse of something that chills me to my core.

It was another face, nothing like hers. It was thin and stony, whereas Mom's face is round and soft. The lips were pulled back in a crooked, hungry smile, and her eyes were squinted and penetrating, not full of life and love. Even her hair had changed color and shape, from Mom's natural auburn waves to black strands hanging limp from her scalp.

"What the hell?" I say, jerking back in revulsion. My stomach heaves and the back of my throat burns from the bile I'm forced to swallow back down. She looks like Mom again, but I know she's not. "Who are you?"

With a slight cock of her head, she laughs once and says, "I'm your mother, you silly goose."

"You're not," I say flatly. She's some sort of hollow version of my mom, an empty shell filled with darkness I can't see but can feel.

"I am, and you need to come with me." She reaches out her hand. I almost take it involuntarily.

"No," I say, moving farther away from her. My back hits the wall. I'm trapped with nowhere to go, nowhere to escape.

"Yesss," the thing claiming to be my mom says, her voice a low hiss. *Hollow Mother,* I think. *That's what she is.* "Come with me, Joana. I'm your mother." She lunges forward and grabs my wrist. Her touch is ice-cold, so cold it feels like my skin is on fire.

I yell in pain and shock and try to pull free, but her grip is too tight. With unnatural strength, she yanks me out of bed.

I hit the ground hard and try to scramble to my feet, but she begins walking, dragging me along behind her.

"Come with me," Hollow Mother says, like a broken record. "I'm your mother."

"Let go of me!" I try to pry her fingers off my wrist, but it's no use—her grip is cemented in place.

"Come with me! I'm your mother!" Her voice rises, both in volume and pitch. She looks over her shoulder and down at me. My mother's face is completely gone, and there's a wildness in the stranger's eyes. She looks manic, like a ravenous wolf about to feed.

I grab the foot of my bed but can't hang on. I try planting my feet into the ground, but it doesn't slow us down at all. I kick and punch her legs, but she doesn't even flinch. She pulls me into the closet. The red room looms large before us, and somehow I know: if she takes me in there, there's no coming back.

"Come with me! I'm your mother! Come with me! I'm your mother! *Come with me! I'm your mother!*"

I feel like a cow being forced into the slaughterhouse, my brain soon to be impaled with a metal bolt, my throat slit ear to ear, my blood drained into buckets, my flesh carved off my bones and ground into red meat.

She steps through the hole and into the red room and pulls me along. The back of my thighs hit the drywall, slowing her for a moment.

It's my first decent chance to save myself, and undoubtedly the last.

I grab the broken edge of the wall with my free hand.

Hollow Mother looks down at me and, seeing my futile attempt to prevent her from dragging me to my death, she laughs. It's a bemused and pitying sound: *Aw, you sweet, poor thing!*

Her condescension sickens me, but she's not wrong. I know I can't hang on forever, but it's either do that or do nothing, and I can't do nothing.

She yanks hard on my wrist and my pinky and ring fingers slip free from the wall, but I manage to hang on just a little longer.

Her smile drops and she stops laughing. She looks mildly concerned, and at first, I think it's because of the fight I'm putting up, but then I follow her gaze and realize she's not looking at me but at the deathwatch beetle.

It's back, perched on the edge of the broken drywall, like it's come to see what all the commotion is about.

I look back at the woman, and something in her face—something in the way she's looking at the beetle—gives me an idea.

I let go of the drywall and raise my hand in the air above the insect, palm facing down.

"No," she says, releasing my wrist, sensing what I'm about to do.

Without further hesitation, I drive my hand down and squash the beetle, feeling it crunch wetly between my palm and the wall.

"NO!" Hollow Mother bellows. She's distracted and distraught, so I seize the opportunity and leap out of the closet, slamming the door shut behind me. I lean my back against it and grip the doorknob tightly, as if I could somehow overpower her if she tries to re-enter the room, but nothing happens. She doesn't turn the knob, doesn't bang against the door, doesn't even make a sound. I take a moment to steady my breathing and collect my thoughts. Still, nothing happens.

Although part of me wants to barricade the closet door shut, I need to know if Hollow Mother is still waiting on the other side. I open the door an inch, just enough to peer inside.

There's nothing there. Hollow Mother is gone. All I see are the hole to the red room and a smear of bug guts on the wall.

I close the door, then have second thoughts and open it wide. If she returns, at least I'll be able to see her coming.

Pitter-pitter-pat.

The sound of quick, nimble footsteps behind me makes my breath catch in my throat. I spin around and glimpse a blur. Something has darted behind the bed. A moment later, I see the top of a head and a pair of eyes peer over the mattress at me.

"Peek-a-boo," whoever is hiding there says.

I yell and jump to my feet. It's a young boy. He drops down, out of sight.

My feet are suddenly damp. I look at the floor and see a trail of wet footprints leading from my bedroom door to the edge of the bed.

It must be the same boy who left a wet trail the first night we moved in. He's been watching me. I shiver, wishing I hadn't thought that. Without knowing his name, *the Peek-a-Boo Boy* pops into my head. He's eight or nine years old, with jet-black hair and pale skin.

"You killed one of her beetles," someone says quietly.

I spin around again and come face-to-face with a girl about my age. She has the same straight, dark hair as the Peek-a-Boo Boy and Hollow Mother.

"She's not going to like that," the girl says. A tear runs down her cheek. She wipes it away, making a mess of her makeup and leaving behind a red smear. But then I realize she's not wearing any makeup. A second tear drops and I see the truth. The girl is crying blood.

They're both dead, I think. *They're both ghosts.*

"She was going to take me in there," I say, pointing at the red room and trying to keep the fear out of my voice, "and kill me."

Red Eyes—the girl—stares at me solemnly and tilts her head to the side. She doesn't say anything, which speaks volumes.

"I'm right, aren't I?" I ask.

She looks slowly at the red room, then back at me. She nods.

Having that confirmed by this girl, this ghost, makes it so much worse. Blood rushes to my head and I feel like I might faint. "Why me? Why does she want me dead?"

A finger rapidly *tap-tap-taps* the back of my shoulder. I flinch, my heart feeling like it's fit to burst, and spin around. The Peek-a-Boo Boy is standing right behind me. He's sopping wet, like a drowned rat.

"Join us," he says, the words bubbling out of his mouth with a lungful of water that splashes on the floor.

A baby begins to wail, but it's silenced almost immediately. I look to my left, unable to believe what I'm seeing. If it weren't happening to me, if someone had recounted these events, I wouldn't believe any of it, not in a million years. There's an old-fashioned wicker crib in the corner of the room. Like a driver gawking at the scene of a fatal car crash, I'm drawn to it. I creep toward the crib. All I see within is a pale-blue baby blanket. It moves once, as if something beneath it kicked. I walk closer. I still can't see anything but the blanket. I take another step. The blanket shifts again. And again. And again. And again. And again. The baby I can't see beneath the blanket is kicking rapidly. It's agitated. It's in distress. Why isn't it crying? Somehow, the silence is worse. *Kick kick kick.*

Then, stillness.

I peer over the edge of the crib.

A tiny hand—discolored gray, drained of all blood—juts out of the crib, straight up in the air. The small fingers curl into a clawed hand, desperately clinging to life.

"Help!" I say as I spin around.

Red Eyes and the Peek-a-Boo Boy look horrified but helpless. They stand side by side, not moving, not speaking. The boy looks like he wants to run far, far away, and the girl's tears run so swiftly that the front of her cream-colored nightdress is soon soaked with her blood.

"Help me!" I say, delirious with panic. "Don't just stand there! We have to help the baby!"

If they're not going to do anything, it's up to me. But before I turn to help, the boy and girl finally do something.

The boy begins to spasm and convulse. Water—even more than before—sputters out of his mouth.

The girl looks at the boy, then me. She reaches her left hand toward me and takes a step forward. The moment her foot touches the ground—*thwack!*—her ankle splits in half, as if an invisible axe has severed it. Blood splatters the floor and she stumbles forward. Her right hand is chopped off at the wrist—*thwack!*—followed by her elbow—*thwack!*—and shoulder—*thwack!* The three severed pieces of her arm fall to the floor. She continues to stumble and lurch forward before her second ankle is hacked off—*thwack!* Next is her right knee, then her left—*thwack! thwack!*—and what is left of her mutilated body lunges toward me.

I stand frozen to the ground with equal measures of fear and disgust.

As she falls forward, her thighs are hacked at the hips and her chest is split clean in half like a thick piece of firewood on the chopping block. *Thwack thwack THWACK!*

Finally, the invisible axe slices clean through her neck with one final *thwack* and her decapitated head spins through the air. It flies straight into my arms. I catch it reflexively and stare down into her dead, red eyes.

Her mouth opens one, two, three times, like a fish out of water. After a few failed attempts to speak, she manages to choke out two words, nearly inaudible.

"Join . . . us . . ."

Her head suddenly bursts into flame and I drop it, horrified beyond words, beyond feeling, beyond the capacity for rational thought. Red Eyes' head bounces and rolls a few feet away, completely consumed in flames. One by one, her trail of bloody body parts light on fire too.

Despite being drenched, the Peek-a-Boo Boy's body goes up in flames next, followed by the crib. The raised baby hand is like a tiny pyre, the flesh melting and peeling away from the bones.

In a matter of moments, the crib is a pile of charred, smoking wood. The boy is nothing more than a charred skeleton. The girl's red eyes dissolve. Her empty eye sockets stare accusatorily at me.

Join us, I hear the ghost of her voice say in my head.

For a moment my bedroom looks like the world's grisliest murder scene, then the remains of the crib and the scattered bones turn to ash that scatters and dissipates in a cold breeze that flows out of the closet, chilling me to my core.

My heart pounds painfully against my chest. *Ta-TUMP-ta-TUMP-ta-TUMP!* It feels like it might never settle.

Breathe, I tell myself. *Just breathe.* With every breath, my heart calms slightly, returning to a more regular rhythm.

I rub my face and look around the room, ensuring I'm still alone. It looks exactly like it did before Hollow Mother entered, followed by the three kids, and my life went from messed up to utter madness.

Join us.

Utter *fucking* madness.

I'll be damned if I let Hollow Mother and the other ghosts in this house take me.

And Peter, I think. *They'll want him as well.*

Without knowing how, I know the truth. They want kids. They want *us*.

But I'm not going anywhere. Not to a new town, nor with them.

I'm staying right where I am. I'm staying right here.

Chapter Eight

THE CLEANSING POWER OF fresh air and sunshine—not to mention a little exercise—is remarkable.

I wipe some sweat from my forehead with the sleeve of my sweater and enjoy the feeling of my beating heart—my *regularly* beating heart—and the euphoria of a runner's high. It was just a short, light jog—it'll be a while before I can go for a full-fledged run—but it's the first time I've been able to do more than walk since my accident, and I want to cling to the endorphins coursing through my veins. They dull not only my pain but also my fear—and I've got plenty of that—as well as the thing that's been nagging me all week: Willem hasn't come to see me. Not in the hospital, and not since I got home on Tuesday, and it's now Sunday—a full week and a day since I fell.

As soon as I turn a corner and Mrs. Cracknell's house comes into view, I slow down to a brisk walk. I wave to Peter and Ash as I pass them on the lawn, stop the music on my iPod and remove my earbuds, and then sit on the hanging bench on Mrs. Cracknell's front porch. It creaks and groans as I swing gently back and forth, kicking off the ground with my feet.

The sounds of the neighborhood—leaves rustling in the breeze, dogs barking in a distant park, a radio playing classic rock as a car passes slowly—mingle with the purr of a lawnmower as Dad mows the backyard.

Peter catches a baseball and swiftly throws it back to Ash. The ball whistles as it cuts a straight line through the air. It makes a loud, sharp smack as it connects with the back of Ash's glove.

"Ow!" Ash says as he pulls his glove off and waves his hand in the air three times. "Where did you learn to throw like that? You play house league?"

Peter laughs and shakes his head. "Nah. Just catch with my dad."

"Really?"

"Mm-hmm. Never really lived anywhere long enough to join a team."

"Must have sucked always moving somewhere new," Ash says in the blunt way thirteen-year-old boys speak to one another. "Always being the new kid."

Peter shrugs, but agrees. "It hasn't been great." He looks at me and smiles. "But we're here now."

A feeling of warmth blooms in my chest and spreads throughout my body. I smile back, knowing I'll need to fill Peter in on Hollow Mother and the others soon. I'd wanted to keep my ability to see Dead Girl in the hospital a secret, but now that the threat is in our home, I can no longer keep him in the dark. But not yet. I don't want to ruin the moment. Peter and I are both making connections, and Dad's first night at his new support group went well. Things are good. I don't want to screw that up.

Join us.

The words have repeated in my head for hours, sometimes in Hollow Mother's voice, sometimes in Red Eyes', and sometimes in the Peek-a-Boo Boy's. Once, in the middle of the night when I woke with a suffocating start, I could have sworn I heard the words spoken in a baby's voice.

Join us.

The three kids, I figure, were siblings, and Hollow Mother was their mom. The Keil family. And now, ever since Mr. Keil killed them all, the kids have been trapped with her, somewhere just beyond the red room. *Come with me, I'm your mother.* Maybe she thinks I am one of her kids. And she doesn't want me to leave.

But where is Mr. Keil's ghost? Moved on, or lying in wait?

Smack!

"Goddamn it!" Ash says. He transfers the ball to his throwing hand and shakes his gloved hand. "Do me a favor and throw a changeup or two, okay?"

Peter laughs. "Sorry, all I've got is a heater."

"And all I'll have is a bruised palm if you don't go a little easier on me."

The front door swings open and Mrs. Cracknell shuffles out into the daylight. "Mind if I join you, dear?" she asks as she sits beside me on the swinging bench.

"And if I say no?" I ask jokingly.

"I'd say welcome to the wonderful world of apartment hunting."

"In that case, I *insist* you join me."

"How magnanimous," she says. "How are you feeling?"

"Better than I have in days," I say without hesitation. "It felt so good to go for a short jog again. My joints were beginning to feel so stiff."

Mrs. Cracknell's back pops and her knee squeaks as she shifts her weight on the bench. "I wouldn't know what that's like," she says.

I smile, then change gears. "I've been wondering about something you said. About the Keils? Do you happen to know how many kids they had before . . . ?" I let my words trail off, not sure how best to finish.

But Mrs. Cracknell doesn't have any problem speaking her mind and addressing the murder. "Before Mr. Keil killed them? Two."

I frown. Maybe the ghosts I saw weren't the Keil kids. Maybe . . .

"No, three," Mrs. Cracknell says. "I don't know how I forgot about the baby."

"Let me guess: a baby, a teenage girl, and a young boy?"

Mrs. Cracknell nods and looks at me suspiciously. "How did you know? Have you been doing some digging?"

Digging? I recall digging my hand through the pile of ashes in the old furnace and finding a human tooth. "Something like that."

"Are you sure you haven't . . . seen anything in the basement?" Mrs. Cracknell asks, looking at me intently.

Before I have time to answer, I hear the last voice in the world I want to hear.

"You. Live. *Here*?" It's Triss, standing on the sidewalk, gawking at me and the house. She looks delighted.

Her face makes me want to throw up. I consider telling Triss that, but settle for a simpler, more direct, "What do you want?"

"Well, I came here to tell my brother that our parents want him to come home for lunch, but now I just want to talk about all of this." She waves a hand at the house.

There's no way she walked all the way over here just to tell her brother to return home. She came to antagonize me, and I know it. "You couldn't have texted him, like a normal person?"

Triss smiles and bats her eyes. "Well, if you must know, since it's on the way, I stopped by Darcy's Diner for a latte. Someone has had to keep your boyfriend company while you've been home alone."

My cheeks burn and I feel my blood pressure rising. The sooner I end this conversation and Triss leaves, the better. "All right, Peter. Time to say goodbye to Ash."

Peter gives Ash a fist bump, then sits on the front steps. Ash joins his sister, looking like he'd rather be with us.

"See ya, Petey," Ash says.

"I don't know about that," Triss tells her brother, loud enough to ensure we all can hear her. "Not after I tell Mom and Dad he lives in the Burlington Kill House."

Damn it. She knows. "It's just a house," I say, my jaw aching from clenching it too tight.

Triss laughs. "You must be joking, right? You think our parents will be okay with Ash hanging out in a dead serial killer's house? Occupied by a crazy old woman who's probably a serial killer herself?"

I stand up so quickly that blood rushes to my head, making me feel a little dizzy. "You don't know anything about her," I say, pointing at Mrs. Cracknell.

"Joana, shhh," Mrs. Cracknell says calmly and quietly. "She's not worth it."

"Oh, is she parenting you now? Where's your own mom?" Triss makes a big show of looking around the yard and up and down the street, and although I don't know how she knows that too, I know what she's going to say. "Oh, that's right. You don't have one."

I take a step forward and suck in a lungful of air, about to unleash hell on Triss, but Mrs. Cracknell stands up quickly and grabs my hand.

"That's more than enough for today," she tells Triss sternly. "It's time for you to go."

"Or what, old woman?" Triss says. "You'll call the cops? I'm not breaking any laws, and I'm not on your property."

"Call the cops? What on God's green earth makes you think I'd do that? Serial killers and the police don't exactly see eye to eye."

A priceless look of confusion and doubt flashes across Triss's face. If I wasn't still so livid, I'd laugh. Triss shakes her head and says, "Whatever. Bunch of weirdos. You were destined to be together. Let's go, Ash." She turns sharply and walks away.

Ash looks at me and shrugs. "I'm sorry my sister is, well, *my sister.*"

"It's all right," I tell him. "You can't be blamed for the way she is."

He nods, then looks at my brother. "Don't worry. I'm sure my parents aren't going to make us stop hanging out."

Peter smiles. "Cool. See ya, Ash."

Ash strolls slowly behind Triss, clearly in no rush to catch up with her.

"Just when I think I can't possibly hate her any more than I already do," I say.

"Some people have a natural-born talent for getting under other people's skin," Mrs. Cracknell says. "But bullies only have as much power as you give them. If you don't rise to her taunts, she'll have no choice but to give up and back down."

"That sounds good in theory," I say with a sigh, releasing the tension built up in my shoulders, "but I honestly don't know if I'm that big of a person."

"Then hit her," Peter says.

It's such an out-of-left-field comment that it takes a moment for it to sink in. "Hit her?" I ask, completely dumbfounded.

He nods like it's the most obvious course of action imaginable.

"Like, in the face? Or a sucker punch to the gut?"

"No," Peter says. "During rugby practice, once you're cleared to play. Tackle her. Hard. Show her how tough you are."

I open my mouth to say it's not a half-bad idea, but stop and turn to Mrs. Cracknell. What would she think of me if I admitted that I wanted to hurt Triss?

She thinks for a moment, and just when I think she's about to scold my brother, she says, "Cutting a bully off at the knees can be an effective approach too."

I nod, feeling better simply from *thinking* of tackling Triss during practice. But as nice as the thought is, something Triss said is still sticking in my side like a thorn. If Willem won't come see me, I'll go see him.

THE BELL DINGS AS I open the door, and the sound of half a dozen conversations and food sizzling on the grill fills my ears. Darcy's is busy today, so busy I see Willem isn't alone. He's got his back to me, jotting down the orders of a group of friends seated at a table in the middle of the diner, and there's also a middle-aged woman working behind the counter. She's wearing a brown jacket and a Queens of the Stone Age T-shirt, a wide-brimmed black hat, and an adornment of oversized rings and necklaces.

Meera, I think, nearly certain.

Since Willem is busy, I make my way to her. As I pass Willem, he senses my presence and turns his head.

"Welcome to Darcy's Diner," he says. "I'll be right with you . . ." His words trail off as our eyes meet. He looks surprised to see me, but I can't tell if it's in a good way or a bad way. "Oh, hey, Pumpkin Spice."

"Hey, Willem." His pet name for me, once cute, annoys me. I tuck a strand of hair behind my ear and take a seat on one of the barstools at the front counter. "Meera, right?"

Meera nods and smiles at me knowingly. "And you must be Joana," she says. "It's nice to finally meet you in person."

"It's nice to meet you too. Thanks again for giving me a job, and then, you know, letting me totally skip out on that job."

She holds up a hand. "Say no more. I hardly consider falling off a fuckin' cliff skipping out on work. There are easier ways to get time off, you know?"

I can't help but laugh. For my first boss, she's nothing like I would have imagined—both her fashion sense and her casual on-the-job swearing. "Well, thanks all the same."

"How are you feeling?" She looks me up and down, as if scanning me for visible damage.

"Much better today, thanks," I say. The scar on the back of my head heats up and pulses, as if it knows it's being talked about. "I think I should be able to return to work soon."

"Only when you're ready," she says, looking around the diner. "But I won't lie, we could use your help. This time of year is always our busiest, and Willem tells me you're both a quick learner and a hard worker—a killer combination."

I was the one who told her that during my five-second telephone interview, but I keep that to myself. Maybe Willem has told her too.

Why has he ghosted me since the accident? I wonder for the umpteenth time.

Suddenly he's standing beside me, handing Meera a slip of paper with the order he just took. "Hey, Jo, what do you know?" He winces. "That was a dorky thing to say."

He's nervous. I could save him, tell him it wasn't too dorky, but instead I keep my mouth shut and let him flounder for a moment. It's petty, but it feels good.

After an awkward moment—made extra awkward by Meera's continued presence (she smiles and appears to enjoy the drama transpiring before her eyes)—Willem says, "So, um, how are you?"

"You'd know if you'd come to see me."

He opens his mouth to reply, then turns to Meera. "Is it all right if I take my meal break now?"

Meera sighs. "Just when things were getting good. All right, fine, take your break. I'll hold down the fort by myself. But be back in an hour sharp, or the missed time is coming out of your share of the tips."

Willem takes off his apron and places it on the counter with a nod. "Don't worry. I won't be a second late."

"Nice to finally meet you, Joana," Meera says with a smile. "Don't fall off any more—"

"Fuckin' cliffs?" I ask. "I'll do my best. And call me Jo."

"Jo it is."

Once out on the street, I immediately drop my indifferent facade and turn on Willem, jabbing him in the chest with my finger.

"What the serious fuck?" I ask, trying to keep my voice level.

"Ow!" he says, taking a surprised step backward. "What was that for?"

"Take your pick! How about not coming to see me once—not *once*—after my accident? Or how about the fact that I've seen Triss a couple of times since I last saw you, and she's had some interesting things to share. She says hello, by the way." My tone drips with disgust and I spit my words out like daggers designed to cut deep.

It works. Willem winces as if in pain, then shoves his hands in his pockets and looks up and down the street. "Do we have to have this conversation here?"

"Yes!" I say, incredulous.

"Okay, look, I'm sorry. I'm an asshole for not coming to see you. I could say I was busy, and I was, but that wouldn't be the truth, and I'm not going to lie to you."

"So, what's your excuse?"

"Not an excuse," he says. His eyes dart left and right, then settle on me, and I see pain in them. "I was scared."

"Scared?"

"Yes, scared. Practically to death. When I first heard what happened, my mind went to the worst place. I pictured your lifeless body floating face down in Lake Champlain and I lost it. I just shut down. Even though I knew you'd survived, my dreams were haunted by the most gruesome images and . . ." He closes his eyes and shakes his head.

"What?" There's still a slightly sharp edge to my tone, but my anger is beginning to dissipate.

He sighs, then continues reluctantly. "I had this irrational fear that if I went to see you, I'd wake up from a dream. A dream in which I thought you had died, but you hadn't. And waking from this dream, I'd find that you actually *had* died." A thin tear slips from his eye and he wipes it away quickly. "It sounds so stupid, and I know it doesn't make sense, but I somehow became convinced that if I stayed away from you, you'd be alive, and if I went to you, you'd be dead."

I take his hand gently and give it a soft squeeze. "I understand," I say.

He opens his eyes and looks at me in a hopeful way. "Really? I don't sound crazy?"

"No, you definitely sound crazy," I say with a smile. "But I get it. After my mom died, I didn't know what was real and what wasn't. In my mind, sometimes she'd be fine, even though I knew she wasn't. I was constantly thinking things like, 'Maybe if I'm really good and clean up my room and brush my teeth and go to bed early tonight, Mom will come back and tuck me in, kiss my forehead, and tell me she loves me.' And I'd clean my room, and brush my teeth, and turn off the light, and slip under the covers, and close my eyes tight, and hope and pray, and then, eventually, I'd fall asleep. But I always woke up in the morning, alone."

"I'm so sorry," Willem says. "How long did that feeling last?"

"It hasn't really stopped," I say. A tightness is forming in my chest and I need to change the subject. "Anyway, you're off the hook for not coming to see me, but the next time I almost die, you'd better be the first person I see when I open my eyes, okay?"

"Okay," he says with a soft laugh. "So . . . Triss visited you?"

My stomach does a flip, and I hate the way the mere mention of her name causes me to feel physically ill. "Not exactly. She came to our house to pick up her brother today, and I saw her in the park before I fell off the cliff."

"What did she say?"

"Enough," I say. "Too much, actually. You two . . . used to be a thing?"

Willem nods. "We did. But we broke it off before summer break."

"Who did the breaking?" I ask, not really wanting to know but also needing to know.

"She did."

"Do you still have feelings for her?"

"What? No."

He answers so quickly that I feel like he's not telling the full truth. And I'm not stupid enough to think there isn't more to the story. But I'm tired and have bigger problems right now than whatever happened between Triss and Willem. Before I can change the subject, Willem laughs.

"What is it?" I ask.

"I just remembered something. You know how I told you some kids dared me to go knock on your door years ago? It was Triss. Guess she's always been a shit disturber."

"Sounds like she's always been a shit. Full stop."

That elicits a burst of laughter from Willem, and I laugh with him. It feels good.

"I need to know more about the house," I say once we've settled. "I need to know more about the Keils."

"Research is my middle name," Willem says, checking his watch. "And I've still got fifty minutes before I start losing my share of the tips. What do you suggest?"

I look up and down the street, then ask, "Where's the nearest library?"

THE FLETCHER FREE LIBRARY, a beautiful redbrick building that looks as haunted as Mrs. Cracknell's house, is just a few minutes' walk from Darcy's. It's busy and lively, which is perfect—hopefully we can do what we need to do without anyone paying us any attention. I'm not exactly in the mood to explain to a librarian I don't know that I've moved into the infamous Burlington Kill House and want to learn more about the family that once lived there. I haven't even told Willem about the ghosts yet.

"It's over here," he says, leading me to a local history room on the first floor.

"Do you come here often?" I ask.

"That sounds like the dorkiest pickup line ever," he says with a smile. "I've lost track how much dirt I've dug up here for articles I've written. Plus, I like to read, and the price is right."

We enter the local history room and wander around. The shelves are crammed with dusty books, boxes are stacked in each corner, and old maps and black-and-white photographs of Burlington cover the walls. Finally, I find what I'm looking for near the back of the room—a microfilm reader. There's a metal filing cabinet beside it with drawers labeled *Burlington Free Press* and date ranges going all the way back to the 1800s.

"What year did the Keils die?" I ask Willem.

He shrugs. "How should I know? A long time ago?"

"Can you check?"

"You don't have a phone?"

I shake my head, not wanting to explain why I don't. He knows enough about me that it should be obvious.

"Sure, give me a sec," he says. He taps and swipes on his phone, then says, "The exact date isn't known, but their bodies were discovered on October 15, 1954."

I scan the dates and open the drawer labeled *JUL 1954— DEC 1954,* then grab the October box. I take out the roll of microfilm, look at the reader, and then back at the film. "Yeah, so, I have no idea how to work any of this."

"Don't worry, I got you," Willem says. He takes the film from me, attaches it to the left spindle, feeds the film around the rollers and through the glass plate, and then winds it around the take-up reel. With a flip of a switch, the lamp turns on and the front page of the *Burlington Free Press* is projected on the screen before us.

"Impressive," I say.

He shrugs. "It's not that hard, really."

"Yeah, but I've probably been to every library in the state, and that's the first time I've seen anyone do that."

"You weren't kidding when you said you haven't lived long in one place, were you?"

"Not really, no."

"Why have you moved so often?"

My default response to this type of question is to change the subject, but I like Willem, and he's not looking at me with pity or ridicule but with genuine interest, so I find myself opening up—not sharing the full truth but a simplified version of it.

"My dad. He . . . he's a good father, but he has his challenges. Whenever we've stayed in one place for a while, he gets . . . squirrelly, I guess." *He hears voices, the dead speak to him, and now they speak to me too.* I leave that part out. "But he seems to like it here, and so do I. Hopefully we get to stick around for longer than usual."

"I get that. My mom gets depressed sometimes. A *lot* of times, actually. She'll be fine one day and then locked away in her room the next and won't come out for days."

We share a look of understanding. "All families are messed up."

He smiles and nods. "That's why it's so important to make good choices when it comes to friends, girlfriends, boyfriends . . ." His cheeks flush and he clears his throat, then quickly adds, "It must be lonely, moving so often."

"You get used to it." It's a little true, and a little lie. You never *really* get used to it. You just get numb to it. "Anyway," I say, turning my attention back to the microfilm reader. "How do you work this?"

He shows me how to move through the pages by turning a knob just below the screen. I scan through the pages until I come to the paper dated October 15, then slow down. There's nothing of interest in that day's paper, and nothing on October 16 or 17 either, but I hit paydirt on October 18. The headline catches my attention first.

PROMINENT BURLINGTON FAMILY SLAIN IN APPARENT MURDER-SUICIDE

There are two black-and-white photographs accompanying the article. The first is a grainy image of Mrs. Cracknell's house with police officers standing on the front porch and a crowd of curious onlookers on the sidewalk. The second is a portrait of the Keil family.

"Oh my god," I say.

Chapter Nine

I'D EXPECTED THIS—CONFIRMATION THAT the ghosts I'd encountered in my room the other night were indeed the Keils. But seeing their faces—their living, breathing faces—staring out at me from the microfilm reader still catches me completely off guard. My heartbeat picks up—*ta-tump, ta-tump, ta-tump*—but even the sudden rush of blood can't fend off the chill spreading through me. The family's eyes are penetrating and cold.

"What's wrong?" Willem asks.

Think fast, I tell myself. "It's just weird seeing the house in this old newspaper, you know?"

Willem nods but continues to frown, trying to figure out what I'm not saying. He doesn't push any further, so we turn our attention back to the screen and read the article together.

> An entire family is dead in what local authorities are calling the grisliest crime in Burlington's history. Sources say that it's believed Abraham Keil, a recently fired entomologist at the University of Vermont, murdered his three

children—Mariah (15), Isaac (9), and Joshua (1)—before poisoning his wife, Sarah, and himself in the family's large home on South Union Street.

Although the bodies were only discovered on Friday, the murders appear to have been committed more than a month ago. A spokesperson for the university confirmed Mr. Keil was fired at the end of the previous academic year for "theft of university property, erratic behavior, and several performance issues." A fellow professor, who asked to remain anonymous, shared that Mr. Keil had begun speaking to himself earlier this year, and that Mr. Keil was rumored to have recently had an affair with one of his graduate research assistants.

In September, Mr. Keil wrote letters to the older children's schools, explaining that his mother was terminally ill and the family would be visiting her in North Carolina for the next few weeks. Around the same time, he also canceled milk and newspaper deliveries, and requested mail to be held at the post office until his return.

The crime scene was discovered when one of Mr. Keil's previous colleagues at the university stopped by his home for an unplanned visit. When no one answered the door, the unannounced visitor peered through a window and saw what he believed to be a splash of dried blood on the floor of the front foyer.

When police arrived on the scene, they forced their way into the house and discovered the suspected blood was only red paint, but then they found Mr. and Mrs. Keil's bodies in the master bedroom. The couple was pronounced dead at the scene.

A neighbor interviewed by the *Burlington Free Press* described Mr. Keil as a quiet, distant man and Mrs. Keil as a recluse. It was not unusual for many days to pass without anyone from the family being seen outside of their house, including the children. Because of this, the neighbor wasn't alarmed by the fact that the Keils' house lights were left on day and night for the past few weeks, only to recently begin burning out one by one. They did not recall hearing any unusual or alarming sounds from the house around the suspected time of the murders.

"Although, if I didn't know Abe had committed the crime," the neighbor said, "I might've guessed the Missus was responsible. She always struck me as an odd duck, but I suppose that's all she was. A little odd. God rest her soul."

John McCurdy, chief of police, did not divulge many details regarding the fate of the couple's children. He stated there is reason to believe they were killed in a much more violent and gruesome fashion than their mother's murder and father's suicide, and that Mr. Keil attempted to dispose of their remains in the basement. Chief McCurdy said it was the most disturbing crime scene he has ever had to investigate in his twenty-seven years as a police officer.

Mr. Keil is survived by his mother, who is alive and well in North Carolina. Mrs. Keil does not have any surviving family.

Willem leans back in his chair and exhales slowly. "That's some grim shit."

I don't reply, my mind racing in a million different directions. It seems clear now that the mother—Sarah—wasn't trying to harm me but to protect me from her husband, Abraham. Just like she must have tried to protect her own kids back in 1954.

I'm your mother.

"I'm not seeing anything like this online," Willem says, scrolling on his phone.

"Can you take a picture of the article?" I ask.

"No need." He points at a sign on the wall: *The Microfilm Reader Is Connected to the Printer. There Is No Charge for Printing.* "Like I said: the price is right." He clicks a few buttons and a printer in the room whirrs to life, spitting the printout into the tray.

The article's words are darker than onscreen, but still legible. The family photograph is nearly completely black, with very little white. The Keils' eyes have been reduced to tiny pinpricks of light that seem to follow me as I pick up the page, making my skin crawl.

Willem studies me closely. "You didn't want to know more about your house just for the sake of it, did you?"

I open my mouth to reply but pause, unsure of which path to tread. My default thought is to lie, to tell him everything's fine and I'm just curious, but that's so far from the truth that it's ludicrous. And I've been carrying so much weight, so much darkness, alone in my mind that I feel like it's about to spill out of me if only given a slight nudge.

"The house is . . ." I say before trailing off. I take a deep breath and finish the sentence quickly before I can change my mind. "Haunted."

For a moment, as Willem stares at me silently, I think he is going to laugh or tell me I'm nuts, but he surprises me. "I believe you."

"Just like that?" I say, yanking my thumb away from my mouth as soon as I realize I've been chewing my nail. "No follow-up questions?"

"No. It feels too . . . personal. Besides, I believe you, no questions asked." Willem looks at his watch and says, "I've still got a little time if you want to grab a coffee or something. What do you say, pumpkin spice?" He smiles and quickly adds, "I'm not calling you that! I'm suggesting we grab a couple of pumpkin spice lattes."

My cheeks flush, red and warm. "Sounds good, and you can still call me Pumpkin Spice."

What pet name do you think he has for Triss? the voice in my head wonders, but I tell it to shut up.

"Cool, but let's go somewhere—anywhere—other than Darcy's. Otherwise, I'll get sucked back into working early. Jo?" He looks over his shoulder, following my gaze. "What is it, Jo?"

I shake my head and feel like crying. *Not here. Not now.* "You don't see her?" I whisper.

He looks over his shoulder and back again, a look of concern spreading across his face. "There's no one there. We're alone."

But he's wrong. We're not alone. Dead Girl is standing a few feet behind Willem. She's staring at me with wide, sad, unblinking eyes, her skin as pale as before. The crack in her skull hasn't magically healed—her brains are still on full, gory display.

She takes a shaky step toward us.

I suck in a sharp breath of air.

"You're scaring me, Jo," Willem says.

I don't answer. I can't. All I can think about is the girl. Who is she? What does she want with me? And although I don't think she's related to the Keils, how did she follow me here?

She takes another step. A rivulet of blood squirts out of her cracked head and runs down her face. She doesn't wipe it away, and the blood pools around her left eye.

"Jo? Please tell me this is some sort of joke."

"I'm not joking," I tell Willem without taking my eyes off Dead Girl. "There's someone behind you."

"Jesus Christ!" Willem jumps out of his chair and whips his head around the room. "There's no one there!"

I stand and take his hand, guiding him across the room, away from the girl.

"She's dead," I say. "And she's coming at us slowly."

"Well, tell her to piss off!" he says, his voice high and shrill.

"I don't think she'd listen."

She takes another step, proving my point.

"What does she want?" Willem asks.

It's a good question, so I ask her. "What do you want?"

She stops walking and tilts her head slightly. She heard me, but did she understand me?

"What's she doing now?" Willem shifts his weight back and forth from his left foot to his right. "Did she say anything?"

I shake my head. "She's just standing there." I point to where she is, but that doesn't seem to give Willem any peace of mind.

Dead Girl tilts her head to the other side, then slowly points back at me, making me feel sick.

"What do you *want?*" I ask again.

"*You* . . ." Dead Girl says, her voice a wheeze, almost more wind than speech. "*Die* . . ." She reaches her arms out and floats straight at me, passing through Willem as if he wasn't there.

Time for flight.

"Run," I tell Willem. He grabs the article out of the printer's tray and follows me as I dart out of the local history room.

"Hey!" a librarian shouts. "You can't run in the library!"

I pick up my pace and run even faster, straight through the lobby and front entrance, only coming to a stop once I'm safely out on the street.

Willem stops beside me, sucks in a deep breath, and asks, "Is she . . . gone?" Another big lungful of air. "Did she . . . follow us?"

I look back at the library, steeling my nerve, expecting to see Dead Girl float through the doors, but she doesn't. A young father grabs his daughter's hand, gives me a concerned look, then hurries away down the street. But no ghost. I shake my head.

"Good," Willem says. "Did she follow you from your house?"

"No," I say, deciding to leave it at that instead of sharing that she followed me from the hospital.

"I always suspected this library was haunted," he says with a shiver. "Was it just me, or did it get really cold really fast in there?"

"It wasn't just you," I say. "It was her. She flew straight through you."

He scrunches his face and arches his back, trying to process what I've said—it's not every day a ghost passes through your body. But then he seems to come to grips with that, and he even manages to crack a smile.

"Cheap date," he says. "I didn't even buy her dinner first."

"Ha, ha," I say, punching his biceps playfully.

With a laugh, he rubs his arm and shrugs. "You sure got out of there quick."

Running away goes against my grain, but how do you fight a ghost? "She was coming straight for me. She . . . she told me she wanted me to die."

"Why? What did you do to piss her off so bad?"

I can only shrug. "No clue."

BEING CLEARED BY THE doctor for no-contact rugby practice is such happy and welcome news that I forget about all the ghosts haunting me. Luckily, after seeing Dead Girl in the library, I've also had a few quiet nights in a row, but I know not to tempt fate by saying that out loud. I don't even like *thinking* it without knocking on wood. But for now, I'm enjoying this sliver of peace and quiet.

"Welcome back," Coach Howerton says. Her smile is full of caution and concern. "You sure you're ready? Rugby isn't a tickle fight."

"I know," I say as I tie my running shoes' laces, seated on the bleachers beside the pitch. "It's a game for barbarians, played by gentlemen . . . and badass bitches like me."

Her smile grows more genuine. "*Badass bitches*. I like that."

I stand up and stretch my neck. "Don't worry about me. I'll be fine."

Coach nods. "I'm surprised to have you back so soon."

"You and my doctor both."

"So surprised—pleasantly so, I should add—that I got you a welcome back present." She hands me a plastic bag that I'd thought contained her lunch.

Inside is a pair of old rugby cleats with clumps of dried mud and grass packed between the studs.

"They're used, obviously," she says.

"They're perfect." I say. "Thank you."

"No need to thank me. They've been in the lost and found for years. It's safe to say whoever they belonged to has moved on and ain't coming back. And I can't have one of my starting players wearing running shoes on the pitch."

Final cuts were made while I was recovering from my fall. Triss, Alicia, and Summer, who all made the team, walk past. Triss overhears Coach, looks at my second-hand cleats, and laughs. Alicia and Summer join her. The trio looks at me with gleeful pity, then pick up a ball and start passing it back and forth.

"Thanks again, Coach," I say, trying my best to ignore Triss and her followers. I take off my running shoes and try on the cleats. They fit like a glove.

"Don't mention it." She looks at Triss with a frown. "Just . . . take it slow, okay?"

"Okay."

"All right team, gather 'round!"

I get to my feet and join the ring of players encircling Coach.

"Today's practice is going to be touch only. Absolutely no tackling. Everyone understand?"

There are many nods and voiced agreements, with most eyes falling upon me. I'm not sure what my teammates are thinking, but it's painfully clear what's running through Triss's mind. The shit-eating grin plastered on her face clearly says *I'm number one again.*

Guess I won't be hitting her today, I think. Peter and Mrs. Cracknell will be disappointed. The thought makes me laugh. *Good things come to those who wait.*

We get started with the basics: warm-up stretches, a few laps around the pitch, and then a bit of toss. I pair up with Laney, who has gotten much better than the first day of gym class and was pleasantly surprised to make the team.

"What was it like?" She throws the ball to me.

I catch it easily. "What was what like?"

"Falling," she says, her wide eyes full of morbid reverence.

"Oh, uh . . ." I spin the ball in the air and catch it a few times as I think back. "It was . . . scary. It happened fast. I remember thinking I might die, but it was nothing like in the movies. No life flashing before my eyes, no light at the end of the tunnel—just an immediate and all-consuming darkness that overtook me after I hit my head. Then . . . nothing." I throw the ball back to her.

"Cool," she says as she catches the ball. "You're like a superhero or something. Like the Boy Who Lived, or the Girl on Fire."

"I didn't do anything," I say, feeling my cheeks turn beet red. "I just fell."

"The Girl Who Fell," Laney says with a wide smile, proud of the name she's just come up with.

"If falling is a superpower, it's a shitty one." But the fall did change me, didn't it? Before I fell, I had never seen a ghost.

I had seen wet footprints and my closet door rattle, and some sort of living memory of Mom and Uncle Roman, but that was it. Then, immediately after the fall, I see Dead Girl in the hospital and, a few days later, Mrs. Keil and her three dead kids in the basement. If there was a way I could give my newfound "superpower" back, I would.

Laney just shrugs and says, "Nothing exciting ever happens to me."

As if that's a bad thing. What I wouldn't give for an uneventful life. I'd settle for an uneventful *week*.

Coach divides us into two sides for a scrimmage. Laney and I are split up, which is a bit of a shame—I haven't had the chance to make friends on the team yet, and I've spoken with her more than anyone else. As fate would have it, Triss and I are also on opposite sides, giving me the opportunity to show her up a little. She whispers something into Alicia's ear. Summer, standing beside me, crosses her arms and sneers at me.

"What are you so pissy about?" I ask her. "You should be happy to have been placed on the winning side: mine." I walk away, robbing her of the opportunity to reply.

Our scrum half rolls the ball into the scrum and their hooker kicks the ball back to their number eight, who picks it up and quickly throws it down their line. They make good progress, running, throwing, catching, and working their way toward our end. They toss the ball all the way to their left wing, Triss, and I'm the last player who can prevent her from scoring a try. She's nearly out of space on her left so she makes a move to cut back to the midfield. I dig into the ground hard and push off, loving how the cleats allow me to change direction so quickly. I reach out to touch her, but she pulls off an impressive spin move and gets past me. I dig into the ground and change course once again, losing valuable time and allowing her to get a healthy head start on me. I pump my arms and force my legs to run as fast as possible. I can't let Triss beat me on my first day back—I simply can't—so I ignore the voice in my head that says *She's too far away, you'll never make it, it's over, give up.* My lungs burn and my heart beats so hard it feels like it's going to punch a hole through my chest. *Ta-tump-ta-tump-ta-tump!*

I make up a little ground on Triss, but not enough. She's too far ahead, and the try line is too close. She's going to score. She's going to beat me.

No, she's not, a new voice in my head says, giving me a much-needed boost of confidence. I kick off the ground as hard as possible and dive headfirst toward her. My hands slap her on the back and I roll as I hit the ground, protecting my head. When I come to a stop, I look up and see Triss standing in the end zone, holding the ball to the ground.

Coach blows her whistle and says, "No try!"

Laney helps me up with a smile as most of the team—both my side and Triss's—cheer.

"That's bullshit!" Triss says. She throws the ball hard to the ground.

"And that's three laps," Coach tells her. "I won't tolerate language like that on my pitch. That was some fancy footwork, both of you. But Joana, no more dives like that for now, okay?"

I nod as I get to my feet, grass stains on my knees and sweat running down my face.

Coach gives me a subtle wink of approval, then turns and sees Triss still standing behind her, glowering at me. "Am I not speaking English? Three laps! Go!"

Triss curls her lip and grunts, then turns and jogs off.

"Let's reset," Coach tells the team, picking up the ball and walking to the right-hand side of the midfield. She organizes us into a lineout and tells Triss, as she passes us on her second lap, to join in when she's finished her third lap. My side's hooker is given the ball, throws it in, and the props lift the flankers to catch the ball. My side wins the lineout and begins tossing the ball down the line, toward me. We get closer and closer to their try line—if they can get the ball to me without an interception or a dropped pass, I'll have a clear path to a try.

You jinxed it, I think as one of my teammates drops a pass. The ball bounces left and right, and Laney is about to scoop it up, but the girl who dropped the ball is able to recover it at the last moment and fires off a desperate pass to me. The trajectory of the throw is a little behind me, so I have to plant my feet and stop on a dime to catch it. I manage not to drop the ball, but stopping has cost me valuable seconds. There's no time to lose. I kick off and begin to sprint.

And collide with a brick wall. My feet leave the ground, my head rings, and I land square on my back, knocking the air out of my lungs. I roll over and wheeze as I struggle to breathe, but somehow—miraculously—I'm still holding the ball.

"Triss!" Coach yells as she runs to my side. "What is wrong with you today?"

I blink and look around, spotting Triss standing a few feet away. She was the wall I ran into. I hate to admit it, but I'm impressed she managed to remain on her feet.

"What?" she says, giving the world's best *I'm innocent* performance. "I came back on the pitch after my laps, like you said, and she ran into me. I didn't tackle her."

Coach sighs and looks at me in concern. "Are you okay?"

With every breath, I feel a little better. My back's a bit sore, but otherwise I feel okay. "I'm fine," I say as I get to my feet.

"Do I need to cancel today's practice?" Coach asks us all.

We shake our heads and say no.

"No contact, *period*!" She turns and looks at Triss pointedly. "You see someone coming toward you, you get out of the way, understand?"

My back pops as I stretch and line up to resume the scrimmage. I do a few arm circles and pat the stiffness out of my thighs, hoping that I can still beat Triss in a race after that hit.

I get my chance to put that hope to the test during the next play. Her side wins the ball and tosses it down the line to her. She takes off like a lightning bolt and manages to get past me. Try as I might, I can't catch her—my back aches and the best I can do is keep pace.

She's going to score a try, but then she slips on a patch of wet mud and falls to her knees, planting her free hand on the ground.

This is it, I think as time slows down. *The perfect opportunity to smash into her, knee-first, making it look like an accident, giving her a taste of her own medicine.*

Triss looks at me barreling toward her like a locomotive, and she must see the grim determination in my eyes. The look of fear that spreads across her face is almost comical.

It would feel good to hit her, to hurt her even, but what would that make me? The smaller person, no better than her. *Be the bigger person*, I hear Dad say, and I jump as high into the air as my legs will lift me. Triss ducks and I sail over her, missing the top of her head by an inch or two. I land on the ground beyond her, roll on the grass, and get to my feet.

For once in her life, Triss is speechless. Shutting her up, I discover, feels nearly as good as hitting her would have.

I place a hand on her shoulder and say, "You're touched."

She gets to her feet without a word, then hands me the ball and walks away. I take the gesture as a small victory.

AFTER SHOWERING AND GETTING dressed, I take time to clean my cleats in one of the changeroom sinks using hot water and a balled-up paper towel. The sink looks like a muddy crime scene, so I take an extra minute or two to rinse most of the dirt down the drain. By the time I'm finished, the changeroom is empty and silent.

I place my wet cleats back in the plastic bag and walk to the bench to grab my backpack.

Footsteps follow behind me.

I spin around. No one is there.

It's the Peek-a-Boo Boy, I think. *Or Red Eyes, or Dead Girl. One of them has followed me here . . .*

"Hello?" I say, hating the tremor in my voice. "Is someone there?"

The footsteps come closer. Then someone turns the corner.

It's Triss. She's alone.

I sigh and hastily grab my backpack to make a quick exit. "Listen, I don't have the time or the energy for this right now, okay?"

She raises her hands. "I didn't stick around to give you a hard time."

Somehow, Triss looks ready for a photo shoot while my

complexion is still flushed from practice and my hair is a mess. It's petty, but I hate her even more for it.

"Oh, really? What, then? You want to tell me how much Willem still loves you? Or how screwed up my home is . . . my *life* is?"

"No, none of that." She shakes her head, glances around the changeroom, and chews her thumbnail. Is she . . . nervous? "Why did you hold back?"

"What are you talking about?"

"You could have run straight into me and made it look like an accident. And after what I did to you, Coach and everyone else wouldn't have even been mad at you."

"I thought about it," I blurt out before my brain tells my mouth to shut up.

"But you didn't hit me," Triss says. "Why?"

I shrug and set my bag down. "I don't know. I guess, I don't want to hurt you, even though you've been a . . ."

"You can say it."

"A total and complete bitch." Even though I think she might punch me in the face, it's worth it. It's like a weight has lifted off my chest, allowing me to breathe deeply for the first time in a couple of weeks.

Triss nods. "That's fair."

I blink and pull my head back, caught off guard by her reply.

She looks at me and says, "Yeah, I'm surprised too."

"Why?"

"Why am I surprised?"

"No, why have you antagonized me since the moment we met?"

"At Darcy's Diner? The day we bumped into each other?

I was pissed off that you weren't looking where you were going. You could've ruined my outfit, my purse . . ." She raises a finger in the air, closes her eyes, and shakes her head. "No, that's not exactly true. That day, I was . . . upset."

"Why?"

"I'd gone to see Willem." She drops her head and her entire face softens. She looks sad and vulnerable. "I asked him to get back together with me."

A part of me—a small part—feels a little bad for Triss. She's never seemed so human as she does at this moment. "And he turned you down."

Triss nods. Her lips quiver and she looks like she might cry, but she quickly regains her composure. "I'm not used to rejection. I mean, look at me." She laughs to make it clear she's joking, and although I'm certain she's still full of herself, I'm shocked to discover she has a sense of humor.

"Anyway, I guess I should say sorry," Triss says with a quick shrug, staring intently at the floor. Apologizing clearly doesn't come naturally to her.

This conversation couldn't be further from anything I could have guessed would happen today, but it feels good. With everything else on my mind, I'm relieved to have one less concern. "So, what are we, like, friends now or something?"

Triss shakes her head. "Let's not get carried away." We both laugh. "But maybe we don't need to be, you know, enemies."

"I've always wanted a frenemy," I joke. "And Peter and Ash?"

"I guess we can't stop *them* from being friends." Her expression turns serious. "But maybe it would be best if they hang out at my house, not yours."

"Willem said you dared him to knock on Mrs. Cracknell's door when you were kids."

She nods and looks a little surprised. "I'd forgotten about that."

"What do you have against her?" I ask. "Some crazy stuff went down in her house years ago, but she didn't have anything to do with that. And she's a little gruff on the surface, but she's actually really nice."

Triss shakes her head and frowns. "It's nothing personal. Just things people said."

"Kids will say anything. Kids make up shit about other people all the time!"

"Not kids. My parents."

"Your parents?"

"Yeah. When I was young. They told me to never go near that house and to avoid Mrs. Cracknell at all costs. When we'd walk past on the sidewalk, they'd grab my wrist so tight their fingers would leave red and white indents in my skin, then pick up the pace and drag me behind them."

"But why?"

"Because of the murders, obviously. What parent would want their kids lingering around the Burlington Kill House? That house is cursed."

"That has nothing to do with Mrs. Cracknell," I say.

Triss's voice drops an octave or two. "You sure about that?"

I open my mouth to respond, but something in Triss's tone gives me pause.

She continues. "Before I started daring other kids to go knock on her door, I did it myself. I was in, like, second or third grade, and I recall seeing her sitting on her front porch as I walked past and later thinking, 'She didn't look so bad. My parents must have been wrong about her.' I had this overwhelming urge to return and knock on her door to prove I was brave enough. So, the next day after school, that's what I did. I knocked, and she answered."

Triss closes her eyes, takes a deep breath, lets it out slowly, then continues.

"The door flew open, and she was standing there *butt-fucking-naked*. I was appalled, disgusted, but also terrified. I'd never seen anyone naked before, and I knew she must have been out of her mind. She had this wild look in her eyes, like she hadn't slept in days, and the things she said . . . Jesus, I've tried, but I'll never forget them."

She pauses, and although I don't think I want to know, I *need* to know. "What did she say?"

"She said a lot. Most of it nonsense, ramblings. But some of it I understood all too well. When her eyes finally found me, she accused me of being one of them. She screamed at me to get out of her head. And she threatened to kill me."

"Are you kidding me?" Triss's story has completely blindsided me. I can't possibly imagine Mrs. Cracknell doing or saying anything like that.

"I wish that I was," Triss says. "She kept telling me I was dead." She points a shaking finger at a spot in the distance, hunches her back, and squints her eyes, impersonating Mrs. Cracknell. "*You're dead. You're dead, you're dead, you're dead!*" Triss drops her finger and then holds up her other hand. Her fingers are curled as if she's holding something invisible, and a tear runs down her cheek. "That's when I noticed what she held, concealed behind her bare-ass back. A kitchen knife, and not one of the little ones. Must have been at least six inches long, and sharp too. My wide eyes stared back at me, reflected in the blade. She raised the knife high and I took off like a shot, screaming all the way home. I couldn't bring myself to tell anyone what had happened. And yeah, I know how all this makes me sound. Why would I send other kids to her door to possibly be butchered and flayed alive? But it helped me cope with my trauma, somehow, and it's not like anyone died."

I shake my head, thinking it was awful of Triss to do that. But then again, we all do things we regret when we're young. *Some of us hide under the bed while our mother is—*

"Shut up," I say, silencing the voice in my head.

"Excuse me?" Triss says.

"Sorry, I didn't mean to say that out loud, and not to you." Triss looks at me warily, so I quickly change the subject. "Mrs. Cracknell wouldn't hurt a fly."

"Just be careful there, okay?" Triss says with a shocking amount of compassion. Wonders never cease.

"I will," I say with a nod, thinking maybe . . . *maybe* I should be watchful of more than just the ghosts.

I sigh. As if I needed another reason to be on guard in my new home.

Chapter Ten

THE BASEMENT IS AS quiet as a mausoleum as I walk down the steps and drop my backpack and rugby cleats in my bedroom. I poke my head into each of the other rooms.

"Peter? Dad?"

No answer. That's weird. Peter might have gone to hang out with Ash after school, but Dad should be home. Victor was in the driveway and I didn't see Dad outside doing handywork.

Thump, thump, thump!

My shoulders tense up and I have to force them back down. I heard footsteps directly overhead, much too heavy to be Mrs. Cracknell.

I creep up the stairs, listening as I approach the door. It's closed, but I can make out a muffled conversation from the other side.

Someone says something like "I'll check." Then I hear footsteps quickly approach the basement and see shadows cast by a pair of feet through the crack between the floor and the door. The door opens quickly. Dad looks down at me and flinches, startled.

"Shit," he says, putting a hand to his chest and gripping his shirt before regaining his composure. "Sorry, Jo. I didn't expect you to be right there. I was coming down to see if you were back from practice yet."

"Yeah, um, I was just coming to see if you were upstairs. What's up?"

"Mrs. Cracknell invited us to dinner," he says. "Only catch is, we have to make it. Come give us a hand."

I shake my head and pat my stomach. "Oh, no thanks. I'm not hungry." It's not true—I'm starving—but after what Triss told me about Mrs. Cracknell, I don't feel like spending much time with her at the moment.

"After practice? I don't believe that for a second. You're a teenager, you're always hungry."

"Yeah, I'm just tired, I guess."

"Is that Joana?" Peter says from the direction of the kitchen.

"It is," Dad calls over his shoulder. "She just got home."

"Well, tell her to get in here! I'm completely out of my element with these potatoes and I need her help!"

Dad looks at me and raises his eyebrows.

"All right, fine," I say, joining Dad in the hall. I leave the basement door open a crack, just in case we need to make a hasty exit. "I guess I could eat."

We enter the kitchen. Peter is standing at the sink, wearing a rose-patterned apron with white frills, peeling potatoes.

"Thank god you're here," he says, his cheeks flushed and his forehead beaded with sweat. "I'm hopeless at this."

"Nonsense," Mrs. Cracknell says. She's standing beside him, chopping the potatoes he's peeled. "You're hope *deficient*, but not hope*less*."

She's using the same knife she pulled on Triss, the voice in my head thinks.

Suddenly, Mrs. Cracknell's clothes disappear and she's standing before me as naked as the day she was born, but old, saggy, and wrinkled. I blink, and when I look again, she's covered in thick, coagulated blood, sliding slowly down her skin. I blink once more and she's raised the knife above her head, ready to bury it in Peter's back. I blink a final time and she's back to normal—just an old lady in her kitchen, fully clothed, no blood, chopping potatoes.

"Ow!" Peter says with a sharp intake of air. He drops the peeler into the sink with a *clang*, then sticks his thumb in his mouth and sucks on it. "Stupid peeler. I cut myself."

Dad moves to help, but Mrs. Cracknell is there first.

"Let's see," she says, guiding his hand down to her eye level and examining it. A bead of blood blossoms on the tip of his thumb, close to the nail. She examines the blood intently, which gives me an odd feeling. My concern grows when I notice she's still holding her knife, but a moment later, she places it on the cutting board. I exhale a breath I hadn't realized I'd held. Mrs. Cracknell wraps Peter's thumb in a washcloth and tells him to hold it tight.

"How bad is it?" Peter asks, looking a little pale, his head turned to the side and his eyes closed tight. He's never been good with the sight of his own blood.

"I think we're going to need to take you to the hospital," Mrs. Cracknell says.

"Really?" Peter asks, a sharp note of desperation in his tone.

"Not even remotely," Mrs. Cracknell says. "It's nothing more than a scratch. Put some pressure on it and it will stop bleeding before you can say knife."

I frown. "That's the second time you've used that expression."

Mrs. Cracknell picks up her knife, looks at it for a moment, then resumes chopping potatoes. "My grandfather used to say it all the time. He practically raised me. Suppose I picked up many of his expressions."

Peter sits down at the kitchen table, gripping the washcloth over his thumb like his life depends upon it. I take over peeling potatoes, keeping a close eye on Mrs. Cracknell. Dad places a baking dish with chicken breasts smothered in cranberry sauce in the oven and sets a timer. I fry some asparagus as Mrs. Cracknell boils and mashes the potatoes, adding a healthy amount of butter and cream cheese to the pot. Enough time has passed for Peter to have gotten over the shock of seeing a pinprick of his own blood, so he sets the table and places the hot food dishes on cork trivets.

"Don't forget the rolls," Mrs. Cracknell says, handing me a bag from a local bakery. "Man cannot live by bread alone, but no dinner is complete without it." Our eyes lock briefly, then she nods. "Yes, that one was my grandfather's too."

I only begin to let my guard down a little after my first few bites. The food is delicious, and so much more satisfying than my standard fare of Cheerios, peanut butter sandwiches, Kraft Dinner, and hot dogs. After my second helping, I feel like I'm about to burst, and excuse myself to use the washroom.

"Use the one on the second floor," Mrs. Cracknell says. "The drain is slow in the ground-level powder room."

"Why didn't you say so before?" Dad asks, sounding a little hurt.

"All in good time," Mrs. Cracknell says, turning her attention back to me. "Up the stairs and turn right. Second door on your left."

After a moments hesitation, I strike out into the unknown. "Thanks. I'll be right back."

Their voices fade away as I walk up the stairs and take a right, passing old paintings in antique frames hung on the walls. Before me there are two doors on both sides of the hall and one at the end of it. It's the only one that's open, just a crack. I can't see anything in the room—it's pitch-black inside. Something about the room, the door, and the darkness gives me a chill, but I shake it off. I'm about to open the bathroom door when, out of the corner of my eye, I think I see something move in the room—a shift in the shadows. I pause and stare but see nothing. The soft rustle of wind, so faint I question whether it's just my imagination, drifts out of the room. I quickly step into the bathroom, turn on the light, and lock the handle, hesitating with my back against the door.

"Get a grip," I tell myself, but I keep my eye on the door, half expecting the handle to rattle. Once I'm done using the toilet, I flush, wash my hands, and splash some water on my face, then look at my reflection in the mirror. The bags beneath my eyes haven't improved since the day we first landed in Burlington. I sigh and rub my eyes, and when I open them again there's a man standing directly behind me.

"Fuck!" I say as I spin around, shielding my face with my forearms.

There's no one there.

I pull back the shower curtain, just in case. The tub is empty.

I examine the mirror, trying to figure out what I mistook for a person, but can't figure it out. Maybe the towel rack? No, it's too low. Feeling a little silly, I swing the mirror open to make sure it's not some sort of trick glass. Behind are three narrow shelves crammed with pill bottles. One of the bottles tumbles out and I manage to catch it before it clatters in the sink. As I place it back on the shelf, I study the bottles' labels. They all have Mrs. Cracknell's name printed on them—her first name is Rose—and although some are recent, others are from five, ten, even twenty years ago.

"Clozapine?" I say, reading aloud the name of the medication printed on the bottle I caught. The name sounds familiar, but I'm not sure why, or what it's for. I close the mirror, picturing the man I thought I saw before, but there's still no one there. I'm about to leave when a drop of water lands on my head.

Plink!

Followed quickly by two more.

Plink plink!

I run my hand through my hair, then look at my fingertips. They're not wet with water. They're slick with blood. I look up. There's a dusty air vent in the ceiling above my head, and it looks like there's something in there, resting against the grill.

Another drop of blood falls. I lean back just in time to see it pass in front of my face and hit the edge of the sink. It splashes and streaks down the side.

"What the hell?" Did some animal crawl into the vents to die?

I grab a plunger from behind the toilet and reach it up toward the ceiling.

What are you doing? my brain screams at me. *Leave it alone!* But I need to know. I need to see.

I'm able to lift the grill an inch or two, but there's something heavy on it, weighing it down. I push a little harder and lift the grill slightly higher.

Something thin and black creeps out of the vent and winds around the top of the plunger handle like a small, probing tentacle. It's a centipede, its legs undulating as it quickly crawls down the handle toward my hand.

With a sound of disgust, I drop the plunger. It clatters to the floor. The centipede falls into the sink, disappearing down the drain as quickly as its legs can move. The vent grate slams shut and breaks open. The thing that had weighed it down comes tumbling out. My reflexes take over and, without thinking, I catch it.

It's a decomposing head. Waxen skin, mouth agape, and empty, bloody eye sockets staring up at me. I recognize the face immediately. Red Eyes. Mariah. The Keils' eldest child.

Her mouth opens to say something, but instead of words, what comes out is another centipede. It crawls over her upper lip and nose, curling into a tight ball in one of her sockets, looking like the world's most fucked-up fake eye.

The food that tasted so good at dinnertime threatens to make a reappearance as I drop Mariah's head in mute horror.

But it doesn't fall to the floor. A man grabs Mariah's head by the hair as soon as I let go. The same man I caught a glimpse of before. The same man I saw in the family photo in the newspaper article. Abraham Keil.

"I'll take that," he tells me as he raises Mariah's head in the air, holding her grayish face close to his own. The sleeves of his button-up shirt are rolled up, revealing long, jagged, bloody scrapes from his elbows to his wrists. "My dear, sweet daughter, you don't look so good."

There's a time for fighting, but this isn't it. I fly out of the bathroom and have taken a few steps down the hall, picking up speed, when I see her.

Dead Girl is standing in front of me, her arms limp at her sides, brains leaking out of her head and splattering on the floor, blocking my path.

"No," I say in disbelief, my own voice sounding distant in my ears. I try to stop but my feet slide out from under me. I fall on my ass and immediately scramble backward to get as far away from her as possible, but I feel like I'm moving in slow motion, not nearly fast enough.

Dead Girl's feet lift off the floor and she glides through the air toward me.

At least Abraham and his daughter's decapitated head haven't followed me out of the bathroom. I get to my feet and run away from Dead Girl, my eyes set on the open door at the end of the hall. I slam into it with my shoulder, drop to the floor in the room, close the door, and push against it with all my weight. I dig my heels into the ground, preparing for Dead Girl or Abraham to break the door off its hinges, but nothing happens. The silent anticipation is somehow worse.

Something knocks on the door three times, violently loud, sending shockwaves through my body and rattling my bones. I yell and push more forcefully, fearing I won't be able to stop whoever's there from barging their way through.

"Joana?" It's Dad's voice. "What's going on? We heard a racket."

Thank god it's Dad.

"Yeah, it's me," I say, getting to my feet. I open the door and see Dad isn't alone. Peter and Mrs. Cracknell are standing behind him, all three looking confused and concerned. I peek behind them but see no sign of Dead Girl in the hall.

"What are you doing in my bedroom?" Mrs. Cracknell asks. She's holding the knife.

What am I going to say? I can't tell them what really happened.

But maybe I can tell them one small *part* of what happened.

"This is going to sound really stupid, but a centipede fell from the bathroom ceiling and landed in my hair." I steal a glance at my fingers, expecting to see the blood that dripped on my head, but my hands are clean. "I totally freaked out, ran down the hall, and hid in here."

"All right, well, everything's okay now," Dad says with a reassuring smile. He flips on the light switch.

"No!" Mrs. Cracknell says in a gasp.

"The centipede is gone . . ." Dad's words trail off as he looks around the room.

Peter and I are speechless too. It's a large room with a king-sized bed and a wall-mounted bulletin board covered in clippings from the *Burlington Free Press*. But what commands my attention are the glass containers. They cover every available surface—tables, dressers, desks, folding trays . . . there are even several on the floor. They're filled with dirt, rocks, plants, and sticks.

Then, one of the sticks *moves*.

It takes my brain a second to play catch-up, but I finally realize it's not a stick but a stick bug. I look at another container and see butterflies hanging off a branch. A tarantula crawls out of a hole in a rock in another. Two scorpions skitter toward each other in the next container, their claws spread wide and their tails raised to strike. Hundreds, if not thousands, of ants march in all directions through the tunnels they've dug in an ant farm.

"They're all full of insects," I say, feeling my skin crawl. I scratch my back and my scalp, feeling like I'm covered in bugs.

Mrs. Cracknell looks at the floor, unable to meet our eyes, as if she's ashamed. "I found them in the basement when I moved in."

"So, you brought them up here . . . where you sleep?" I ask.

"No, not at first. All these containers were empty. I think the bugs had gotten out somehow, or maybe Mr. Keil let them out before he did . . . what he did. They had taken root in the walls and infested the house. That's probably why I got such a good deal on it. Well, that and the murders, of course. But truth be told, I felt a little bad for the insects—in a way, I'd moved into their home, after all. So, I learned how to trap them, and one by one I filled all these." She places the knife down on the table and presses her fingertips to the glass of the stick bug's container, and it slowly makes its way to her. "They were always more active at night, so keeping the containers in my bedroom made it easier to collect them. With time, I came to care for them, and their larvae, and on and on. I guess living a life alone will make people seek comfort and company in any number of strange and unusual places."

I can't help but feel a little sorry for her. Did I really think she was some sort of knife-wielding maniac, like Triss would have had me believe? That she was going to kill me and my family, cut us up into tiny pieces, and feed us into the furnace to reduce us to ash and teeth? She's just an old lady—a little gruff, but lonely. The thought that she'd answer the door naked and threaten to kill Triss is unfathomable; Triss must have been trying to mess with me.

"I couldn't trap *all* the insects, of course," Mrs. Cracknell says. "Many are still loose, but I promise they won't harm you."

"Like the deathwatch beetles," I say.

She nods and adds, "And the centipede you saw in the washroom. Can you show me where it came from?"

We leave the bedroom, and I can't say I miss it. I don't have a phobia of insects, but a room filled with them? No, thanks.

I'm the first to enter the bathroom. "It dropped out of—" I stop talking as soon as I look up.

The vent is closed. But it was open, broken, when I ran out. And the plunger is tucked back behind the toilet. I had dropped it on the floor. Did I imagine all of it? The blood, the centipede, Mariah's head, Abraham? Even Dead Girl?

"Dropped out of what?" Peter asks.

"Um, the vent."

"I'll take a look," Dad says, stepping up onto the counter.

My heartbeat picks up, *ta-tump, ta-tump, ta-tump.* What if her head is back up there again? I clench my fists, wanting to look away but powerless to do so.

He runs his fingers over the edges of the vent cover, poking and prodding, before stepping back down off the counter. "If there are still any centipedes up there, I can't get to them now. The cover is sealed shut. I'll get my tools."

All I can think is *How? How, how, how?*

"It can wait," Mrs. Cracknell says. She gives me a pointed look, but I can't figure out her meaning. "Neither the insects nor the house are going anywhere any time soon. Besides, it's time for dessert."

If there's one thing I know about my dad, it's that he hates leaving a job until later. But he can tell from Mrs. Cracknell's tone of finality that she won't be swayed, so he reluctantly nods and steps out of the bathroom. Mrs. Cracknell follows him.

"You okay?" Peter whispers as we hang back a moment.

I nod and say, "Mm-hmm."

Back downstairs in the kitchen, Mrs. Cracknell serves us apple crisp with vanilla ice cream. I take small bites I barely taste, trying to pretend like a ghost didn't just talk to his daughter's decapitated head while I stood mere inches away, watching in mute horror. Or that Dead Girl wasn't waiting for me when I ran into the hallway.

Where are they now? The rational part of my brain tries to tell me they weren't real . . . but I can still feel their eyes on me.

I place my spoon down, not able to stomach another bite. The remaining ice cream melts into a white puddle that soaks into the apple crisp. A headache begins to pulse at the front of my forehead. Closing my eyes doesn't help. There are two things I want above all else—to keep my family safe, and to hang desperately onto the little sliver of stability we've found here in Mrs. Cracknell's basement apartment—but those wants are at odds with one another. After what I've seen this evening, I know, deep down, that I can't have both. I have to pick one.

By the time everyone else has finished their dessert, I've made my choice.

Chapter Eleven

"MY DEAR, SWEET DAUGHTER," I say later that evening, back in our apartment, "you don't look so good."

Dad and Peter sit and stare, silent and still. Peter's eyes are almost as wide as his mouth, and Dad . . . well, Dad looks like he's going to cry or punch a hole in the wall. Maybe both.

"Guys, say something," I implore them. I can't take the silence any longer.

Finally, Peter speaks. "That is so fucked up."

Dad doesn't scold him for swearing. He just looks around the room, shaking slightly.

"He actually said that to her *head*?" Peter says.

I nod and lean back on the couch, exhaling loudly. Telling them about my encounter with Abraham in Mrs. Cracknell's washroom—and, before that, finally filling them in on the night Sarah and her children appeared in my room—has completely drained me. I feel like a net trying to hold water, only the water is my spirit, my soul, my *everything*.

"Do you see them all the time?" Peter asks. He glances over his shoulder. "Are they here with us now?"

"No, most of the time I don't see them. Sometimes I feel like I'm being watched, but that's probably just my nerves getting the better of me."

"Where do they go when you can't see them? And why do they decide to appear when they do?"

"Your guesses are as good as mine," I say.

Peter sighs. "This is a lot."

"No kidding." I wish that was everything, but it's not. I take a deep breath and dive in, knowing if I don't finish this now, I might not ever. "There's one more thing. After I fell off the cliff, when I woke up, I saw someone in my hospital room. A girl, standing behind you both. She was dead. And she . . ." I look at Dad, wondering how he'll react to what I say next. "She followed me here."

The words have barely left my mouth when Dad says, "Goddamn it. I knew we shouldn't have come here."

"To this house?" I ask.

He shakes his head and rubs his face. "To this city."

"Why? What is it about Burlington that made you avoid it all these years, only to come back now?"

Dad shakes his head again as he looks away and crosses his arms. "Forget it. Forget I said anything."

"No chance," I say.

He cranes his head back as if taking note of me for the first time. "Excuse me? I said, *forget it*."

But I'm not backing down, not this time. "I just told you all the crazy shit I've been dealing with, and you're going to sit there and stonewall me? I don't think so."

This time, Dad doesn't immediately shoot me down. He hesitates, and I know he's weighing the pros and cons of giving us some answers.

"All right, fine," he says, his voice low and gruff, like sandpaper on rough wood. "I used to live here a long time ago."

"How long ago?" Peter asks.

"Before either of you were born." He sighs, then adds, "That's not true. You were both born here, in the same hospital where Jo was taken when she fell off the cliff."

"Was Mom . . " Something sticks in my throat. I clear it before finishing the question. "Killed here?"

He closes his eyes, frowns, and nods.

That's why he didn't want to come back for so long, why Burlington is just about the only city or town in the entire state we've avoided since we started moving. The thought of settling here must have been too painful. The wound caused by my mother's murder is still not fully healed, and Dad must have a thousand memories of her here.

A sudden question pops into my head and I blurt it out even though now might not be the best time. "Have you ever heard or seen Mom since she died?"

"No," he says with a tone of such finality that I don't question him any further.

"All those years we spent moving from town to town," I say, thinking back on our past, trying to add up all the places we've lived and quickly losing count. "All the while avoiding Burlington. What brought you back now?"

Dad thinks about my question for a moment, his brow furrowed, his eyes thin slits. "We had lived practically everywhere else in Vermont."

"Why not leave the state?" Peter asks. "New York, Massachusetts, New Hampshire—"

Dad cuts him off. "New Hampshire? Wash your mouth

out with soap!" He maintains his serious, gruff expression for a few seconds before a smile slowly spreads across his face and he laughs.

His joke isn't particularly funny, but I haven't heard him laugh in far too long, and the sound is infectious. Before long, Peter and I are laughing with him.

"It was actually this house that pulled me here," he says once we've settled down. "I saw it in the paper, and the opportunity seemed too great to pass on, no matter how painful my memories of Burlington are."

Something isn't lining up about his story. "But you found the listing when we were in Darcy's Diner, the first morning we arrived. Your coffee cup formed a circle around it."

He shrugs and offers me a half-smile. "Maybe that was a little less than spontaneous."

"What?" I'm not mad, just surprised.

"I wasn't sure I'd be able to go through with it and move back here, but as soon as we drove into town, I knew."

"Knew what?" Peter asks.

I have a feeling I already know. It's how I felt when we arrived too.

"This was home." Dad sighs, a long, drawn-out sound filled with equal parts sadness and regret. "But that doesn't matter. We can't stay now that Jo has the Whisperings." He looks us both over, and although nothing about this conversation has been easy, it looks like a weight has been lifted off him. Sometimes the simple act of making a decision—especially a tough one—can be liberating. "We need to leave now."

Even though I know in my heart it's what we need to do, it pains me to hear it said aloud. And although I'm accustomed—

deadened, even—to picking up and leaving in the middle of the night, this one stings.

"Can we, maybe, leave in the morning?" I ask. "I'd like to see Willem one more time, tell him what's going on, so he doesn't think I ghosted him."

"I wouldn't mind telling Ash the same thing," Peter adds hopefully.

My dad's lips bulge as he runs his tongue over his teeth. He doesn't look thrilled by the request, but he doesn't shoot it down immediately either. "Fine. But we'll share a room, just to be safe. Mine—*not* Jo's."

I can't say I'm thrilled by the prospect of the three of us sharing a bed, but I can't say I want to spend the night alone, either. A similar but slightly more appealing arrangement is sleeping on the floor in Dad's room, so I grab my bedding and pillow and dump them in a pile beside his bed. It doesn't look like much, but it's soft and warm. And we're together.

"You sure you're all right down there, Jo?" Dad asks from the far side of the bed.

"I'm fine," I say, staring up at the ceiling. There's a brown water stain above my head, similar to the heart-shaped one in my room.

Peter peers down at me from his side of the bed. "Let me know if you see any insects and, um, want to trade places."

"I'm fine, and there aren't any insects." *Yet*.

"That's good," he says, and I wonder if he's talking about the lack of insects, or that I didn't take him up on his offer. "Did you know everyone swallows an average of eight spiders in their sleep each year?"

With a shake of my head and a roll of my eyes, I shift onto

my side. "That's a myth—people don't swallow spiders while asleep—and again, there aren't any bugs down here."

Right on cue, an earwig skitters out from beneath the bed. I strike immediately, slapping the floor and feeling crunchy bug bits squish under my palm.

"What was that?" Peter asks. "Was that a bug? Did you just squash a bug? That was a bug, wasn't it?"

"Relax, it was just a muscle spasm." He's already on edge, and if I tell him what really happened, we'll all get even less sleep than we're currently destined to.

Dad is the first to drift off, his heavy breathing filling the room. Peter is asleep soon after, their snores forming the most irritating harmony one could possibly imagine. I envy them. My sleep is rarely so peaceful. The ceiling stain seems to shift slightly every time I take my eyes off it. I examine my nails, practice deep-breathing techniques, even count stupid sheep, but none of it helps. I can't stop thinking about everything that happened today. Abraham, Mariah's decapitated head, and Dead Girl all appear in my mind whenever I close my eyes.

Something shuffles and I look around warily, not sure I'm going to like what I see. But it's only Peter. He's sitting up in bed. His eyes are open, but they're unfocused, like he's not seeing anything.

"Peter?"

He doesn't answer, move, or even blink.

"Peter," I say again, a little louder.

Still, nothing.

He's sleeping. With his eyes open, which makes my skin crawl. He swings his legs off the edge of the mattress, stands up, and walks into the hall like a robot.

"No," I say under my breath, not wanting to wake Dad. I stand up and follow my brother, exiting Dad's room just in time to see Peter enter mine.

I race to the doorway and see Hollow Mother—Sarah—begging Peter to hide in the red room with her. Before I can do or say anything to protect my brother, Abraham steps out of the shadows and chops an axe clean through Peter's neck with one brutal blow. I stand rooted to the ground, unable to move, unable to think, unable to comprehend what I'm seeing, but painfully aware of the most harrowing feeling of pain and hollowness I've felt in thirteen years currently filling my chest. My brother's head hits the floor and rolls across the hall, painting the walls red with his blood, and comes to a stop at my feet. He looks up at me—his eyes are no longer unfocused but full of life, wide and fearful, and I see something else in them too. They're questioning, accusatory. His mouth opens and closes, opens and closes, opens and closes, and the most horrendous, wet, choking sound gurgles out of the back of his throat. He's not trying to breathe—he's trying to speak, but it sounds like his mouth is full of blood.

"Your . . ." he sputters. "Fault . . ."

Abraham, suddenly standing right in front of me, grabs a fistful of Peter's hair and yanks his decapitated head high in the air like a hunting trophy, like he did with Mariah's head. The scrapes on Abraham's forearms pulse with coagulated blood. He laughs, his booming voice reverberating in my eardrums.

Peter continues to stare at me, his accusatory look heating into anger, as a steady stream of blood waterfalls to the floor. My socks soak it up, turning my feet red.

"Your..."

His skin turns yellow, then gray, then black.

"Fault..."

His eyes become bloodshot, such a dark red that I can no longer see his pupils.

"Your..."

His tongue hangs limply out the corner of his mouth, bloated and pulsating, turning an angry shade of purple. Pulse, pulse, pulse. I can't look away from it no matter how much the sight sickens me. Pulse, pulse, pulse. I can't even move; my feet are cemented to the floor. Pulse, pulse, *pop!* It explodes with a wet spray, leaving behind a wreckage of flesh that looks like a shriveled meat balloon. He clenches his jaw and bites down hard, severing what's left of his tongue. It falls to the ground with a loud slap. I kick it away in disgust. His blood has soaked halfway up the legs of my pajama pants.

"*Faaa...*" His head rocks back and forth three times, building enough momentum to reach my face. He opens his mouth wide and clamps his teeth down, biting into my nose. Blinding pain shoots through my face and I pull back as hard as I can, screaming and crying and shaking with adrenaline. My skin tears. Blood runs over my lips and chin. The final thread of flesh that holds my nose to my face rips free and I fall to the ground. Peter chews my nose three times, then swallows. My mangled wad of flesh pushes through the gaping hole where his neck used to be and falls to the ground.

I feel faint and dizzy, but just as my vision is growing dim, both Abraham and Peter's head disappear, as does all of my brother's blood. The hall is empty. I rub my face and feel my nose right where it should be. The vision was so vivid that I thought it was real.

At least Peter's okay. But then I realize he might not be. He sleepwalked into my room and hasn't come out. A wave of panic rolls through me as I race through the hall.

Thud, thud, thud. The sound comes from inside my room. I enter but don't see Peter. I hear the thudding again, from within the closet. I fling the door open and find my brother. He's just standing there, his back to me, hitting his head against the wall above the hole in the drywall.

"Peter?" I ask.

He doesn't answer. *Thud, thud, thud.*

My hand trembles as I reach out and touch his shoulder. I feel him, so this can't be another vision.

You felt your brother bite your nose off, I remind myself.

Thud, thud, thud.

"Peter!" I say more loudly, as I place my other hand between his forehead and the wall. He continues to rock back and forth, but my hand softens his blows. I hold his chin and guide him to face me.

"Mom?" he says, looking at me but still not seeing me.

I shake my head. "No, Peter. It's me, Jo. Your sister."

"Mom," he says again, looking straight through me.

I glance over my shoulder. There's no one there.

"You're sleepwalking. You're dreaming. Let's get you back to bed." I take his hand—his skin is cold and clammy—and lead him out of the closet. Before I close the door, I see—no, I *think* I see—a blur of movement in the red room. I pick up my pace, wishing Peter would move faster, but he's shuffling his feet like a zombie. I begin to feel better once we're safely back in Dad's room.

"Mom," Peter says one final time as I guide him down beside Dad. He closes his eyes and rolls over onto his side. Hopefully he won't wake up again for the rest of the night.

I lie back down on the floor and stare at the ceiling again, wondering if I'll get any sleep at all. I must doze off, though, because some time later—maybe an hour, maybe less, maybe more—I open my eyes and the pale blue shaft of moonlight on the wall has shifted a few feet.

Something tickles my arm. It's a spider, crawling toward my shoulder. I brush it off quickly with a shiver of disgust. It lands on the ground and skitters into the shadows.

Was it headed for my mouth? I wonder, wishing Peter hadn't put that thought in my head.

Something tickles my arm again. Another spider, or maybe the same one. I brush it off and it scurries across the floor. Déjà vu.

With a sigh, I roll onto my side and face the wall, pulling my blanket all the way up to my neck, hoping that will be the end of it.

But then, the spider returns. Its legs poke and prod me through the blanket.

That's it! I dart my hand blindly in its direction. It's fast—my fingers graze its bony back as it retreats.

That wasn't a spider, I think as I sit up and look around.

There's no sign of it.

For once, you're right, the voice in my head says, imploring my brain to listen, willing my mind to clue into what touched me. *That wasn't a spider. It was a hand. A* human *hand.*

Dad and Peter are lying stone-still, sound asleep. There's no one else in the room. If it was a hand, who touched me, and where did they go?

Under the bed. It's the only place someone could hide so quickly. I force myself to look, hoping I see nothing but darkness and dust bunnies.

But there's a woman there, staring out at me with a wide grin. She raises a finger to her lips and makes a *shh* sound, smiling all the while. It takes me a moment to realize it's Mom.

"Round and round the garden, like a teddy bear," she says. "One step, two step, tickle you under there!" Her hand darts out and scratches my arm. Her touch doesn't tickle; it stings. I suck in a sharp breath and pull back. With a frown, she withdraws her hand as if slapped. "What's wrong, sunshine? Aren't you happy to see me?"

There's one thing I'm certain of immediately. This ghost or vision hiding under the bed, waking me with a tickle in the middle of the night, isn't my mom.

But the longer I look at her, as tired and weary as I am, I slowly stop caring. She looks like Mom. She sounds like Mom. She even smells like Mom.

A smile slowly spreads across her face, as if she can hear my thoughts. "Of course you're happy to see me."

The desire to be closer to her, pressed up tight enough to feel the rise and fall of her chest, to hear the gentle beat of her heart, suddenly overwhelms me.

Mom smiles even wider. Unnaturally wide. She slides back, creating a little extra space between us, and pats the floor. "Come closer," she coos. "Come join me under here."

I'm helpless to disobey and waste little time slipping out from under my blanket and sliding on my back under the bed. It's such a tight squeeze that my nose presses against the bottom of the bedframe.

Mom slides an arm under my back, wraps me in a tight embrace, and pulls me in close to her.

I don't feel her chest rising or falling. I don't feel her heartbeat. But I don't care. It feels good to be held by her again.

"I've missed you, Mom," I say, grabbing hold of her forearm and pulling it tighter against my chest, as tight as possible. I close my eyes and smile.

The room is silent. If it weren't for the feeling of my mom's arm in my hands, I'd wonder if she had disappeared. But I still smell her—only, her normal scent now has a hint of lavender. In fact, I think the lavender is being used to cover something up. Something sharp and rancid, like rotting meat. I'm about to repeat what I said, assuming Mom didn't hear me when I told her I've missed her, when she finally answers.

"I'm not your mother."

I open my eyes and begin to turn my head to look at her, but at that moment either Dad or Peter shifts their position in the bed and the underside of the box spring presses down into my face, pinning me in place.

"What?" I say, icy dread quickly spreading through me.

"*Too-ra-loo-ra-loo-ral*," she says in a singsong voice. "I said, I'm not your mother."

I suddenly feel trapped. I *am* trapped. The bed is pushing down on me and not-Mom is holding me in place. I look down. The skin of her hand looks gray and papery, like an old, abandoned wasp's nest. I try to pry her fingers off me, but it's as if they're made of cement.

"Let me go," I say, but to no effect.

Someone in the bed shifts again, and I gain enough space to turn my head. I expect to see a ghost beside me, but it's still Mom. Only her skin is all-over lifeless, like her hand, and her eyes are cloudy.

"I'm not your mother," she says again and again. With every word, she dies before my eyes. Her skin flakes off her bones. Her teeth blacken and fall out of her mouth. Her hair grows wispy and white. And her eyeballs roll back and disintegrate, leaving wide, dark, empty sockets. "I'm not your mother, I'm not your mother, I'm not your mother . . ."

I pull and push and try desperately to free myself, but nothing works.

Her body has deteriorated so much that it crumbles in on itself.

I scream. As if she was inside my mom's body the whole time, Hollow Mother is lying in her place, covered in Mom's ashes.

"*I'm* your mother!" she says, tightening her hold on me and pulling me deeper under the bed.

"No!" I yell, trying to rip her hand off me, but it's as useless as before. I grab hold of the bedframe. My arms strain and my fingers feel like they might rip clean off, but I manage to slow her progress. "Dad! Peter! Help!"

"He's coming," she whispers in my ear. "I'll keep you safe, but you must come with me. Come with your mother."

Stomp! Stomp! Stomp!

Footsteps. I can feel the reverberations in the floor. Sarah stops pulling me and falls still.

"Stop it right now," she says to whomever has entered the room.

Stomp! Stomp! Stomp!

"How *dare* you!" she says, her words full of hatred. She releases her grip on me and slides out from under the bed.

I worm my way to the edge and peer out at the room, fearing what I might see. But I see nothing. There's no one standing in the room, doorway, or hall, and Hollow Mother has vanished. Was that Abraham I heard enter the room? Sarah wasn't happy to see him, and must have led him away. I drag myself out and stand up, feeling my back go snap-crackle-pop as I straighten it.

Dad and Peter are both in bed. Somehow, they've slept through everything.

Dad rubs his face, blinks, and squints at me. "Jo? What's wrong?"

"Nothing," I say. It's easier to lie. "Had a bad dream, that's all. Think there's enough space in the bed for me?"

He's too tired to answer but holds the sheet up for me to get in. I slide into the middle of the bed, a tight squeeze, but it beats spending the rest of the night on the ground, staring into the darkness under the bed.

I keep a close watch on the open door, half expecting to see Sarah or Abraham return, but after a while—how long, I can't say—my eyes grow heavy, and the world darkens, tilts, and slips away.

Chapter Twelve

"PUMPKIN SPICE!" WILLEM CALLS out with a smile as soon as he spots me. "What brings you into Darcy's so early on a Saturday morning you're not scheduled to work?"

I've gone over this conversation a dozen times. And yet, as I slowly approach the counter where Willem is standing, I find myself at a loss for words.

Willem's smile falters, then falls from his face altogether. "What's wrong?"

This is why I've avoided making relationships, so I wouldn't have to say goodbye to someone I genuinely like. My pulse quickens and my cheeks flush. *Just say it*, I tell myself, but the words still refuse to come.

Willem leans in closer and drops his voice to a whisper. "Is it the ghosts? C'mon, what happened?"

"It's not the ghosts," I say, then shake my head. "I mean, it *is* the ghosts, but it's not just that. It's . . ." I look at the floor, unable to meet his eyes, and spin my ring. "I'm leaving."

"What? When?"

"Today," I say. "As soon as I return home."

For a moment, Willem looks confused. Then an expression of grim understanding dawns on his face, and he nods soberly. "I hoped this day wouldn't come, but I suppose I always knew it would. Things must have gotten really bad."

"You have no idea."

"Where are you going?"

I shrug. "Don't know yet. We never do, until we get there."

Willem pours a drink and hands it to me. The steam rising from it carries strong notes of nutmeg and cinnamon. "One last pumpkin spice latte. On the house."

"Thank you," I say. "Maybe it doesn't have to be the last. I could come back to visit."

He smiles half-heartedly. "Yeah, of course." He stands up a little straighter. "I'll let Meera know. She's going to be so mad you're quitting that she'll probably fire you."

I laugh. "I'll give her a call whenever I land wherever I land." I scan the diner, just to make sure she's not standing behind me. "It's for the best she's not here. I don't know how many goodbyes I can handle in one morning."

"Don't forget to swing by Triss's house on your way out of town," he says sarcastically.

"Actually, Triss and I kind of came to a mutual understanding."

"Seriously?"

I nod. "Shocking, right?"

"Shocking?" he says. "That's the understatement of the century. I wouldn't be more shocked if the floor suddenly disappeared and we fell into a bottomless pit."

"At least then I wouldn't have to leave." A sudden thought pops into my head. "Before I go, can I use your phone one more time to look something up?"

"More research?" he asks, handing me his phone. "You're speaking my language."

"You still have that article we printed at the library?" I ask as I google *too-ra-loo-ra-loo-ral*.

"Of course. You want it back?"

"No need. You can keep it as a memento."

"I'll read the murder article fondly every time I think of you."

"How romantic," I say, already beginning to miss our dorky flirting. I hand his phone back.

He looks at his screen and frowns. "What's *Too-Ra-Loo-Ra-Loo-Ral*?"

The bell on the front door chimes behind me.

"An old lullaby made famous by Bing Crosby, apparently. Sarah Keil sings it often, so I was curious. It's about a child who misses their late mother." I can't help but wonder if it's not a coincidence Sarah is singing that particular song to me.

Someone shouts my name urgently. It's Peter, walking quickly toward us, his face twisted with worry.

Something is wrong. Really wrong. My stomach drops and I feel lightheaded.

"What is it?" I ask him, my voice sounding distant to my own ears, feeling as if I've been submerged in ice-cold water.

"It's Dad," he says. He closes his eyes, looking like he's going to be sick.

"What?" I say loudly. "Peter, tell me. What happened to Dad?"

Peter takes a deep breath and shakes his hands. "He fell. He's . . . in the hospital."

I'VE SAT IN THE uncomfortable hospital chair for hours, my back and legs growing stiff, watching the sun cut across the sky and disappear behind the buildings across the street. Not only was Dad taken to the same hospital as me, but he also ended up in the exact same room I stayed in after my fall. The same room where I first saw Dead Girl. Fate is funny sometimes, which is a nice way of saying fate has a sick sense of humor. The type of humor that finds great pleasure in slicing you open from your throat to your waist, emptying your insides—guts and soul alike—and turning you into a hollow shell.

Yeesh. I need a break. I need sleep.

"I'm going for another walk," Peter says, standing up and stretching backward with his hands on his hips. "You wanna come?"

"Wish that I could," I say, looking him up and down and feeling every single ounce of his pain. "But I'm afraid that if we both leave, the nurses might lock the door and refuse to let us back in."

"They won't let us stay all night."

I nod. "But the longer we stay here, the better."

Dad snores loudly—not a peaceful sound but a choking sound that causes him to cough and sputter. He rolls over and falls back asleep. The pain medication they've given him has knocked him out hard. When he's not sleeping, he's barely coherent.

They're keeping him overnight on account of the concussion he sustained when he fell from the top of the ladder doing one last home repair for Mrs. Cracknell. He hit the side of his head on the porch railing on his way to the ground. "I'm lucky I broke my fall with my head," he said with a slow smile as he filled us in on what had happened. "Would have hit the ground a lot harder if I hadn't." Broke his right leg in three places and earned himself a cast as a reward.

Peter looks at Dad, asleep, and shakes his head. "What was he doing, repairing the gutters? We were about to leave!"

I sigh. "It's part of who he is. Leave no job undone."

"Well, he should never have used Mrs. Cracknell's ladder. She said herself that it wasn't steady, that it was as old as Methu . . . some old guy."

I don't have the heart to respond. The ladder was old and rickety, true, but I have a feeling it wasn't to blame for Dad's fall.

"Anyway, the hospital's halls are calling me. You want anything from the vending machine?"

"No, thanks."

Peter steps out of the room and closes the door with a *click*, leaving me alone with Dad. He's not much company at the moment, so my thoughts grow loud and troubling. My skin is itchy and hot, knowing the path my mind is about to tread. I don't want to think these things, but I'm helpless not to.

Dad's fall wasn't an accident. In Mrs. Cracknell's house— the Kill House—there's no such thing as accidents. His fall was intentional. He was pushed; I'm certain of it. It could have been any of the ghosts—they're all messed up in their own ways—but my money is on Abraham. He wants us to stay. Permanently.

"Don't know you," Dad mumbles in his sleep, rolling over on his side and squeezing the pillow in the crook of his elbow like he's trying to choke the life out of it.

Weird dream, I think, but then a sudden thought chills my blood: What if he's not dreaming? What if he's *hearing*? What if someone's *whispering*?

I scan the room for shadows, or someone *hiding* in the shadows. Out of the corner of my eye, I catch a tiny blur of movement, but it's just the sleeve of Dad's coat, hanging from a hook on the wall and rippling in the breeze blowing through the open window. No Dead Girl—no ghost, period.

Dad sits up suddenly with a sharp breath, making me flinch and swear. His eyes are wide, staring at the wall. I look, but there's nothing there.

"Dad?"

He doesn't respond.

"Dad!" I say more loudly.

Nothing. It's like I'm not even in the room.

"Goooo . . ." he says, his voice low and rough, drawing the word out impossibly thin. "Awaaaay . . ."

I rush to the bedside and shake his arm. "Dad!" I say again, louder this time. It works—he finally snaps out of the drug-induced mind trap he'd fallen into. He shakes his head and rubs his hand over his face, then looks at me in confusion.

"Jo?" he says. "What happened?"

"You were dreaming," I say, hoping that's true. "You freaked me out."

"Sorry." With a deep breath and a few soft grunts of discomfort, he eases himself back down to a prone position. He flicks the IV bag that's pumping a steady drip of morphine into his veins. "This stuff is messing me up, making my dreams seem real and reality feel like I'm dreaming."

"Without it, you'd be in so much pain."

"That might be preferable to how foggy my head is." He places his fingertips to his forehead, gingerly, and closes his eyes. "No more. When this bag is done, I'm not letting them refill it."

"Has anyone said how long they think you'll be here?"

He doesn't give any indication that he heard my question, so I'm about to ask it again when he finally opens his eyes. "The doctor said I'll probably be discharged tomorrow." He gives me a pained look that has shifted from physical to emotional. "I'm sorry, Jo."

It's clear what he's thinking, because I'm thinking it too: Peter and I will need to spend at least one more night in the Kill House, on our own.

"It'll be fine," I say, shaking my head. "Peter and I can take turns sleeping if we need to."

"It's not just tonight," he says. "With a broken leg, I'm not going to be a very appealing handyman-for-hire. I don't even think I'd be able to drive us to a new town with this cast. I'm hoping Mrs. Cracknell takes pity on us so we can stay in the basement apartment a little longer, and I can do some less physical jobs around the house as I heal. But as soon as possible, we split."

"How long?"

"I don't know. Two, maybe three weeks?"

Time is a funny thing. If I'd been told yesterday afternoon we'd be leaving Burlington in three weeks, I would have been upset and said that's barely any time at all, but now, today, I'm desperate to leave and three weeks feels like an eternity. I've said my goodbyes and made peace with the move, so now I just want to go.

"We'll be okay," I say, not because I believe it but because there's no alternative—at least, not one I'm willing to accept. Regardless of whatever comes our way, I have to keep a positive attitude. Things will be better once Dad returns home, even with his leg in a cast. One night without him. Just one night. "We'll be okay," I repeat.

He smiles and says, "You're the strongest, toughest person I know, Jo. Stronger and tougher than me."

"How high are you?" I say with a laugh, but his words stoke a feeling of warmth and pride in me. It's a small boost at a time when I need it most. Maybe, just maybe, we *will* be okay. "I'm going to get a drink of water, but I'll be right back."

Dad nods and closes his eyes as I slip out of the room. I walk to the water fountain at the end of the hall as quietly as possible, not wanting to gain the attention of the nurses out of an irrational fear they'll ask me to leave if they see me. After a long drink cold enough to burn my throat pleasantly, I walk back to Dad's room.

"What do you want?" I hear him demand from within.

I quicken my pace and enter the room.

"Go away!" Dad says, sitting bolt upright in his bed. "You're not welcome here!"

"Dad? Who are you talking to?" There's no one else in the room—at least, no one else I can see.

Dad lays back in bed, looking exhausted but relieved. "I think he's gone."

"Who's gone?" I ask desperately.

Dad turns to face me, a look of confusion written clearly across his face, as if he'd forgotten I was there. He regards me with a frown, then asks, "You didn't see him? You didn't *hear* him?"

"No!" Abraham, the Peek-a-Boo Boy, the fucking Boogeyman—I didn't see a soul.

The seconds tick by, marked by the *beep-beep-beep* of the monitor tracking his vitals. Finally, he speaks. "Shit."

"What?"

He lays his head back and stares at the ceiling. "I heard an old man—*the old man*, the one who has followed me to every town and city. Always desperate enough to hurt us to get whatever it is he wants, and this time he sounded more desperate than ever. Now that he's found me, it's only a matter of time before he returns. But that's not what scares me most." He turns and looks at me again, and I see genuine fear in his eyes. "What scares me most is you had no clue."

"Why does that scare you?"

"Well," Dad says, speaking slowly like he needs to spell things out for me. "I can hear ghosts again, but you can't."

"Oh," I say, sitting back in my chair as the full weight of what he's implying hits me. "Shit."

He nods. "You fall, hit your head, and my ability transfers to you. And not only that, but you can see the Whisperings too. I fall, hit my head, and the ability transfers back, but like before, I could only hear the ghost." Dad sighs. "The only constant is change."

"Does any of that make sense?" I ask, my head spinning.

"Jo, *none* of this makes sense. Never has. But that doesn't make any of it any less real."

I shrug, trying to suppress the desperation that's bubbling up within me. "All right, fine. Maybe I can't hear or see ghosts anymore. Back to old times, right?"

With a sigh, he says, "We didn't live in the Kill House before."

And finally, the other shoe has dropped.

I have to return to the Kill House. With Peter, but without Dad or the Whisperings. How can I protect us from something I can't see? From something I can't even hear?

"Maybe the ghost was gone before I entered the room," I say, not sounding entirely confident in that theory.

"Maybe," Dad says, his tone equally doubtful.

"What did I miss?" It's Peter, standing in the doorway, a half-eaten Oh Henry! bar in his hand, staring at us with a look of confusion and concern.

IT'S NEARLY MIDNIGHT. The street is eerily silent and still, like the neighborhood is holding a collective breath. But not the house. The house feels alive in a way I can't quite put my finger on. Is it the windows, watching me and Peter as we hesitate on the sidewalk? Is it the walls, expanding and contracting, a trick of the moonlight, like a giant pair of lungs? Is it the door, waiting to open wide, hungry to swallow us whole?

Don't be ridiculous, I tell myself. It's my imagination, and only my imagination.

But the evil that dwells within the house is most certainly not only my imagination. Part of me feels a momentary surge of relief remembering I've lost the Whisperings, but then I remind myself that it's better to know, better to see, no matter how terrifying that might be, just like leaving the hole to the red room open ever since I uncovered it.

"I don't want to go inside," Peter says.

"Neither do I," I say, wrapping my scarf around my neck and shivering from the chill in the air. "But we can't stay out here all night either. We'll freeze."

"I know." Peter scans the street. His eyes land on Victor, and his face lights up. "Why don't we sleep in the car?"

"Because . . ." I let my words trail off, unable to think of any reason not to. "That's actually not a bad idea. It'll be cold and uncomfortable and absolutely perfect."

Peter beams with pride, then his expression falters slightly. "Do you have the keys?"

"Damn it, no. Hopefully Dad didn't have them in his pocket when he fell." Hopefully, they're where he always leaves them, hanging on the wooden key hook in the kitchen.

Peter tries each of the car door handles, just in case. He looks at me apologetically, as if he's personally responsible for the fact that Victor is locked, or maybe because it was his idea to sleep in the car, but more likely because we both know I'm going to be the one who needs to enter the house to look for the keys.

"I'll go," I say, a sickening sensation spreading through my gut.

"I can come too," he offers.

I place a hand on his shoulder. "Thanks, but it's better you stay out here. You'd only slow me down."

It's probably not true, but he doesn't argue. "Be fast."

"I always am." With a nod, I walk resolutely to the side of the house, fearing that if I slow down for a moment, I'll get cold feet and chicken out.

Get inside. Get the keys. Get out.

I unlock the door, open it, and slip inside, closing the door slowly and silently behind me. It's as dark as a crypt. I pause and listen but hear nothing. Because there's nothing to hear? Or because I've lost the ability?

I shake my head and creep quickly down the stairs, not daring to turn on the lights, desperate to remain hidden. It's not a rational thought—I don't think the dead need light to see—but I don't care. I'm not exactly in a rational frame of mind.

Get downstairs. Get the keys. Get out.

Creak-creak-creak. Each stair groans under my weight. I wish I were lighter. I wish I could float. I wish I could move through the house without making a sound. *Creak-creak-creak.*

I reach the hallway floor, thankful for how solid and silent it is.

Get down the hall. Get the keys. Get out.

I might not be able to float, but I can practically fly. I run fast, covering the short distance in record time, hardly making a sound.

Get in the kitchen. Get the keys. Get out.

I rush through the kitchen doorway and reach for the keys.

Get the keys—

My hand slaps the wall where the keys should be hanging.

"What? No!"

I fumble around in the dark, refusing to believe that the keys aren't there.

But they're not. The hook is empty.

"No, no, no, no."

Where could they be? Dad never has them when he's not driving. Dad never puts them anywhere but on the hook.

Creak.

I hold my breath, my entire body going rigid at the sound. It came from behind me, somewhere down the hall.

The seconds tick by slowly. One, two, three . . . I don't hear the sound again. I don't hear anything.

Again, I wonder if that's because there's nothing to hear, or if—

"Shut up," I whisper, immediately regretting speaking out loud.

My mind races, trying to formulate a plan B, but I come up empty. It's clear Peter and I can't spend the night in the house—I've practically lost my mind in the span of thirty seconds—and we have nowhere else to go. Without the keys, we can't sleep in the car . . .

No. I'm unwilling to accept the keys aren't somewhere in the house. Maybe Dad left them in his room, or they fell out of his pocket and slipped between the couch cushions in the family room, or . . .

Or maybe someone else is to blame. Maybe Abraham moved them. Another way to prevent us from leaving. Another way to trap us.

I shake my head, despair washing over me like a cold shower. The keys could be anywhere.

Forget the keys. Get out.

I turn—

Get out.

enter the hall—

Get out!

and run—

Get!

straight toward—

Out!

Hollow Mother.

I try to stop so quickly that my feet slide out in front of me and I fall to the ground, landing hard.

She's coming toward me, shambling, head down, hair hiding her face.

I scramble backward desperately.

Without the Whisperings, how can I see her?

Her hair parts as she takes another step, and I see her face.

It's not Sarah. It's Mrs. Cracknell. I feel foolish for mistaking her in my panic, but I'm also relieved.

"Thank goodness it's you," I say as I get back to my feet. "I think I had a heart attack."

She doesn't respond. Her eyes are open but unseeing. She's walking in an odd, halting pattern. I wave my hand in front of her face—she doesn't even blink. She's sleepwalking. Before I can step aside, she bumps into me and, without waking up, continues to mindlessly push against me, like she's trying to walk *through* me. I put my hands on her shoulders and gently turn her around, then guide her back the way she came. I need to get her back to bed safely, then I'll get out.

The stairs to the main floor groan twice as loudly as the side-entrance stairs. I keep my eyes on the openings between each one, feeling like something might reach through and grab me at any moment, but we reach the main floor without incident. I'm not out of the woods yet, but at least I'm a little closer.

"Hammer, hammer . . ." Mrs. Cracknell mutters as we enter her bedroom.

A bedside lamp has been left on, providing enough light for me to avoid tripping over a pile of clothes on the floor. Several insects scurry in their glass containers, watching me as I get Mrs. Cracknell to her bed. I pull back the sheets and lay her down. She goes willingly, rests her head on the pillow, and her eyes flutter, then close.

"Hammering . . . always hammering," she says before falling asleep. She doesn't look peaceful—her brow is creased and her lips are drawn tight.

I look down at her sadly. The life she's lived, here in this house, alone for so many years with nothing but insects for company—not to mention the medication behind her bathroom mirror. "Sleep well. I hope . . . I hope you're okay."

Her breathing begins to grow heavier, steadier. I pinch the lamp's knob to turn it off, then pause. Something has caught my attention—one of the newspaper clippings pinned to the bulletin board on the wall.

BURLINGTON WOMAN SLAIN BY BROTHER
Family in shock and mourning

The article is dated October 15, 2007. I don't read any further. My focus is on the pictures. There are three of them. The first is a picture of a small bungalow in the country with a roll of yellow police tape stretched from a tree to a street sign that says *Ticonderoga Rd*. The second is my uncle's United States military photo. And the third is a family portrait. *My* family portrait, maybe one of the last pictures taken of the four of us together.

I pull the article free from the wall and stare at it in shock. Tears come freely—I do nothing to stop them. The clipping trembles in my hand. I feel like I should sit, but the voice in the back of my head implores me to get out of the house as soon as possible. I silence the voice. Although I've only ever seen a few pictures of Mom, and never this one, my focus isn't on her. My focus isn't on me or Peter either, both so young and innocent. It's on Dad.

He's wearing a white, short-sleeved button-up shirt, tucked into khaki pants, and a thin tie. I've never seen him dressed like that. His hair has been combed and parted neatly, and his beard is trimmed. But it's more than just his clothes or his hair. It's his face. He looks so young. He looks so happy. The deep wrinkles that now cover his face aren't yet a whisper on his skin. There aren't dark bags hanging beneath his eyes. His smile is wide and genuine. My heart breaks at the sight—I honestly can't recall ever seeing him look like this. It's a painful reminder of the life that was robbed from him when our world was turned upside down with one swift blow.

Mrs. Cracknell snores loudly, jostling me out of my thoughts and causing me to jump. I quickly fold the clipping and slip it into my pocket, then leave her room and close the door. I hurry toward the front door—there's no way in hell I'm going back down through the basement.

Something shiny catches my eye before I leave. On the front hall table are Dad's keys. How they got there, who can say? But I have a sinking suspicion that the ghosts are to blame. Why? Probably just to screw with me.

Laughter comes from the darkness behind me. I turn but there's no one there. Once again, I hope my imagination is getting the better of me. Best to leave before anything *else* gets the better of me.

I grab the keys that shouldn't be there and rejoin my brother on the sidewalk.

"What happened? Why'd you come out through the front door?"

"Get in and I'll tell you," I say, unlocking the car doors. I turn the key in the ignition and Victor revs to life.

"We're not going to sleep here?" Peter asks.

I shake my head. "I know where we can go for the night."

Chapter Thirteen

THE HOUSE ISN'T HARD to find. Ticonderoga Road isn't very long, and the houses hidden among the trees are large estates with welcoming faces, well-maintained lawns, and expensive cars parked in the driveways. All except one.

Our house. Well, our old house.

It's clear it's been abandoned since my family moved out, leaving behind possessions we didn't have time to pack and memories too painful to bear—memories that would haunt us no matter where we landed.

The white paint has peeled off the wood-slat walls, making the house look like it's been skinned alive. The windows are boarded up and a couple of two-by-fours are nailed across the front door. The yard is a jungle of waist-high weeds, alive with the buzzing of insects. There's a hole the size of a kiddie pool in the roof.

How has the city left the house to sit and rot? How has it not been bulldozed and replaced by a new, modern house—a home filled with a large, happy family blissfully unaware of the horrors that took place thirteen years ago?

Count your lucky stars it's still here, I tell myself. All the same, now that I'm seeing the house with my own eyes, I'm questioning why I thought coming here was a good idea.

Mom, I remind myself. *If you couldn't be close to Dad tonight, you wanted to be close to Mom. You wanted—needed—closure. And if you can't get closure, you'll settle for a few answers.*

"So this was our home?" Peter asks.

"This was our home. I won't think any less of you if you want to stay in the car," I tell him. We're standing on the gravel driveway, Victor parked between us. I'll admit the car is still looking like an appealing place to sleep.

Peter shakes his head. "You think I'm going to stay out here all night? Alone? No way."

"Yeah," I say. "Didn't think so." I turn my attention back to the house. A cool breeze kicks up some leaves and sends a shiver down my spine. My feet feel like lead.

"If we're doing this, let's do it," Peter says, seeing me hesitate.

I smile and nod. If he hadn't spoken, would I have stood outside until morning? Maybe. I take a step, my knee creaking as it bends.

"You shouldn't be here," someone says from between the trees to our right. It's an old man's voice, full of phlegm and venom. The first panicked thought that springs into my head is that it's the old man who has followed Dad since Mom died, and who just showed up in his hospital room earlier this evening.

I tense, and scan the woods, my heart hammering. *Ta-tump! Ta-tump! Ta-tump!*

"Who's there?" I ask.

The old man steps forward into the light of the house's clearing, and my attention immediately zeroes in on what he's holding. Pointed at my chest, shaking in his tight grip, is a double-barreled shotgun.

"Holy shit," I say, raising my hands above my head.

Peter puts his hands up too, looking at me with wide, fearful eyes, then back at the man.

"I said, you shouldn't be here!" the man says, his voice rising to a shout. His robe is untied, revealing his boxer shorts and nightshirt beneath. He looks tired, angry, and scared—a dangerous combination.

"All right, all right," I say, trying to remain calm. "We just took a wrong turn and got a little lost, but we'll get back in our car and—"

"Bullshit!" he barks, spit flying from his cracked lips, jutting the shotgun toward us for emphasis.

"Please," I whimper as a tear slips down my cheek and my thoughts pinwheel out of control, picturing his finger squeezing the trigger, a great blast of light and a thunderous roar, the feeling of my feet lifting off the ground as my chest explodes in a meaty spray.

"You came here on purpose, that's clear as day," he says. "Just like all the other rubberneckers over the years, waking me and my wife in the middle of the night with your hooting and hollering while you get your sick thrills. I'm done with it!" He changes the aim of the shotgun from my chest to my head.

My mind is a blur, a nonsensical swirl, a mass of thoughts without sense.

"Silas?" a new voice calls out from behind the man. A woman who sounds as old as him.

The man—Silas—doesn't appear to hear her. His finger tightens on the trigger.

A light turns on, illuminating the front porch of the house next door and the old woman standing there. Dressed in a nightgown and with hair in rollers, she scans the area with a small flashlight and then folds her arms across her chest for warmth, looking confused.

"Silas?" she repeats, louder than before.

Her voice finally gets through to Silas. His finger relaxes slightly on the trigger, and he glances over his shoulder. "Edith, go back inside. I'm handling this."

Edith's flashlight finally lands on us, and she sees me and my brother for the first time. Her expression immediately turns from a frown to a wide-eyed look of worry and concern. "Silas! Good lord, what are you doing? Those are *children*."

"Huh?" he says. He knuckles his eyes, blinks a few times, and squints at us. A look of shock temporarily lights up his face, but he's quick to shake his head, as if he's already made up his mind about me and my brother and isn't willing to veer off the path he's treading. "They shouldn't be here. They're up to no good."

"Even if that's true," Edith implores as she approaches us slowly, "that gives you no right to scare them to death."

He was going to kill *us to death*, I think, deciding to keep that to myself. If Edith can talk her husband down, who am I to get in her way?

"We weren't here to cause any trouble," Peter says, breaking the silence.

"Peter—" I say, about to tell him to stop talking, but he cuts me off.

"No! We might as well tell them why we came so we can get out of here."

Silas and Edith stare at Peter expectantly, waiting for him to continue. Silas lowers his shotgun, so I nod at Peter to continue.

"We used to live here, long ago. I was just a baby, and my sister was only four. We've never been back but we're in a bit of trouble and had nowhere else to go."

Edith cocks her head to the side as she works things out. "Are you . . . are you the Guest children?" She looks down and thinks hard for a second, then snaps her fingers, raises her head, and points at us. "Joana and Peter, right?"

I nod eagerly, a feeling of relief washing over me.

Edith touches her husband's arm. "Silas, these are Jack and Isabelle's kids."

He aims the shotgun at the ground in front of his feet and looks at us in utter shock. "Well, holy shit."

"Language," Edith says, whacking Silas's arm. She then hits him a second time.

With a wince, he asks, "What was that one for?"

"For nearly shooting our old neighbors."

There are *many* things I'd like to say to that, but we're not dead and Silas is still holding his gun, so I bite my tongue once more.

At least he has the decency to look genuinely apologetic. "Yeah, right. Sorry about that."

"It's okay," I lie.

"I'm still so sorry about what happened to your mother," Edith says. "She was a lovely woman. Simply lovely. What sort of trouble are you in?"

I jump in before Peter can answer. The truth worked before, but I don't think it would have the same effect now. Instead, I offer a tweaked version, making the situation more dire than it is so hopefully the old couple will leave us alone. "Our dad—Jack—is in the hospital. They . . . don't think he has long."

"Oh, I'm sorry," Edith says. Her tone is so genuine, so instantly hurt, that I feel a little bad for lying about Dad dying.

But I plow on. "Thank you. He asked us to come here. Said he had hidden something sentimental inside but never had the chance to come back to get it."

"What is it?" Silas asks.

"I'd rather not say. It's, you know, private. But he hopes to see it—hold it—one last time before he . . . before he . . ." I cover my face with one hand and whimper.

"Right, of course," Silas says. "Let us help you look. It's the least we can do after . . . you know." He looks at his shotgun, then back to us.

I'm about to politely decline, but Edith speaks first. "I don't think they want us to do that, Silas. They need to be on their own, but listen . . ." She looks at us with such a serious, penetrating stare that I nearly take an involuntary step backward. "You hear or see anything . . . *unusual*, anything at all, you come straight over to our house. Okay?"

As I try to process her meaning, I nod.

"Good," she says, then hands me her flashlight. "Here, you'll need this."

"Thank you. I'll make sure to return it when we're done."

Edith shakes her head, a sad look slowly spreading across her face. "No, my dear. You keep it. I have a feeling you're not going to want to stick around any longer than necessary after you find what you're looking for."

THE NAILS HAMMERED INTO the boards over the door are rusty, and the wood is damp and soft. It doesn't take much strength to pull everything down.

I squeeze the doorknob, then pause. "Last chance to sleep in the car."

"Are you kidding me?" Peter says, offended I'd even ask.

I want to tell him I'm only looking out for him, that we don't know what we'll find inside, and that being here will likely raise painful memories. But he's not a little kid anymore. He's old enough to make his own decisions.

"All right," I say, and turn the knob.

The door swings quickly into the house, pulling me forward, as if someone had opened it from the other side. I take a few jerky steps into the front foyer before coming to an abrupt stop, hearing footsteps retreating down the hall.

"Did you hear that?" I ask Peter.

He joins me slowly. "Hear what?"

"Someone running away as soon as I entered."

He looks around the foyer, down the hall, and up the stairs. "Probably just the echo of your own footsteps."

I frown and give him an *Are you serious?* look. To prove me wrong, he cups his hands around his mouth and says, "Echo!"

His voice bounces off the walls in answer. *"Echo, echo, echo . . ."*

Maybe he was right, which makes me feel a little better. I feel silly, but I remind myself that I've been living with ghosts for the past few weeks, and it's understandable if I'm a little extra jumpy—especially here.

I've thought about what happened in this house often. Despite that, I've long wanted to return. But now that I'm here, I fear I made a mistake. Some things are best left buried, both metaphorically and literally.

Ta-tump. Ta-tump. Ta-tump.

It's my heart. I know that—I can feel it beating in my chest—but it seems like the sound is coming not from within me but from without.

Ta-tump. Ta-tump. Ta-tump.

It sounds like it's coming from the walls.

Ta-tump. Ta-tump. Ta-tump.

No, it sounds like it's coming from overhead.

Ta-tump. Ta-tump. Ta-tump.

Now the heart is beating in the floor, its pulsating rhythm reverberating up through my feet, my legs, and my spine, straight into my skull.

"Jo?" Peter is looking at me with concern. "You okay?"

"I'm fine," I say with a fake smile, spinning my ring. I'm about to add something stupid, like "C'mon, let's go," or "No time like the present," but then I have a change of heart and shake my head. "Actually, no. I'm not fine. Even though I've lost the Whisperings, I can't stop hearing things. I feel like we shouldn't have come here, but I don't know where else to go, so . . ." I spread my arms, not exactly sure how to finish the sentence.

"So . . ." Peter says, picking up my sentence where I left off. "No time like the present."

I laugh sharply.

"What'd I say?"

I put my hand on his shoulder. "Just the right thing." I tilt my head toward the hall. "C'mon, let's go." It's not until the words have left my lips that I realize that was the other stupid thing I didn't want to say, and I laugh again. Peter gives me a sideways glance like I've lost my mind. We walk on.

The air smells musty, as if mold has infested the walls. I feel like I'm walking through a swamp, meeting resistance with every step, my feet sticking to the ground. I know it's probably just my lingering reluctance to go any farther, but it's an odd sensation, as if something in the house is trying to stop me from continuing.

Get out, get out, get out!

"This is so weird," I say, mostly just to hear my own voice instead of the one in my head.

"What is?"

Everything, I think. "Being back. I was so young the last time I was here I probably wouldn't remember anything if it weren't for the dreams that have kept this house alive in my head. But everything's exactly as I remember it." The floral wallpaper, the hall table where Mom stored her purse, the hook on the wall where Dad always hung the car keys. Only, there's no purse, no keys, no Mom, no Dad. No life. I feel like I've walked into a morgue, not a house. "Mom and Dad are everywhere here. At least, my memories of them are."

"I hope he's going to be okay," Peter says with a frown.

"Hey, he will be. I promise." I don't have any way to know that, but I feel it in my bones.

Peter nods, but he doesn't look entirely convinced. "Dad told me he heard something odd just before he fell," he says softly.

"What?"

"Someone humming something like *too-ra-loo*. And he thought he also caught a hint of lavender, even though there's none growing in Mrs. Cracknell's garden."

Just then something slips out of the darkness and comes straight at us. Scurrying, black, and squeaking. Rats. Four or five. My breath catches in my throat as I leap to the side of the hall. Peter presses beside me and we watch with revulsion as the rats scurry past in a row. The last one makes a sudden, unexpected turn and scurries onto my foot and up my shin. I scream and kick the air, sending the rat sailing. It hits the opposite wall and falls to the floor. It flips to its feet, opens its mouth wide, looks at me with rage, and hisses.

"Come near me again and I will stomp the ever-loving life out of you," I say, my voice a low growl.

For a minute I think the little prick is going to make another run at me, but then it scurries after the others.

"That was crazy," Peter says. "Why'd it try to climb you?"

"No clue," I say. A shiver racks my body as I imagine the rat getting past my knee. What I wouldn't give for a scalding hot shower and a bucket of antibacterial soap. My heart is practically pounding up my throat and out my mouth—*ta-TUMP-ta-TUMP-ta-TUMP*. I don't want to stay in the hall, so I lead my brother into the family room, one of only a few rooms on the main floor.

It's like a museum, everything exactly where it was when we lived there. More memories flood my mind, so vivid I can see them filling the room, like watching a living movie. Young me and Mom snuggle on the small checkered couch, reading a picture book together; beside that, Dad sits in his battered recliner chair, watching a baseball game after work with young me sound asleep on his lap; and all four of us sit on the red rug in the middle of the floor, opening presents, smiling, and laughing, a lit Christmas tree in the corner of the room bathing us in a warm glow—young me sneaks a glance at the fireplace in the hopes of catching a glimpse of Santa Claus.

"You seeing any of this?" I ask Peter.

"Seeing what?"

"Us."

He shakes his head, and we carry on.

As we pass through the kitchen, I see another mix of memories. My parents making us pancakes for Sunday breakfast; singing "Happy Birthday" to me while carrying a cake with a lit candle in the shape of the number three; and bringing in a tray of hamburgers and hot dogs from the backyard barbecue on the Fourth of July.

In the dining room, Mom and Dad take care of some paperwork while I draw pictures, a box of emptied crayons fanned out on the table; Dad paces the room holding Peter pressed against his chest, the first night bringing my brother home from the hospital, patting his back and humming gentle lullabies; young me helps set the table with the place settings reserved for company and special occasions, Mom following behind and straightening the cutlery. *You know all this pomp and circumstance is completely unnecessary*, Dad says, waving an arm at the table. Mom smiles and says, *I know, but I like it. It's for me, not your brother.*

They're setting the table for dinner with Uncle Roman. Could this memory be the night he . . . ?

I know the answer as surely as I know what I'm going to see when I go upstairs. It's my curse to relive this night over and over and over again, but it's also a small blessing Peter isn't seeing what I'm seeing. For the hundredth time I consider leading him out and driving far, far away, but I know I can't.

Leaving won't change a thing, but staying and facing my fears and regrets might.

We complete our slow circle of the first floor, ending back in the front hall where we began. I place my hand on the banister post and aim the flashlight up the stairs. Dust particles dance in the light. Peter places his hand on top of mine.

"We don't have to go up there," he says. "We can stay down here—you can sleep on the couch, and I'll take the floor."

"I wish we could," I say. "But I have to go."

He opens his mouth to protest, or offer another alternative, or tell me he can't go any farther, but then he nods. "Yeah, I know."

I lead the way. Each stair groans underfoot—first under mine, then under Peter's.

Creak-screech.

Creak-screech.

Creak-screech.

Creak-tump!

I come to an abrupt stop. Something didn't sound right. It sounded like the beat of a nervous heart. Or something louder, like a long-handled tool, a splitting maul, being used as a walking cane. I look back reluctantly, relief washing over me when I see we're still alone.

"What is it?" Peter asks, glancing over his shoulder.

"Nothing," I say, knowing he likely won't buy that even though it's true . . . I think. "C'mon."

We reach the top and pause. There are four doors. Two are closed—a small bathroom and the linen closet. Two are open slightly—my parents' bedroom, where Peter slept in a crib, and a second bedroom, closest to the top of the stairs.

"This was me," I say as I push the door open, overcome by emotions. There's the small bed where Mom and Dad tucked me in with goodnight kisses and I first heard my uncle walking up the stairs in the middle of the night. There's the space beneath the bed where I hid my most precious toys and keepsakes, and where I hid myself instead of doing anything to help my parents. There's the floor where I built toy train tracks and drew pictures on multicolored construction paper and tried to do somersaults, and where Uncle Roman bashed in Mom's skull like a ripe watermelon. The wooden floorboards have been permanently stained a deep, dark red—the bloodstain is painfully visible in the light of my shaking flashlight.

The hair on the back of my neck stands on end and my stomach clenches as if I've just gone over the steepest part of a roller coaster. I have the uncanny sensation that we're no longer alone in the room, that someone is standing directly behind me.

My blood is ice as I turn to see who's there, suddenly filled with the irrational conviction that one of the Keils has followed us.

But it's not them.

It's someone I've never fully allowed myself to believe I'd see again outside of my dreams and hallucinations, not even here in this house.

"Mom," I say.

Chapter Fourteen

"JELLY BEAN," MOM SAYS. Only she would know her nickname for me—not a hallucination, and not Sarah Keil pretending to be my mom.

It's really her.

She spreads her arms and I rush to her. She wraps me up and holds me tight, and although she feels ice-cold, I've never felt warmer.

"What?" Peter says in utter disbelief. "Mom is here? Like, really here, not just . . ." He taps the side of his forehead and I understand his meaning. *Not just in your head?*

I wipe tears from my cheeks and nod. He can't see her, which pains me. "Will he be able to feel you? If you hug him?"

Mom shakes her head sadly. "No, if he can't see me, he won't be able to feel me either."

But I'm not giving up that easily. Peter deserves this too. "Sit on the bed," I tell him, and he does. Then I guide Mom to sit beside him, and I sit on her other side and hold out my hand. "Here, take my hand." He places his hand in mine, and

I guide it to Mom's lap, then transfer it to her hand and squeeze both of their hands together. Mom looks at me skeptically, but I ignore her. "There, do you feel anything?"

Peter closes his eyes and concentrates. He tilts his head and says, "Our hands are clasped?"

"Yes," I say.

He opens his eyes, looks at the space between us, and his lips twitch into a slight smile. "I think I feel her."

I'm not convinced, thinking he might be tricking himself into *believing* he can. But even if that's the case, does it matter? Perception is reality, and it's not like she's not there—she is. If he thinks he can feel her, isn't that all that matters? Doesn't that make it real to him?

Mom slowly slices her hand out of Peter's and turns to face me. "You finally came. I'm so happy you can see me."

"Yeah, I . . ." I let my words trail off, realizing I still have the Whisperings. I can still see ghosts.

"How long have you had the gift?"

The "gift." Before this moment, that's not how I would have described it, but now, I wouldn't trade it for anything.

"Only a couple months, but Dad's had it since . . . well, he's had it for longer. We call it the Whisperings."

"It's a good name. So few have it. You always were a special one, Jo."

I wouldn't call falling off a cliff and waking up with the ability to see ghosts special, but I keep that to myself. Instead, I'm suddenly overwhelmed by a lifetime of grief and guilt, and I begin to sob uncontrollably. My body heaves, the tears practically pour out of me, and I bend over in my mom's lap. It's not pretty, but I'm powerless to stop it.

"There, there, baby girl," she says soothingly, stroking my hair and rubbing my back.

I feel four years old again. Her touch fills me with a sense of security and comfort as real as the warmth from being bundled up in a thick, soft blanket.

"It's okay," she says, smiling down on me. "Everything's okay. We're together again, and that's all that matters."

I struggle to stop sobbing and then catch my breath. "But it's my fault."

"What is?"

"Everything," I say. "All of this. All the shit we've lived through these past thirteen years, always on the move, living in crappy apartments, never being able to have anything resembling a normal life. And at the top of the list, your death."

Mom's face suddenly becomes stern. She shakes her head stiffly. "No. That wasn't your fault. How can you even think that?"

"Your blood is on my hands," I say, looking at my palms and half expecting to see them coated in red. "I should have come out from under the bed, but I didn't. I just lay there uselessly, doing nothing when I should have been doing something, anything."

"Jo, you were four years old, practically a baby. There was nothing you could have done."

I shake my head, unable to meet Mom's eyes, not in this moment of weakness. "But there was. All I needed to do was come out, and we would have been okay. Uncle Roman said so."

Mom scans the room quickly. "Don't say his name aloud, not here." She gently cups my chin and makes me face her, her expression soft and warm. "He wouldn't have let us go. That was nothing but another one of his twisted lies. Your uncle wasn't well, and there was nothing you could've done to save me. But what you did do—staying under the bed—saved *you*."

"What do you mean?"

"It gave me the chance to slow him down. And it bought the time needed for your father to find us, and to stop his brother before he could do anything to you and Peter."

"But you had to give your life—"

"And I would give it again and again if I could, if it meant protecting you," Mom says, cutting me off abruptly. "That's my duty as a mother. You need to say it."

"Say what?" I look to Peter before remembering he's only hearing one side of this conversation. I can tell he's trying to be respectful, but he looks as confused as someone watching a movie on mute and with only half the screen working.

"That it wasn't your fault," Mom says.

I nearly laugh. Not out of humor, but surprise. "I don't know what you mean."

"It's not your fault, Jo, and I want to hear you say it."

I shake my head and tuck a strand of hair behind my ear. "No. I can't."

"Why not? It's the truth, and I don't think you're going to believe it until you say it."

"It's silly, and . . ." I hesitate, trying to think of an excuse. I finally land on one, but it's not one I want to admit: I still don't believe it *is* the truth, no matter what Mom says.

But realizing that gives me pause. Like Mom said, I was only four years old when my uncle killed her. Did I seriously expect that I could've done anything to stop him? Do I truly believe that he would have let us go if I'd come out from under the bed? I've been carrying this baggage for most of my life, and it's heavy. I test setting it down, and it feels good. I feel light, lighter than I've ever felt.

I can still be a fighter, but it's okay to be a flighter sometimes. And there was nothing I could have done.

"It's not my fault," someone says, and it takes me a heartbeat—*ta-tump*—to realize it was me.

I look at Mom and she looks at me. I smile. She smiles back, twice as wide. I cry, and so does she. We hug again, and when we part, she looks at me and Peter.

"That's what I've been waiting all these years to hear," she says.

Ta-tump. Ta-tump. Ta-tump.

For a moment, I think I can hear her heart, but that's not it.

Ta-tump. Ta-tump. Ta-tump.

It's footsteps.

Ta-tump. Ta-tump. Ta-tump.

Familiar footsteps. Coming up the stairs. *Ta-tump.* Down the hall. *Ta-tump.* Entering the bedroom. *Ta-tump.*

Uncle Roman, his splitting maul in hand. It isn't bloody—not yet.

"Little pig, little pig, let me cave your skull in," he says.

"Not tonight," Mom says, her smile refusing to fade. "Not ever again."

Uncle Roman looks confused, like he was expecting Mom to do or say something different, likely something consistent with what she's been doing and saying for the past thirteen years. He drops his splitting maul to the floor with a loud *ta-tump* and narrows his eyes inquisitively.

"Goodbye, Jelly Bean," Mom says. She squeezes my hands.

"I love you. Always have. Always will. Tell Peter, and your dad too. I'll see you all again one day, but hopefully not too soon." With a final, wistful smile, she begins to fade. I can see Peter through her, and then, a moment later, I can't see her at all. And I know she's finally moved on. On the surface, it seems like I helped her, but in reality, she helped me.

"Huh," Uncle Roman says, reminding me he's still there. "Never thought I'd see the day your bitch mother left me."

I look at him in utter contempt. Every fiber of my being flares with red-hot fury, an anger that threatens to consume me.

"But a door closes, and a window opens," he says, raising his splitting maul above his head. "Guess I'll have to settle for finally killing you." He takes a heavy step forward and swings the splitting maul straight for my head.

I raise my hands to block the blow, knowing how pointless that is. The gesture won't even slow the splitting maul down before it turns my face into a splattered wall-stain of blood and flesh and broken bone and teeth.

But now that I know Mom is waiting for me, I'm no longer afraid to die.

The sledgehammer side of the splitting maul passes through my hands, then through my head, but I don't hit the floor. My hands are fine. More importantly, so is my head.

Uncle Roman takes an off-balance step as he completes his home run of a swing. He looks at me, then at his splitting maul, then back at me. Equal measures of confusion and anger populate his expression, like he doesn't know what happened but he's certain he's pissed off about it. "What the fuck?"

At first, I don't know what happened either, but understanding dawns on me quicker than him. Like Mom, he's fading.

I can see through him, and his splitting maul too. These past thirteen years, he's remained here so he can kill her, night after bloody night.

"With Mom gone," I say, speaking with disdain, "I guess you no longer have purpose here."

"No!" he bellows, raising his splitting maul once more and lunging at me.

"I hope you don't find a single shred of peace where you're headed," I say, waving my hand through his chest. His body dissipates and swirls in the air before disappearing.

Gone. My uncle is *gone*. Tears run down my cheeks, and I wipe them away messily. The bastard is finally gone.

That's how you beat a ghost, I think. *You find out what's keeping them here, and you take it away.*

It takes me a bit of time, and a very odd look from Peter, to realize I'm laughing. I not only found the closure I sought but some answers too.

"Jo?" he asks hesitantly, like he's not sure he wants to know what's going on. "What happened?"

I rub my face, take a deep breath, and look around my old bedroom one final time. "I'll tell you on the drive back to Mrs. Cracknell's house." After a moment's consideration, I add, "*Our* house."

Chapter Fifteen

TREES AND STREETLIGHTS, our only companions this time of night, line the streets as we drive home. The listless sway of the trees and the electric buzz of the lights makes me feel a little dispirited. The city feels like a ghost town this time of night.

An epic yawn forces my mouth wide like a lion's. I rub my eyes and tighten my grip on the steering wheel, remembering that I haven't slept in a day, and it's been one hell of a day. I maybe, probably, *definitely* shouldn't be driving, but we have to get back—the longer we're away, the longer I think Dad and Mrs. Cracknell are in danger. I blink and refocus on the road ahead. Not much longer now.

"That's Ash and Triss's house," Peter says as we pass a nice-looking two-story home. A second-floor bedroom light turns on as we pass.

Other than that, Peter hasn't said much since I caught him up on what happened back in my old bedroom.

"You okay?" I ask, stealing a sideways glance at him.

He shrugs. "Yeah, I guess. Just feel bad. Mom's been attacked every night for years. It's messed up."

"No kidding," I say. "But at least it's over now. She's at peace."

"I wish we'd known sooner. We could've done something."

"Beating ourselves up about it isn't going to do any good," I say, trying to sound reassuring. "What's past is past, and there's nothing we can do to change that. What we *can* change is everything that lies ahead."

"You sound just like Dad."

"I was thinking the same thing as I said it." I smile at Peter, and he smiles back.

"So, what lies ahead?" he asks.

Uncertainty? Failure? Inevitable death? These words pop up in my mind, too depressing to voice. I think a moment longer before a more concrete response comes to me.

"Well, now that I know I can still see ghosts, I can confront Abraham. But it would be best to try to speak with the kids again first. Hopefully we can figure out why they're all still here so we can help them move on."

After a moment, Peter says, "You really think Dad is in danger, even in the hospital?"

"I don't know," I say with a defeated sigh, wishing for the hundredth time that he hadn't fallen. We could've been on the other side of the state by now.

Something Peter said, back in our old house, suddenly comes back to me.

"Hang on. You said Dad told you he heard someone humming 'Too-Ra-Loo-Ra-Loo-Ral' and he smelled lavender just before he fell off the ladder?"

Peter nods. "Yeah, that's what he said as we waited for the ambulance to arrive, but he was in and out of it, and half of what he said was nonsense."

I frown so hard my forehead hurts, thinking of the obvious while refusing to accept it.

"What is it, Jo?"

"If that's true, I think Sarah pushed Dad, not Abraham. And if *that's* true, we've got things all wrong. Sarah is probably the killer, not her husband." The dots in my head connect quickly, sketching a picture I feel foolish for not seeing earlier. "And that might explain why the kids are still here. They want to set the record straight."

Peter shakes his head.

"What?"

"How often do you hear of a mom killing her own kids?"

"Not often, but it happens sometimes." I have no way of backing that up other than some vague recollection of someone once telling me about a mother who drowned her kids in a bathtub—second-hand information at best, but it seems to be enough to help Peter consider the idea instead of rejecting it completely.

"Maybe, I guess," he says.

"Like I said, I need to speak with the kids . . . hopefully without them falling apart and bursting into flames."

"Great," Peter says. "Another one-sided conversation for me to listen to."

Count yourself lucky you can't speak with the dead, I think, not looking forward to what's to come.

IT'S A LITTLE PAST three in the morning when we pull into the driveway. After I kill Victor's ignition, the night is eerily silent. I peer into Mrs. Cracknell's windows, but see no movement, and all the lights are out.

"What is it?" Peter asks.

"Nothing," I say, but something doesn't feel right.

I unlock the door to the basement apartment. It was only a few hours ago that I found the car keys by the front door, but it feels like days have passed. Once I'm in, I shove the keys as deep as possible in my jeans pocket and think, *Let's see you hide them from me now.*

"You'll give me plenty of warning if you see or hear one of them, right?" Peter asks, entering after me and closing the door.

"Of course," I say, thinking that the ghosts don't typically give me much advance notice.

Everything is dark, gray, and murky. It's like the house has been drained of color, sapped of life. I don't want to turn on all the lights, announcing loudly that we're home, but I also don't want to trip in the darkness and break my neck. Fortunately, I still have the flashlight Edith gave me. Peter stays as close as possible as we descend into the bowels. The stairs groan and creak beneath our feet, and I'm so focused on what lies ahead that it takes me a moment to realize there's the sound of three sets of footsteps—ours, and a third behind us.

I stop dead and spin around, aiming the beam of light back up the way we came.

"Is someone there?" Peter asks in alarm.

"I don't see anyone," I say.

But then I hear a new sound. Not footsteps on creaking stairs, but a voice.

"*I'm coming . . .*" someone unseen hisses from above. Slowly, a shadow materializes as it flows through the door.

She's back. Dead Girl. I can't tell if she's seen us yet, and I'm not sticking around to find out.

"Hide," I whisper urgently, putting a hand on Peter's back and guiding him down the remaining stairs, through the hall, and into the family room. He looks surprised but knows better than to argue. We drop to our hands and knees and squeeze between the back of the couch and the wall. It's tight but we fit, just barely.

"Who is it?" he asks.

"Her," I say, watching the door and wishing I'd closed it.

"Her *who*? Red Eyes? Hollow Mother?"

I shake my head. "Dead Girl."

"What does she want?"

I shake my head and press a finger to my lips, telling him to stop talking. If we have any hope of remaining hidden, we need to be silent.

Dead Girl appears in the doorway and scans the family room. I stop breathing and close my eyes tight, hoping she didn't see me. Hoping she can't hear me.

"I know you're in here," Dead Girl says quietly. "Where are you?"

Can she hear my heartbeat? *Ta-tump-ta-tump-ta-tump!* It feels like it's about to explode. Can she hear the blood coursing through my veins, making my extremities burn and my eardrums throb? Can she hear my panicked thoughts screaming inside my head?

I open my eyes a sliver, peek around the edge of the couch, and see her feet. Bare, pale, splattered with blood, and creeping toward us. A small lump of brain hits the floor with a splat.

She might not have seen us yet, but she knows where we are.

I can't take it any longer. I feel like I'm about to crawl out of my own skin. No more hiding. I stand up.

"What are you doing?" Peter asks in concern.

I ignore him and face Dead Girl. We're only two feet apart. Close enough for her to reach out and dig her nails into me. Close enough for me to smell the reek of death rolling off her in waves.

"What do you want from me?" I demand.

She continues walking without answering, closing the gap between us.

My brain shouts at me to run, but I stand my ground, refusing to give her another inch.

"I said, what do you want from me?"

She takes another step. Our skin touches. A chill instantly spreads through my entire body, firing up all seven trillion of my nerves. My breath catches in my throat. I can't move. It's how I imagine rigor mortis would feel, only I'm still alive and my lungs and heart are still working. And holy shit—is my heart ever working.

TA-TUMP-TA-TUMP-TA-TUMP-TA-TUMP!

And then, as effortlessly as if she's slipping into a nightgown, Dead Girl slips into *me*.

It's the trippiest feeling imaginable, defying all logic and rational thought. I'm two people at once, both me and her. I'm seeing through my eyes, but I'm also seeing through her eyes seeing through mine. Moving together, we hold up my hand and regard it in awe—such a simple thing, my hand, made wondrous by our coupling. My heart hammers, as does hers, beating for the first time since she died, the two creating a double beat. Her thoughts fill my brain—all manic wonder and joy at being "alive" again—but the one thing I don't seem to possess are her memories. Somehow, I know without a shadow of doubt that she doesn't have access to mine, either. Other than that, we are one.

"This is *incredible*," we say. We run a hand through our hair and sigh in utter bliss as our scalp tingles. All the ways I've ever touched myself have never felt so good.

"Agreed," we reply. "Absolutely incredible."

Peter slides out from behind the couch, staring at me like he's never seen me before. In a way, he hasn't.

"Jo? What's up with you?"

We laugh and smile. "Peter, brother," we say, then fall into another laughing fit. "I have a brother! I always wanted . . . well, I always wanted a *sister*, but I'll settle for a brother."

"You're scaring me," Peter says, raising his hands and backing away from us. "Seriously, what's wrong with you?"

"Nothing," we say, and nothing is, but it dawns on me—Joana Guest, not Dead Girl—why Peter is freaked out. It must look like I've lost my ever-loving mind, serious enough to require psychiatric help. "I'm going to tell you something, but you have to promise you won't get all weird."

He frowns but stops backing up. "I'm not sure I can promise that."

"That's fair," I say. "Dead Girl entered the room, and then . . . she entered me."

"What?" Peter says, looking as confused as if I'd just told him I'd been elected president. "What do you mean, *entered* you? Like, possessed you?"

"Exactly," I say, and then Dead Girl adds, "My name is Alice, by the way."

"What should I do?" Peter asks.

"Nothing!" I say. "I'm fine. She—Alice—hasn't possessed me to hurt me, and she hasn't been following me to hurt us either. I know that now."

He doesn't look convinced, but his concerned expression has softened a little. "So, what does she want?"

After a moment of silent deliberation, Alice says, "I want help."

"Help with what?" I ask.

"Crossing over," she says as if it's the most obvious answer in the world, like she can't believe I even had to ask.

"Why me?" I ask. "How can I help you?"

"You can hear me," she says. "You can see me."

The Whisperings, I think, and Alice nods. She can hear my thoughts, just as I can hear hers.

"Before I flowed into you, I could hardly even speak, thanks to the accident."

I wonder if it would be rude to ask her how she died before remembering she can hear my thoughts.

"I don't mind," she says. "It was a long time ago. My dad took me to a double feature, *Rosemary's Baby* and *Night of the Living Dead*, at the drive-in theater. He didn't care for horror movies but knew how much I loved them. He had to watch them through his fingers, but he stayed awake for both, for me. He was exhausted, so I offered to drive home. I'd just gotten my driver's license, and although I didn't have much experience, I promised I'd drive slow and safe. He didn't love the idea, but he was so tired that he finally gave in and handed over the keys. I drove home, slow and safe like I promised, along a country road. It wasn't long before Dad was snoring softly beside me. I was starting to get a little tired myself and wanted to get home, so I sped up, thinking Dad wouldn't ever know."

Alice pauses and frowns, her face—my face—pinched and pained. I don't have to be in her head—or rather, she in mine—to know what comes next will be near impossible for her to recount.

"Out of nowhere, a thick fog descended upon us, flowing between the trees like tentacles, obscuring my view of the road ahead. I thought I should slow down, or pull over, until the fog dissipated, but I kept going. I thought we were alone, and in a way, we were—there wasn't another car anywhere near us—but of course, you're never really alone in the woods. Suddenly, a moose as tall as a bus barreled out of the forest and across the road. I swerved, narrowly avoiding the moose's hind legs. The car careered off the road. I tried to turn again, spinning sideways into a large tree. We came to a sudden, screeching, jarring stop. A thick branch smashed through the window and cracked my head open. I died instantly, feeling no pain. I didn't see a white light, like in the movies. Instead, I saw *everything*. My blood-soaked, lifeless body. My dad, his mind foggy as he wiped blood—some his, mostly mine—off his face. I can still hear his tortured scream when he turned and saw what was left of me, his only child, slumped in the seat beside him. The sound haunts me to this day."

"Holy shit, Alice," I whisper. "I'm so, so sorry."

"Yeah, me too," Peter says, his voice low and lifeless.

Alice closes our eyes and nods. "Then a white light did appear. It swallowed me up and took me away. But I came back. Dad blamed himself. Still does. Says he shouldn't have let me drive, shouldn't have fallen sleep. He even says he shouldn't have taken me to the movies, like there was any way he could have known what was going to happen that night. He stopped working, started drinking. My parents split up a year later. He's . . . he's tried to end things a few times, but thankfully he hasn't been able to go through with it. If I could just talk to him, tell him it's not his fault, tell him I'm fine, maybe then he'd be . . . not okay, but . . . I don't know. Better? But he can't see or hear me."

"That's why you need my help," I say.

We nod again, and she says, "When you first saw me in the hospital, I knew you could help me. You're the first person to have seen me since I died, so I've been following you ever since. I can't give up. I won't give up."

I respect that. If my dad was suffering, and there was anything I could do to help—even after death—I'd do it. Nothing would stop me.

"You're a fighter," I say, and Alice smiles. "I'll help you. I'll speak with your dad."

"Thank you," Alice says, our face and voice both beaming. "Thank you so much. I'll find you when the time is right, but right now, someone else is waiting."

I take an involuntary step forward, feeling like something is ripping through me before realizing something is ripping *out* of me. It's Alice, slipping out of my body. It's like our souls have been glued together, but finally, after a little effort, she breaks free and is standing before me once again. I feel lighter and colder, and although I wouldn't want to live with someone else inside me permanently, in a weird way, I already kind of miss it.

But the pleasant sensation is replaced quickly with the ice-cold realization of what Alice said.

"Someone is waiting?" I ask. "Who?"

Alice points toward the bedrooms, then leaves the way she came.

I look down the hall, a pit forming in my gut. I don't see anyone, but I know that means nothing. Far too often, people are hiding in plain sight.

"Has she left?" Peter asks.

I nod. "But there's someone else."

"Who?"

"I don't know."

"Where?"

"I don't know that, either." I tear my eyes away from the hall and look at Peter, hating how scared he looks. As stressful and terrifying as all this is for me, it must be worse to be left in the dark like him. "Somewhere down the hall. If I had to guess, my bedroom."

"Well—"

"Don't say 'No time like the present' again," I say lightheartedly, cutting him off.

"I wasn't going to say that," he says, a touch too defensively. "I was going to say . . ." His eyes dart to the ceiling as if the end of his sentence might be found there. When he can't think of a lie, he sighs in mild frustration. "Fine. I was going to say 'No time like the present.'"

I smile, victorious. "I know you too well, little brother."

"Shut up," he quips.

I laugh and lead the way.

The brief feeling of levity, teasing my brother just like old times, evaporates as soon as I enter the hall. It's much colder than the family room, and the temperature seems to drop with every step I take. But that's not what bothers me. It's the *not knowing* that's truly terrible. Not knowing who's waiting for us. Not knowing what lies ahead. And more than anything, not really knowing what to do.

I quickly look into the kitchen and two of the three bedrooms as we pass. As I expected, they all appear to be empty. It's weird being back here without Dad. Seeing his bedroom, with his pajamas hastily strewn across the unmade bed, sends a sharp pain through my chest.

Faintly, I hear a baby crying in my room. *Joshua*, I think, *Mariah and Isaac's little brother*. Then footsteps, running across my bedroom floor. The door flies open and Isaac comes to a quick stop before me.

"Please, help," he says desperately. "It's my brother. He can't breathe. He's turning blue!" Isaac grabs my hand and pulls me desperately.

As I follow Isaac, a voice pushes through the noise in my head, reminding me that Joshua is well beyond saving, but the thought quickly dissolves, overpowered again by blind panic.

We barge into my room. Mariah is standing in the corner, her back to us. She's shaking violently. I can't see her face, but I hear her weeping. Goosebumps cover my skin, and my stomach drops with the sudden suspicion that this is wrong, this is a trap, but then she turns, sees us, and her eyes go wide.

"Help," she says. "Oh god, please help!" She's holding Joshua tight to her chest, bouncing him up and down. His body flops around like a rag doll, arms and legs limp. His face is pinched tight with pain, but he's not making a sound. He's no longer *turning* blue—he's well past that. His entire head is more of a dark purple, like a fresh bruise.

My brain switches to autopilot and I take Joshua from Mariah. She gives him up willingly, eager for someone to save him, to save *them*. Unsure what to do, I bounce him three or four times in my arms, but nothing changes, and I fear that if I bounce him any harder, I'm going to break his soft neck. I cradle him in one arm and poke and prod in his mouth, searching for blockages, but find none.

"Shit, shit, shit, what do I do?" I say, more to myself than anyone else. Can I perform CPR on a baby? Even if that's possible, I've never taken first aid and have no idea how to do it. But then I remember something I saw on a TV show once. A baby was choking on a piece of fruit, so her parent flipped her on her belly and smacked her back until the food flew out. *It's worth a shot.* I flip Joshua over and begin hitting his back. One, two, three, four, five. How many times should I hit him before checking to see if anything has come loose from his throat? Six, seven, eight, nine, ten. What if he's not choking? Eleven, twelve, thirteen, fourteen, fifteen. What if he simply stopped breathing? Sixteen, seventeen, eighteen, nineteen, twenty. What if he's already dead?

He is already dead, I think again as I turn him face-up to check his mouth.

I nearly drop Joshua to the ground. There is something there—not in his mouth, but over it. An adult hand, reaching around from behind me, covering Joshua's mouth and pinching his nose tight.

I grab the hand and try to pull it free, but I can't. I squeeze the fingers and try to pry them free, but whoever is suffocating him is too strong. Blind desperation overtakes me, and I dig my nails into the back of the hand, splitting skin, tearing flesh, and scraping bone. Everything peels off the hand easily, too easily, and blood pours freely in the wake of my nails, flowing over Joshua's face. It works—the hand finally releases Joshua's nose and pulls away. I turn to see who was attacking the baby, but there's no one behind me. Just Mariah and Isaac to one side and Peter to the other. They're watching me intently, seemingly unaware that there was anyone else in the room just a second before.

Joshua cries. I turn my attention back to him. The blood that had covered his face when I ripped into the hand is gone, and his color is no longer purple but a healthier-looking red. He screams and wails as he desperately sucks in air, his arms raised to the sides of his face, his hands clenched in tiny, shaking fists.

I hand him back to Mariah, confused, relieved, and shaken. There's no blood on my hands, no skin under my fingernails.

Mariah cradles her baby brother tightly. She hastily wipes some tears from her cheeks, and I realize she's crying blood again, like the first time I saw her.

"Do your . . . eyes always do that?" I ask, not wanting to be insensitive, but my curiosity is killing me.

"I have haemolacria, bloody epiphora, but it's fine." She looks down at Joshua and smiles. "You saved him. Thank you."

I nod, but I'm still not sure what I did. "There was a hand covering his face. Did anyone else see the hand?"

I'm met with blank stares from Mariah and Isaac, and a perpetually confused look from Peter.

"It was an adult hand," I say. They might not have seen the hand, but I did, and I have a pretty good idea of who it was. "It was your mom. She was suffocating Joshua, just like she did so many years ago, right? Your dad didn't kill you, like the newspapers reported—she did."

Mariah shakes her head, unable to meet my eyes.

"She killed each of you, one after the other, and got rid of your bodies." I try not to picture Sarah dismembering the kids, but it's too late: the image is already filling my head, and it's far grislier than anything I've ever seen on TV.

"No," Mariah says, still shaking her head in denial. I can't blame her. I'd be in denial too.

"Yes," I say, pressing on. I'm sure this is painful for them, but it's better to push forward now, while we have this time alone. Their parents will likely be here any moment. "When we moved in, she tried to trick me into believing she was my mother. Reeking of lavender, she sang 'Too-Ra-Loc-Ra-Loo-Ral' and tried to take me into the red room behind the closet. And when my dad was pushed off a ladder, the air was filled with the scent of lavender, and he heard someone singing the same lullaby."

"You're right," Mariah says softly.

I knew it. I knew I was right.

But Mariah continues. "She did push your dad. And she did try to take you. But she didn't kill us."

"What?" I say. "But I was certain—"

"You didn't let me finish," Mariah says, cutting me off. "She didn't kill us . . . alone."

"Alone?" I say, my mind reeling. "What do you mean?"

"They did it together." Mariah's words hang in the air between us like laundry left out on a line to dry. "Mom and Dad. They both killed us. They sawed our bodies into pieces small enough to feed into the furnace, here in the basement, as we watched. When they were done, they killed themselves." She raises her head and meets my gaze, staring intently at me. "And you're next."

Chapter Sixteen

"YOUR PARENTS DID ALL those horrible things together?" I ask, rubbing my forehead. I'd convinced myself the person to fear was Sarah, then Abraham, then Sarah again, but I had never paused to consider that I should fear them *both*.

"Yes," Mariah says.

She doesn't appear willing to say more, but I need to know one thing.

"All these years . . . it's bothered you that your murders were attributed to your father—and only your father—hasn't it?"

Mariah and Isaac don't answer. Their silence is all the answer I need. That's why they haven't moved on, I'm certain of it, but I have no idea how to help them.

I hear a door at the top of the stairs open. Is it one of the Keils? Or Mrs. Cracknell? I ready myself for anything as the sound of footsteps approaches, but I'm not ready for who appears in the doorway.

"Ash?" Peter says, sounding as surprised as me. "What are you doing here?"

"I couldn't sleep and saw you drive past my house," he says, looking back and forth between us. "Not only was it suspicious for you to be out so late, but I could tell from the glimpse I caught of the looks on your faces that something was wrong. Really wrong. And I knew I wouldn't be able to fall back asleep until I figured out what was going on—plus, I thought you might need some, I don't know, help or something—so I biked over here. I knocked, but no one answered." He takes a deep breath and wipes some sweat off his face. "One of you really needs to get a phone."

This is bad. "You shouldn't have come here."

"Why?"

I look at Mariah and Isaac. Their faces are drawn with worry. They know better than anyone why Ash, another kid, shouldn't have come to the Kill House. But how do I explain any of that to someone who has no idea?

"I'll fill you in later, Ash," Peter says, wisely sidestepping Ash's question. "But you have to go. Like, right now."

Ash looks a little confused, and a little hurt. "But I came to help you."

"Trust me, there's nothing you can do to help," Peter says.

"Maybe there is. Tell me what's going on and we'll see."

This is taking too long, and every second that Ash is here, he's not only putting himself in greater danger but he's putting *us* in greater danger too. What would get a thirteen-year-old boy to leave as quickly as possible? I blurt out the first thing that pops into my head.

"My period came earlier than I expected, okay? And I needed to rush out to the pharmacy to buy some supplies."

It works—Ash looks startled and embarrassed—but only for a moment before he begins to question my story. "So you woke Petey to go with you?"

I sigh, trying to think up a fresh lie to get me out of the first one. But my train of thought is halted when I smell a hint of lavender.

"Oh, no," Mariah says, whipping her head to the side and staring at the closet with wide eyes.

"Run! Hide!" Isaac shouts.

I don't have time to run or hide. I don't even have time to warn Peter and Ash. Sarah rushes out of the closet, wraps her arms around Peter, says, "Come with me, child," and drags him backward. His eyes bulge and he screams in terror.

"What the hell?" Ash yells, watching Peter be pulled against his will by an unseen force.

Mariah, still holding Joshua, runs from the room. Isaac has disappeared and I have no idea where he's gone.

I take a furious step forward, prepared to do everything in my power to stop Sarah from taking my brother, but I'm stopped dead in my tracks. Big, burly, scarred arms wrap around me from behind, squeezing me tight. Abraham's hold on me hurts, the way Sarah's touch hurt the night she tried to drag me into the red room, which is where she pulls Peter. They disappear from sight.

I struggle and squirm and try to break free, but Abraham is too strong. He looks from me to the red room, and then back to me.

"I wouldn't, if I were you," he says, his voice loud and piercing in my ear. His breath smells of pipe smoke. "That's the last place you want to be with my wife."

"My brother is in there," I say through gritted teeth.

"For now," Abraham says coldly. "Not for much longer."

"Who are you talking to?" Ash says in utter disbelief. He's slumped on the floor in shock, his back against the wall and his knees pulled up tight to his chest.

A loud *thump*, the sound of something being struck, comes from the red room, followed by a *thud*. Sarah emerges a moment later. There's no sign of Peter.

"If you've done anything to him," I say, hot tears running down my face.

"You'll what?" she asks with a smile. "Kill me?" Her gaze lands upon Ash, and her smile widens. She clasps her hands together and takes a step toward him. "Oh Hello, there."

"You better not do anything to him, either," I say.

Sarah looks at me and laughs. The fact that she doesn't even feel the need to reply makes me feel helpless, enraging me.

"You can't keep us here forever," I say.

Turning her attention to her husband, Sarah says, "Did you hear that, Abe? We can't keep them here forever."

He grunts in response and tightens his grip on me, forcing more air out of my lungs. Every breath hurts. I feel like I might pass out.

"You couldn't be more wrong, child," Sarah tells me. "Dead wrong. This is our forever home, and not even death can take it away from us, or us away from it."

"Stop calling me *child*," I say, tasting bile creep up from the back of my throat.

"But that's what you are," Sarah says.

"Not yours."

"You will be," Sarah says, a malicious gleam in her eye.

"We've wanted to grow our family for ages," Abraham says. "And then, finally, you came into our lives."

"*Grow* your family? By killing kids, like you killed your own?"

"We had no choice," Sarah spits out, suddenly agitated. She takes a deep breath and attempts to regain her composure. "The world is a cruel place and death comes for us all. Dying here, together in this house, was the only way we could protect them. The only way we could protect ourselves."

I only got under her skin for a moment, but it felt good. And it told me something about Sarah, pointed out a sore spot. She believes what she and her husband did was fair and just, but she still doesn't want to be confronted with the cold, hard truth that they killed their kids. She wants to put a spin on it—she *saved* them.

"Speaking of which," Sarah says, sharing a knowing look with Abraham. "It's time."

Abraham nods at the bed. Sarah returns his nod, then begins walking playfully around the room.

"Come out, come out, wherever you are!" she says, looking high and low, searching behind furniture and clothes and pillows. She comes to a sudden stop at the foot of the bed. "Peek-a-boo! I see you!" She drops to her hands and knees, reaches far under the bed, and pulls out Isaac. He comes kicking and screaming, unable to overpower his mother.

My stomach flips, causing me to dry retch. This is familiar—all too familiar—to me, too similar to my own traumatic memories.

"Let me go!" Isaac screams, his face beet-red. "Let me go, let me go, let me go!"

"Stop resisting, child," Sarah says. "You're a dirty little boy, and it's time for your bath."

"No," I say, knowing where this is headed and feeling powerless to prevent it.

"Joana, please tell me what's happening," Ash says miserably. I'd forgotten he's still in the room.

"I can't," I tell him truthfully.

Sarah pulls Isaac out of the bedroom and down the hall. His cries mix with her humming the tune of "Too-Ra-Loo-Ra-Loo-Ral."

Abraham drags me to the door, then stops and looks back. "We can't leave you here," he tells Ash.

Despite not being able to hear the dead, Ash seems to sense that something bad, really bad, is about to happen, and he looks terrified. Abraham grabs Ash in a headlock and pulls us both out of the room. Ash makes an awful gurgling sound. If he could scream, I'm sure he would. I, on the other hand, am beginning to feel screamed out. My insides ache and my soul hurts.

Ash struggles against Abraham all the way to the bathroom, where Sarah has taken Isaac, but I remain limp. Like a fly trapped in a spider's web, it's better to conserve my strength. I'm going to need it.

Water gushes out of the tap, rapidly filling the tub. Isaac is still desperately trying to get out of his mother's snare, but he's losing steam and has nothing to show for it.

"Shhhhh . . ." Sarah whispers softly. "There, there, sweet child. You have to be cleansed." Once the water level has nearly reached the edge of the tub, Sarah turns off the tap. "In you go now."

Abraham gives my neck a squeeze and angles my head so that I'm forced to watch. I could close my eyes, but I'm convinced that would somehow only make it worse, hearing but not seeing.

"Please," Isaac says, tears and snot and spit mixing on his cheeks, lips, and chin. "Please." He stops resisting. "Please."

Sarah lifts him easily and places him in the bathtub. The water rises and flows over the edge, pooling on the floor. "Please, please, please. No, Momma. Don't do this."

My heart shatters into a thousand tiny pieces. Watching him give up the fight, resigning himself to desperate begging, is horrible beyond words.

"It's for your own good," Sarah coos, placing her hand on his forehead. "Now, lay back and let Momma wash all your worries away." She pushes his whole head underwater. He closes his eyes and doesn't try to stop her. A few small bubbles flow from his nose, breaking the surface with tiny *pops*.

I know this is not really happening. It's a glimpse from the past and Isaac is already dead, not dying. I tell myself all of that, repeating it in my head with the cadence of a steady drumbeat. But it doesn't matter. Seeing it for myself, a child being ruthlessly murdered by his own parents, is tearing me apart. My entire body shakes. I want to kill Sarah and Abraham and burn down the house and destroy everything all around us.

Just wait, I tell myself. *The time will come.*

The silence in the bathroom is interrupted only by the gentle *plink, plink, plink* of drops of water falling from the bathtub faucet.

Isaac's eyes flash open and he begins to thrash about in the tub, splashing water in every direction. His mother pins him down.

"Only a moment more," she says sweetly. "You're so close, and then you'll be done, and this will all be over."

Until the next time she drowns you, I think, picturing my mother being murdered each night by my uncle until I finally helped her move on.

Isaac stops kicking. His body spasms and twitches like an irregular heartbeat. *Ta-tump. Ta-tump. Ta-tump, ta-tump. Ta-tump. Ta* . . . And then he falls still. Three small bubbles drift out of his mouth, the final breath of air he held in his lungs. His lifeless eyes remain wide open, staring up at us from his watery grave. His stare is both accusatory and melancholic.

Sarah drains the tub and lifts her son's body out, laying him on the floor with his head in her lap. Gently, she towels his face dry, runs her fingers through his hair, and gives his forehead a kiss. I watch as if in a trance, feeling hopeless and dejected.

"There," Sarah tells Isaac's lifeless corpse. "That wasn't so bad, now, was it?"

"You're a monster," I say. "Both of you."

"Am I?" Sarah asks, her question genuine, not angry or sarcastic. "Is it monstrous to want a lifetime—no, an *eternity*—of love and happiness with your children? To free them of all the horrors and pain and suffering of this world?"

"But why?" I ask. "How is this"—I spread my arms wide—"any better than living a normal life, like everyone else, and dying when it's your time? How could you both be so heartless, so cruel?"

Sarah moves so quickly that Isaac's head slides off her lap and hits the floor with a hollow thud. She flies straight at me, grabs me by the hair, yanks my head back, and holds her face inches from mine, her eyes wild, her teeth bared. "And leave them all alone? To fend for themselves? Never! The world would chew them up, spit them out, and pick its teeth with their bones. *That's* heartless. *That's* cruel. What we did was *love*." She releases my hair, rubs her face, and then straightens her dress, trying to regain her composure.

In the short silence that follows, I ponder her words, feeling she revealed more by what she didn't say than what she did. "Leave them all alone," I say, repeating her words bitterly. "You didn't kill yourselves from the guilt of what you had done to your children. Your marriage had fallen apart—your husband's mental health was suffering, he was sleeping with an assistant, and he had been fired. You were going to commit suicide all along, and so was he, so you decided to kill your children first."

Sarah doesn't answer. She doesn't even look at me. Abraham's grip on my arm loosens, but not enough to escape. Ash, also still held by Abraham, is pale and listless, looking like he might faint at any moment.

"What did you do?"

It takes me a moment to realize the person who asked the question isn't in the bathroom, but in the hall. Mariah, holding Joshua, is staring at Isaac as if seeing him dead for the first time. Maybe, in some way, she is. Ghosts seem to be stuck in some sort of perpetual time loop, reliving the worst, most traumatic moments of their lives. If that's not cruel, I don't know what is, but there's no sense entering another debate with Sarah.

She reaches a comforting hand out to her daughter. "Mariah. There you are, my love. Come here."

"What did you *do*?" Mariah asks again, her lip quivering. A single, bloody tear breaks free and rolls smoothly down to her jaw.

"I did what I had to do. I saved your brother. Come closer, so I can save you and Joshua too."

"Save us?" Mariah says, her voice cracking. "You killed him! How is that saving us?"

Sarah holds her wet, empty hands up, palms out, as if trying to show Mariah she's innocent and trustworthy. "I know this is hard to understand, but believe me when I say your brother is in a better place now, and we'll all be joining him soon. And when we do, we'll have no cares, no worries. Nothing will be able to harm us. Most importantly, we'll be together forever, happy once more, and no one will come between us ever again."

"No," Mariah says, shaking her head and taking a step backward.

If only she hadn't telegraphed what she was about to do—if only she'd run away as fast as possible—maybe she would have had a chance at escape. But it doesn't matter. I'm watching a play that's already been written. The Keils are the actors, the house is their stage, and they're no more in control of their own destinies than a character scripted on a page.

"No, I won't let you hurt him," Mariah says, shielding the back of Joshua's head with her hand.

Sarah looks ready to pounce. "Abraham, get them!"

Mariah finally turns to run, but too late. Abraham lets go of me and Ash—Sarah grabs us before we can get away—and gives chase to Mariah. His footsteps are like thunder pounding on the floor, so heavy I feel the reverberations where I sit. After three strides, he has her and he pulls her hard to the floor. She manages to protect the baby during the fall but can't hold onto him. Joshua rolls a few feet down the hall and wails in distress. What I'm watching might be like a stage play, but that doesn't make the baby's unbidden cries any easier to listen to. The sound is so heartbreaking, so awful, that I might rip my own ears off if that would stop me from hearing it.

Mariah tries to scramble away from her father, but he pins her to the floor.

"Let me go!" she screams, thrashing wildly, but uselessly, beneath him.

I know what comes next, but he appears to be hesitating. He's looking at her with a lack of emotion, but I feel like it's an act, like he's suppressing something else that's going through his head.

Maybe Mariah picks up on it too, maybe she's at the end of her rope, or maybe she genuinely thinks she has a chance at escape—whatever her plan is, she digs her nails into her father's forearms, just below his elbows, and drags her hands down viciously. She tears long, deep cuts into his skin and blood runs down his arms in rivulets.

Abraham doesn't let go of Mariah. He doesn't flinch or even make a sound. It's like he feels no pain. But he frowns, squints his eyes, and pinches his mouth. He looks sad.

"It will be better, Daughter," he says slowly, "if you can't see what's to come."

Mariah's eyes go wide in terror. She shakes her head.

He grabs the sides of her head—at first, I think, to stop her from shaking it, but no. He places his large thumbs over her eyes—she closes her lids—and then, without hesitation, presses down brutally.

Pop! Pop!

Mariah screams.

Joshua wails.

My stomach heaves and I throw up. It's nothing more than liquid and bile, burning the back of my throat and puddling near my feet. The world takes on a shimmering, muted tone, and everything sounds muffled. I feel like I'm about to faint. What's happening no longer resembles a play—it's too real, too awful, and is taking too big a toll on me, physically and emotionally. I just want to leave. I just want everything to stop. I just want my dad.

But even if I could get away from Sarah and Abraham, Peter is still in the red room. And I could never leave without him.

Blood oozes out of Mariah's ruined eyes. All the fight has left her. She's moaning but no longer struggling, no doubt in a massive amount of shock.

In one swift and powerful motion, Abraham lifts Mariah's head up and then slams it back down to the floor. The back of Mariah's head cracks, and she falls still.

"Take her to the cold cellar," Sarah says.

Abraham stands, looks down at Mariah's body, and then drags her through the hall to my room, trailing blood on the floor.

That's why I felt a cold draft coming from my closet—the red room used to be a cold cellar. Why did the Keils paint it red?

You know why, I think, wishing I didn't. Especially since my brother is in there.

Abraham steps out of my room, alone, a moment later. He walks to Joshua, who's cried himself hoarse, and picks him up gently. "Shh-shh-shh," he whispers as he steps into Peter's room. He places his hand over the baby's face a moment before they disappear from view. I'm not thankful for much at the moment, but I'm thankful I can no longer see them—a small mercy. A moment later, Joshua's cries stop. And a moment after that, Abraham re-emerges, the baby bundled in a blanket, one small hand hanging limply out of the wrap.

I thought I had nothing left, no more ability to feel emotional pain, but seeing Joshua's lifeless hand breaks me yet again.

But I also feel my resolve slowly begin to return. I've gotten through watching the worst of it, and I can't let these parents—

these monsters—go on doing what they've done to their kids night after night.

"We need to hide the evidence," Abraham says.

"That's not part of our plan," Sarah says. "There's no need. Once we join the children, it doesn't matter what we leave behind. It doesn't matter what people think. It—"

"We *need*," Abraham says, pointedly cutting his wife off, "to hide the evidence."

Sarah sighs, knowing this is a battle she's not going to win. "Okay."

It seems clear that, while obviously not mentally well, Abraham was not as committed to this plan as his wife was. Or maybe he's simply having regrets now that they've done what they've done. Because Sarah is right—after committing suicide, what would it matter whether they had hid the evidence or not? They'd done what they had set out to do, and they shouldn't have had any way of knowing what people thought of them.

However, they didn't move on, and they *did* learn what people thought of them. At least, the kids did. They know that everyone blamed their dad, and their dad alone, for the murders. They want the truth to come out; I'm more certain of that than ever. So, if I can find a way to ensure Sarah gets her fair share of the blame, then maybe the kids will move on.

My mind races. The reason Sarah and Abraham have stayed here is to be with their kids for an eternity.

Holy shit. That's it.

Get rid of the kids, get rid of the parents.

"On your feet," Sarah barks at me.

I quickly comply. Better to not put up a fight just yet, but instead let Sarah think I'm broken. "Ash, get up."

"What is even happening?" he says dejectedly.

"Get up!"

He blinks and focuses on me, then stands.

Abraham takes Joshua through my room and into the closet. Sarah leads us after them. I feel nauseous at the prospect of what I'll see in there—hell, the very thought of simply entering the red room makes me feel physically ill—but at least I'll also see Peter again. I hope he's okay.

"In you go," Sarah says, pushing me and Ash into the closet, past the broken drywall, and into the red room.

The sickness I felt before is nothing compared to the stomach-flipping sensation of entering the red room. Although he can't see what I see, Ash is overcome by the vibe of the room and has the same reaction I do. His face pales, he gags, and then he vomits in the corner where Sarah releases him. His body begins to shake, and not just from throwing up but from the cold. A shiver runs up my spine, its chill spreading across my back like winter frost on a window.

But there's one thing I'm thankful for. Peter is lying in a heap beside the wall. He's unconscious, but his chest is rising and falling, so at least he's still breathing.

"What happened here?" Ash asks, wiping bile off his chin with the back of his sleeve.

More like what's about to happen here. "Nothing good." A puff of frosty air blooms out with my words.

"Is Petey okay?" he asks, his eyes finally landing on my brother.

"He'll *be* okay."

Mariah and Isaac's bodies are on the floor across from us, their backs propped up against the wall and their heads leaning against one another. Abraham lays Joshua across their laps. If it weren't for all the blood, it would almost look like they'd fallen asleep that way. That's easier to swallow than the truth. If only I could trick myself into believing it.

Consistent with the residual haunting that's been playing out before my weary eyes, the red room looks like it did back on the night all this awful shit went down. It isn't empty. It isn't red, either. The cinderblock walls are gray and covered in metal shelving that's full of assorted tools—hammers and screwdrivers and glass jars filled with nails and screws. Instead of using their cold room to preserve food, Abraham used it as a tool room.

Which explains why they brought the bodies here.

We need to hide the evidence.

Another shiver races up my spine, but this one isn't caused by the cold.

Abraham grabs a pair of old handsaws from the shelf. He hands one to his wife.

"The sooner we start," he says, walking toward his children, "the sooner we'll be done."

Chapter Seventeen

PETER GROANS, SHIFTS, AND rolls over. His eyes flutter open. He groans again, rubs his face, and sits up. "What happened?"

What happened? I don't know how to answer that. I *can't* answer that.

But I also can't stop the images from flashing through my head.

Rusty saw blades pressing into skin.

Flesh tearing.

Blood spilling.

Bones breaking.

Bodies splitting.

Piles forming.

And then, everything being fed, piece by bloody piece, into the old furnace. The smell of burnt meat was so thick it filled the back of my throat. I can still taste it.

I can't bring myself to share any of that with Peter, so instead I share what happened to him, then add, "And the Keils killed their children. They've been doing it ever since the night they all died, just like Uncle Roman did to Mom."

"Why didn't they kill us?" Peter asks.

"I don't know, but I think the events of that tragic night had to play out just like they did so many years ago," I say, twisting my ring. "But I have no doubt they'll be back for us soon."

I can't help but think of all the people around the world who have been murdered over the years and wonder how many of them have been forced to relive the worst moment of their existence, night after night, with no end in sight. It's a horrible thought.

Peter wipes his forehead, and his hand comes away bloody. "Is this mine?"

"I think so," I say, recalling how he nearly fainted when he scratched himself with a potato peeler. The last thing I need is for him to pass out now.

He wipes his hand on his shirt and shrugs. "Guess the sight of my own blood doesn't bother me much anymore."

I exhale with relief.

The cold room once again looks like it did when I first discovered it. Once the kids' bodies were gone, Abraham removed his table and tools, and Sarah scrubbed the floor and walls. But she couldn't completely remove the bloodstains, so they covered them by painting everything red. At one point, Sarah chastised Abraham for spilling some paint upstairs near the front door. Then, once they'd finished, the Keils disappeared, the cold room of the past became the red room of the present, and Peter woke up. A few minutes before that, Ash, physically and mentally exhausted, had fallen into a fitful sleep.

"He's a good friend," Peter says, looking forlornly at Ash. "He shouldn't have come."

"Agreed." But I can't help thinking that, since he *did* come, we can make use of his presence somehow. I've been pondering how to convince the Keil kids that we'll get the truth about their parents out to the world, and I know simply telling them we'll do it won't be enough. Like Mom needing to see me with her own eyes, Mariah and Isaac need to see proof that the truth of their story will be told. And to do that, although I hate the thought of putting anyone else in danger by bringing them into this hellscape, I need Willem.

The corner of Ash's phone is peeking out of his pocket. I pull it out gently, not wanting to wake him. I manage to get it out and hold the screen up to his face, unlocking it.

"What are you doing?" Peter asks.

I open his contacts app and scroll through it. I knew I wouldn't find Willem's name and number, but I have a backup plan. "I'm going to call Triss." I tap on her name and hold the phone to my ear.

She answers on the fifth ring with a groggy, "What do you want, Ash-hole?"

"Triss, this is Joana."

"Huh? Joana?" Her voice perks up. "What are you doing with my brother's phone? Why are you calling me so early?"

"I can't tell you everything right now—I don't have enough time and none of it would make sense—but your brother came over to our house. He's in trouble. So are Peter and I. I'm not going to lie—it's really bad."

"What's going on? How bad is it? It's that old woman, isn't it?"

"Triss, listen. I'll explain everything later, but right now we need your help."

There's a moment of silence on the line, and I imagine Triss is taking a few seconds to wrap her head around what I've said. "Okay, yeah, of course. Tell me what to do."

"I need you to call Willem, tell him what I've told you, and tell him he needs to come here as quickly as possible. And this is the most important part: he needs to bring the newspaper article we printed at the library and a copy of the school newspaper."

"This is so messed up," Triss says quietly, more to herself than to me. "All right, got it."

"And Triss," I say, knowing she won't listen to a word of what I'm about to say, but I need to say it anyway. "Please don't come here with Willem. It's not safe."

"Forget that," she says without hesitation. "My brother is there. I'm coming."

"I know," I say. Turns out, we're not all that different, me and Triss. "Be fast." I hang up and slip Ash's phone back in his pocket.

"I get it," Peter says with a nod. "I know what you're planning. Where are the Keils now?" he asks.

"I don't know. Sarah and Abraham disappeared after they did . . . what they did. As for the kids . . ." I shrug. "I assume they'll be back, but I have no idea when. Hopefully by the time Willem gets here."

As if on cue, I hear a door open, followed by footsteps coming down the stairs. For a fleeting moment, I allow myself to think it's Willem and Triss, but that would be impossible.

"Joana?" Mrs. Cracknell calls. "Peter? Are you here? Are you okay?"

Oh no. This complicates things. What if the Keils return now? Mrs. Cracknell won't be able to see them. She won't be able to protect herself. And I need another person to worry about like I need a hole in my heart.

I open my mouth to implore her to go back upstairs, but

don't manage to get a single word out. A cold, wet hand slaps over my mouth, stifling my voice. I taste blood—not mine—as whoever has silenced me drags me across the floor. The back of my head and shoulders slam against the wall beside Peter. He looks like he's about to yell, but the same person covers his mouth too. Although my head throbs and my vision spins, I see Sarah seated between us, her back against the wall, still covered in her kids' blood. Smiling, she pulls Peter's head to one breast, then mine to the other, pressing my face hard against her blouse.

"Shh," she says. "Where are your manners, children? Let's not scare off our gracious host."

"I know someone is down here," Mrs. Cracknell calls out, her voice a little closer.

"That's it," Sarah says quietly. "Come join us. There's always room for one more."

"Jo?" Mrs. Cracknell says, sticking her head in my bedroom and giving it a quick scan. She sees the empty bed, and I think she's about to turn and leave, but then she peers at the closet and frowns. "What the devil?" She walks to the closet, looking at the drywall damage, not yet seeing us.

"One or two more steps," Sarah whispers eagerly, like a child playing hide-and-seek who *wants* to be caught.

Mrs. Cracknell runs her finger along the jagged edge of drywall and takes a step into the red room.

"Now!" Sarah shouts gleefully.

Abraham suddenly emerges from the shadows of the closet and wraps his arms around Mrs. Cracknell. She screams as he lifts her off the ground, and I know how confusing and terrifying what's happening to her must be.

But she stops screaming quickly, far quicker than I would have imagined. She's still "floating" a foot above the ground, and I have no idea how she regained her composure so quickly.

"We," Mrs. Cracknell says, looking directly at the empty space where Sarah is sitting, "had a deal."

What? She can see the Keils?

Sarah laughs, a hollow sound without any joy in it. "Who's the more foolish? The fool, or the fool who believes the fool?"

Wait a minute . . . *what?* She's working *with* the Keils?

Something inside Mrs. Cracknell breaks. The outrage falls from her face and she looks sad and defeated. "We are all fools if we live long enough. But I'm ashamed of myself for having trusted you."

"I can't help doing what I'm going to do to these kids," Sarah says. "It's in my nature."

My throbbing head is spinning now too, filled with questions swirling around like debris in a tornado. My tongue is burning with things I want to say, but I still can't talk with Sarah's hand covering my mouth.

Ash has woken up and is staring at Mrs. Cracknell. Peter whimpers, the sound muffled by Sarah. It dawns on me that with my ear pressed hard against Sarah's chest, I should hear the rhythm of her heartbeat, but I hear nothing.

Like Alice, I think. *She had no heartbeat until she entered my body and felt my own. But even without a heartbeat, Alice felt things, both emotionally and physically.*

Sarah will feel things too. Including pain.

I bite Sarah's palm as hard as I can, feeling my teeth break skin and tear through flesh, hitting bone.

She yells and withdraws her hand, then slaps me hard across the face.

I slouch to the side, cupping my stinging cheek, and my head hits the floor.

Sarah grabs the back of my neck and forces me to look up at her. "Remember your place. If you dare lash out at me again, I'll break your neck, just like that." She snaps her fingers an inch from my eyes. *Crack!*

"Go ahead," I say, tasting the blood pooling on my tongue. "You're going to kill me anyway, aren't you?"

Sarah's sneer is replaced by her typical smile. "Yes, but I'll kill your brother first and make you watch. And if you think he'll die peacefully, think again."

I nod and remove my hand from my cheek. It still stings, but it was worth it. I can talk again—not just with Sarah, but with Mrs. Cracknell. I turn and face her. "You're in on all of this?"

She shakes her head, conflicted. "No, Joana, of course not. Like you, I see the dead, and I have had an uneasy truce with the Keils for forty-three years. I've left them alone, and they've left me alone. Until recently, all was well and fine. But time bows to no one, and I could no longer keep this house from beginning to fall into disrepair. I needed to rent out the basement apartment, but I didn't want to put anyone in harm's way, so I told you to not do any repairs down there and made a deal with the Keils. Leave my new tenants alone, and I would donate the house to the city after my death *if* they agreed to designate it a heritage property, protecting it from demolition." She turns to face Sarah, her eyes narrowing and her lips pulling back like a dog about to snap. "But now that you've broken our agreement, I'll have no choice but to destroy the will I've prepared and have this house bulldozed."

Sarah laughs. "How will you do that with a broken back?"

A momentary look of confusion passes over Mrs. Cracknell's face.

Sarah and Abraham share a knowing look.

In one swift motion, Abraham raises Mrs. Cracknell up in the air, lifts her legs so she's perpendicular to the ground, bends his knee, and brings her down with as much force as he can muster.

The *CRACK* that fills my ears is sickening. I cover my face and scream, hearing Peter and Ash make similarly shocked and appalled sounds.

But not Mrs. Cracknell. She's as silent as a stone, and falls like one too, as Abraham releases her body. She hits the ground hard and lies in a heap, facing the wall. I pray to see her chest rise and fall, but she doesn't appear to be breathing.

"You fucking asshole!" I say, my voice catching in my throat. "What did you do?"

"By protecting the house," Abraham says, his voice stony, "I protect my family."

Mrs. Cracknell still hasn't moved. It takes an agonizing moment to allow myself to realize she never will again.

"But you didn't have to kill her," I say. "She would have done what you wanted in order to protect us."

"Maybe," Sarah says. "Maybe not. Now we don't need to wonder." She looks around the room, then at Abraham. "I don't see her spirit. Does that mean . . . ?"

He scans the room too, then nods. "She's moved on."

"Guess she didn't care about protecting you, after all," Sarah tells me with a grimace.

Through her actions, Mrs. Cracknell made it clear that she cared about me, Peter, and Dad. She didn't deserve to be killed, and especially not in such a horrible, violent way.

It's one more reason to stop the Keils. Mrs. Cracknell's death is fuel on the fire already raging within me. I open my tightly clenched fist to wipe tears from my face, wondering when the Keil kids will return. Without them, I can't get rid of their parents, so I have to hope they're back and somewhere in the house.

If they're not coming to me, I'll have to go to them, wherever they are. I look at Sarah and Abraham. There's just enough space between them for me to rush out of the red room. If they catch me before I get away, I won't get another chance.

I'll get out of the room, I think.

Not necessarily, the voice in my head rebuts.

I'm faster than they are.

You don't know that.

I'm faster than anyone on my rugby team, even Triss.

You're still not one hundred percent after falling off the cliff.

I've also never needed so desperately to be fast, I think with a nod, silencing the voice. *I'll get out. I* need *to get out.*

"Hey, Peter," I say, having made up my mind and wanting him to know I have a plan. "I'll be back before you can say knife." I get to my feet and sprint past Sarah and Abraham, toward the hole in the wall. She yells and he lunges, but I manage to avoid them by the skin of my teeth—the tips of Abraham's fingers graze my back, but he's too late and I take off like a shot. Through my room, down the hall, and up the stairs. Into the front foyer, the dining room, the kitchen, the first-floor hall, and past the bathroom. The kids aren't there—*maybe they're nowhere* yet—so I double back the way I came. Up the main stairs to the second floor. I pause at the top of the stairs, catching my breath and listening. Other than my own rapid heartbeat—*ta-tump-ta-tump-ta-tump*—I don't hear anyone else, not the Keils giving chase, nor the kids returning, nor Willem or Triss.

"Where are you?" I ask the darkness.

"Joana," the darkness replies.

I nearly jump out of my own skin and turn to see Mariah and Isaac, holding Joshua, standing at the end of the hall. They look "normal" again. No longer drowned and bludgeoned and hacked to pieces and burned in the furnace.

"Can you help us?" Mariah asks.

"Yes," I say, my sense of relief nearly overcoming me. "That's why I came to find you."

"How can you?" Isaac asks, his voice thick with skepticism. His last living memory is of his mother drowning him in the bathtub while his father stood by and watched, so he has every right to be doubtful. He and his sister both.

"All of this—you trapped here, being killed time and again—only ends if the truth comes out and you move on. If you move on, so too does your parents' purpose for remaining here. If you move on, so will they. Until you accept that, you'll be stuck here in a never-ending loop, but once you move on, your parents won't be able to hurt you ever again."

"How can you be certain?" Mariah asks.

"The same thing happened to my mom. She was murdered by my uncle thirteen years ago, and he finally moved on when she did, just last night." I can't believe that happened a few hours ago—it feels like an eternity.

Mariah shakes her head. "But how can you convince the world of the truth? We watched as the police overlooked obvious evidence and declared that our father alone killed his entire family, and every journalist accepted that as an unchecked fact."

"The world has changed. People no longer trust the police without question like they once did, and anyone with a computer or a phone can share news the way only the media used to be able to."

Mariah and Isaac don't reply, eyeing me with doubt. But I knew it wouldn't be easy convincing them—they've been stuck here so long, and their reality has been the only truth they've known.

At the bottom of the stairs, the handle on the locked front door rattles. Willem peers in through the small window in the door, his hand pressed against the glass above his eyes. He turns and speaks to someone—Triss.

Perfect timing, I think with relief.

The doorknob turns again, slowly, and the door swings open.

How did they unlock it?

They didn't. It's opening on its own.

No, not on its own.

As soon as Willem and Triss set foot in the house, Sarah and Abraham appear out of the shadows to the left and right of the door. Sarah grabs Willem and Abraham grabs Triss. My friends yell and scream as they're suddenly restrained by invisible hands with preternatural strength.

No, I think with despair. We were so close. I found the kids. They were ready to believe we could help them move on. Willem is here with his backpack slung over one shoulder, and I assume the articles I asked Triss to make sure he brought are within. I want to cry. I want to fall to my knees and scream and tear my hair out. I want to give up.

As bad as the situation is, it gets worse. Peter and Ash appear in the basement doorway.

"Triss!" Ash yells when he spots his sister. He takes a quick stride toward her.

"You better stop him!" Sarah says, not angrily, but bemusedly. She tightens her arms around Triss, who hollers in pain.

"Ash, stop!" I shout. He does, looking up at me in confusion. "One of the ghosts has your sister. The other has Willem. They'll hurt them if we do anything."

"Oh, we'll do a lot worse than *hurt*," Sarah says.

I ignore her. She's taunting me. And she has the upper hand, so I don't want to give her the satisfaction of seeing the agony I'm in.

"Nice of you to bring us two more children," Sarah tells me, eyeing Willem and Triss up and down like a snake trying to decide which mouse to eat first. "We're going to be one big, happy family." She hugs Triss tightly.

"Who is *touching* me?" Triss asks with a whimper and a squirm.

"What's happening, Jo?" Willem asks desperately.

"It's the ghosts," I say. "Mr. and Mrs. Keil. They killed Mrs. Cracknell, and they're going to kill us too." I feel reprehensible—worse than I've ever felt in my life—for having led them both straight into this spider's web. Asking them to come here signed their death warrants, and for what? To walk in the door? To get close, but not close enough?

Sarah runs her face along Triss's shoulder and inhales deeply without breaking eye contact with me, then wrinkles her nose. "I think she could use a bath." She grabs Triss by the hair and drags her toward the basement stairs.

Triss screams in agony, clutching at the invisible hands pulling her to her death.

Peter and Ash, frightened, jump out of Sarah and Triss's way.

I can't stand by and do nothing. If I'm going to die, better to die trying to save the people I love than to stand by and wait for my turn. I clench my jaw so tightly I fear my teeth might crack as I run down the stairs.

I only get halfway before Sarah stops in her tracks, eyes wide with surprise.

Not because of my sudden resolve.

Because of Mrs. Cracknell. She flies through the basement door and collides with Sarah, stopping me in my tracks too. Triss is knocked free and falls to the ground. Mrs. Cracknell, amazingly, remains on her feet. She and Sarah twist and turn a few times, and when they come to a halting stop, Mrs. Cracknell is standing behind Sarah with her arm tightly pinned around her neck.

"You're not going to hurt another child," Mrs. Cracknell says. "Not in this house. Not anywhere."

I've never seen Sarah look concerned, but she looks it now. It's glorious. Mrs. Cracknell has obviously inherited the same supernatural strength the Keils did in their afterlives, and Sarah is now being force-fed a spoonful of her own medicine.

Abraham throws Willem to the ground and charges to help his wife.

Mrs. Cracknell pulls Sarah, kicking and screaming, down into the basement. She meets my eye, gives me a slight nod, and then disappears.

I catch her meaning. She can't stop them. She can only slow them down. She's bought me some time, and I intend to use it.

I race down the rest of the stairs and grab Willem's backpack. "You okay?" I hurriedly ask without breaking stride, and he nods. I unzip the bag, finding what I need within, as I run back up the stairs. I hand Mariah the old newspaper article and tap it desperately.

"See?" I say. "We dug this up at the library. Read this part about your neighbor—it casts a little doubt on your mother's innocence."

Mariah scans the article quickly, looking surprised. "We didn't think anyone had any suspicions about her."

I plow on, my anxiety growing with every passing second. I don't know how long Mrs. Cracknell will be able to keep the Keils away, but I doubt I have much more time. "And look at this." I hand her the article from the school newspaper. "My friend Willem wrote this." I point at him—he's gotten to his feet and joined Triss, Peter, and Ash at the bottom of the stairs. The four of them are looking up at me with very different expressions: some hopeful, some scared, and some like I've lost my mind and am talking to the wall.

"He's a journalist?" Mariah asks.

"Yes," I say. *Not the type you might think, but technically speaking, sure, he's a journalist.* "And he can help get the truth out about what happened to you and your brothers."

This is it, I think. *This is what the Keil kids need to move on. And then their parents will be forced to move on too, and not a moment too soon.*

But Mariah hands the papers back to me, takes a step back, and shakes her head.

I feel like I've swallowed a lead balloon. "What's wrong?"

"It's all so . . . unbelievable. You speak like there's a way anyone can just share news across the world. And you expect me to believe he's a journalist? He's the same age as you and me."

"Mariah, we don't have time for this," I say. "You have to trust me! If there was any other way I could show you, I would . . ."

There *is* a way. The same way Dead Girl, Alice, showed me what happened to her. Mariah has to see things with her own eyes. No, she has to see things with *my* eyes.

Before I stop to wonder if it will work, I step into Mariah.

"What are you doing?" she asks in shock as we fill the same space.

Knowing possession takes more than a ghost simply passing through someone living, I open my mind and prepare to bare my soul, but it doesn't feel like it felt with Alice. It just feels . . . cold.

"Mariah," I say. "Possess me."

She doesn't possess me, but she doesn't step away either.

"Please, I *need* you to possess me," I say. "It's the only way I can prove to you that we can help you."

Still nothing. Why isn't she doing anything to save herself? If the tables were turned, what would it take to convince me to act?

The answer hits me immediately. Peter. I would do anything for my brother.

"Do it to help your brothers."

Isaac bounces Joshua in his arms, looking on silently.

"All right," Mariah says softly.

My entire body freezes at once, as if someone has injected liquid nitrogen directly into my veins. For a moment, I can't breathe. My heart pounds a furious beat. *TA-TUMP-TA-TUMP-TA-TUMP!*

Although it's the second time I've been possessed, I haven't gotten used to the feeling yet. I don't think I ever will. Once again, it's a little uncomfortable and trippy as hell, but it also feels fantastic—thrilling and comforting in the best possible way.

"This is incredible," Mariah says, using my mouth. "My heart." She puts my hand to my chest and laughs.

Like with Alice, she can't see my memories, but since she has access to my thoughts, I have a feeling they'll carry more weight when I *show* her my plan.

As our hearts beat together as one, I share how we can help. "We'll write as many articles about your family as it takes and send them to the local newspaper. Even if they don't publish them, we'll post them online for everyone in the world to read. Even if I have to stand on a street corner and hand out copies, I'll do it. I'll do anything."

There's a series of *thuds* and *bangs* from the basement, followed by an animalistic yell that sounded like Sarah.

"To help me?" Mariah asks.

"No," I say, not unkindly, but truthfully. "To help my brother, just like you want to help your brothers. You see, Mariah? We both want the same thing."

Sarah and Abraham flow through the basement door with the force of water raging through a burst dam. I quickly look away, and Mariah uses my eyes to look at her brothers. A tear—hers—runs down my cheek. I wipe at it and look at my fingers, expecting to see blood, but the tear is clear.

"They've suffered enough," I say. "So have you. Let me take it from here. You three need to move on. It's time."

As her parents rush up the stairs, Mariah agrees with a nod of my head. "Okay," she says softly.

She steps out of my body, and although she was only in there briefly, I instantly feel lighter, like my feet have lifted an inch or two off the ground.

Mariah gets between me and her parents, who come to a sudden stop.

"Step aside, Mariah," Sarah says, her voice like steel.

"No," Mariah replies.

A ripple of confusion and disbelief passes over Sarah's face, soon replaced by a slow-burn fury. "What did you say to me? I'm your mother, and you will do as I command. Now, step aside."

Mariah wavers, and for a moment I fear she's going to back down and let Sarah pass, but then her body goes rigid. She raises her head and stares her mother in the eye. "*No.*"

Sarah opens her mouth to respond, but no words come out. She's speechless, a sight I never thought I'd see.

Mariah continues, emboldened. "You're not going to kill anyone ever again. Not me, Isaac, or Joshua, nor Joana, Peter, and their friends. That all ends tonight. *Your existence* ends tonight."

Sarah spits out a laugh, then finds her voice again. "You stupid, foolish, insolent girl." She takes a threatening step up the stairs, gripping the banister so tightly I think she's going to crack it in half. She smiles and nods maniacally, her eyes wild and wide. "I will make you pay. I will make you suffer. You will cry, and you will writhe, and you will beg, and *all* of it will be bloody. When I'm done with you, you'll wish you *could* move on, and you'll never disrespect me like this again."

She climbs another stair, but Mariah raises her hand palm out, stopping her mother yet again.

"That's where you're wrong," Mariah says. "I *can* move on. I could have moved on anytime, I just didn't know it. But Joana has shown me the way. She's lit the path for me."

"What are you talking about?" A slight quiver in Sarah's venomous tone tells me she's scared.

Mariah points at her mother. "They're going to expose you. They're going to tell the world that Dad didn't kill us alone, that you did it together."

"So what if they do?" Sarah says. "I couldn't care less."

"No, but we could," Mariah says, pointing at her brothers. "The indignity of the way we died—the way we were killed—and no one knew the full truth. That's why we've been unable to move on from this eternal nightmare."

"Enough!" Sarah screams, lunging forward and grabbing Mariah. She storms past and knocks into me hard. The side of my head strikes the newel post. Stars explode in my vision as I fall to the ground.

"I'll be back for you," Sarah says. "After I teach my daughter a lesson. After I clean these wicked thoughts out of her skull." She drags Mariah down the hall.

"No!" Isaac says, but Abraham is on him in a flash, dragging him and Joshua behind Sarah and Mariah.

Through the pounding haze filling my head, I feel a desperate sense of déjà vu. It's happening again. Sarah and Abraham are going to kill their kids again, but this time, when they're done, they're going to kill us too.

"No, they're not," I say, realizing after the words have passed my lips that I've spoken them aloud. I shake my head, get to my feet shakily, and hurry down the hall, past Abraham and straight into Sarah, occupying the space where she stands. I open myself to her—body and soul—and feel my spirit latch onto hers. I don't wait for her to possess me—I possess *her*. Our hearts beat together as she sucks in a choking gasp of air, arches my back, bends my neck so I'm facing the ceiling, and yells in shock.

"What is this?" she shouts, using my mouth.

Sarah is the last spirit on earth that I want to be so intimately close to, but I was desperate, out of options. And it worked—Mariah has freed herself from her mother's grasp and moved a safe distance away.

"This?" I say. "This is me doing what's right. This is me stopping you from hurting your children ever again."

Sarah takes a step forward and I'm pulled along with her. She tries to take a second step, but I anticipated it this time, and manage to hold back. I feel Sarah straining to move my left leg. I flex my thigh muscles and hold out for a few seconds, but then she overpowers me, and we take another step forward, toward her daughter.

I look at Mariah, and our eyes meet. I open my mouth to tell her I can't do this much longer, so she needs to move on, but Sarah forces my mouth shut to prevent me from speaking.

But Mariah catches the meaning in my desperate, silent stare, and nods her head. She takes a deep breath, relaxes her body, and closes her eyes. After a moment, she smiles and says in awe, "I can see the light. It's beautiful." She opens her eyes and looks at her brothers. "Isaac, can you see it too?"

Isaac closes his eyes and smiles. "I can. It's so bright and warm."

Mariah laughs with relief, her eyes beginning to well up with red tears. "Thank you, Joana." I've never seen anyone look at me with such gratitude in my life.

She closes her eyes again. Takes a step forward. Holds out her hand as if someone is leading her away. Says, "Nana . . ."

And disappears.

"No!" Sarah shouts, the word drawn-out and tortured. I begin to laugh, knowing full well how crazy I must sound, but not caring in the slightest.

Abraham tightens his grip on Isaac, but he can't stop his son from following Mariah. Isaac fades, and with him, Joshua. In the blink of an eye, Abraham is holding nothing but air.

"No," Sarah says again, but this time the word is short and defeated. I slouch and feel like my body just shrunk a little, as if I'd been filled up with a helium balloon that has just deflated. "No, no, no, no. You bitch. I'm going to kill you, and I'm going to make sure you suffer." She swivels my head left and right until our gaze stops on the others, still standing at the foot of the stairs. All four look spent, physically and mentally.

"But first," Sarah says, "I'm going to kill them with my bare hands. Or rather, with *your* hands."

I grab the banister railing and try to force my body not to move, but Sarah overpowers me yet again. We run down the stairs jerkily, clumsily, but also quickly.

"Joana, what are you doing?" Willem asks in concern.

I try to stop Sarah from speaking, the same way she stopped me from speaking before, but can't. Why hasn't she crossed over yet?

"I'm going to claw your eyes out with my fingernails," she says through me, "bite through your jugular with my teeth, and stand over you as you bleed out on the floor. But first, I'm going to kill him." I turn sharply at the bottom of the stairs, grab Peter around the neck, and push him hard to the floor.

He lands heavily on his back and wheezes. Sarah keeps her hands—my hands—squeezed tightly around his neck.

I force a quick glance to my left. Abraham has grabbed the others and is holding them back. Sarah forces my gaze back to Peter. His face is already turning red and he's looking up at me in pain and shock.

"I forgot what it feels like to hold someone's life in my hands," Sarah says.

Peter's mouth opens and closes, making the most pathetic and soul-wrenching choking sound. His face is taking on a purplish hue.

Sarah doesn't relent, smiling down at my brother as she uses me to crush his windpipe. "To feel that life slipping through my fingers," she continues, "like the sand of an hourglass."

Peter stops fighting. His eyes roll back in his skull.

"With every second, that much closer to death," Sarah says. "Tick, tock, tick, tock, tick, tock."

Something small and dark scurries toward us from the floorboards—a deathwatch beetle. It taps the floor: *ta-tump ta-tump ta-tump*. If I could reach it, I could kill it, send Sarah into a rage . . .

"Not this time," Sarah says, preventing me from squishing the bug. "And besides, you're out of time. Your brother already has one foot in the grave."

The sun rises fast, impossibly large and bright. It streams through every window and fills the house with its blinding light.

No, not the sun. Something even larger, even brighter. But what could possibly be larger and brighter than the sun? Sarah and I reflexively close my eyes as a comforting warmth washes over us.

Holy shit, I think. *The light is the light. The proverbial light at the end of the tunnel. It's working. Sarah is passing over.*

"If I go, I'm taking you with me," she says, reading my thoughts.

I try to force her out of my body, but she latches on. I scream, feeling a hundred, a thousand—no, a million tiny hooks digging into me throughout my insides. It's her soul somehow fusing with my own, and it's fucking excruciating, more painful than anything I've ever experienced, more painful than words could possibly describe.

Ta-tump, ta-tump, ta-tump.

I open my eyes. The deathwatch beetle has crawled onto my chest and is tapping directly on me. Beyond it, through the blaze of white light, I can just make out the faintest silhouettes of Peter, Willem, Triss, and Ash. I try to speak, try to tell them *everything will be okay now, you have nothing left to fear*, but before I can say a single word, I feel my soul being ripped unwillingly out of my body. The light becomes all-consuming.

Sarah has moved on, and true to her word, she has taken me with her.

Chapter Eighteen

I'M DEAD.

It's not a question but a statement. I don't speak it out loud, but I hear the words as if I had. I'm standing on light, the sky above is light, and there's nothing but light in every direction as far as I can see.

I'm alone.

Hello? I call out, saying but also not saying the words. *Anyone?*

No one answers.

I take a step forward, and although there's nothing solid beneath my feet, I don't fall. I take another step, and another, and another, but I get nowhere. There's still nothing but never-ending light all around me.

Where am I? Purgatory? Limbo? Heaven or hell?

It's none of those, someone says.

I spin around, startled by the sudden appearance of the voice. Upon seeing who's there, my heart skips a beat.

Mom, I say, lunging into her arms and wrapping my own around her, squeezing tightly.

Hello, Jelly Bean.

Feeling her warm skin pressed against mine, I wonder if I actually *am* dead, or . . . ?

You're dead, Mom says, as if reading my mind.

You heard my thoughts? I ask.

She nods. *We can hear everyone's thoughts here. There's nothing to hide, and no need for secrets.* With a warm smile, she adds, *Here, we're free.*

What is this place?

The In-Between.

Do you . . . live here?

Mom shakes her head. *No, I came to collect you. Loved ones always do, when someone dies.*

Where are you going to take me?

Onward, is all she says, and for me, that's enough. I take a deep, cleansing breath, and realize I've never felt this relaxed, this carefree, in my life. I'm with my mom, and nothing can hurt me. I'd follow her anywhere.

Except . . . a thought pops into my head and wriggles around my brain, like a small cemetery worm in search of its next meal. *I wasn't supposed to die today.*

Mom cups my face and gives me a look both happy and sad. *Oh, Jelly Bean. We all die precisely when we're meant to. Not sooner, not later. If it hadn't been your time, you wouldn't be here.*

I frown and shake my head, trying to work something out. What she said makes sense, but it also doesn't seem quite right. *But . . . I don't think it* was *my time.*

Tell me how you died, Mom says without sadness or grief—without any emotion at all.

I think hard, trying to recall what happened. The light is

making it hard to remember, as if it's filling my mind and cleansing all memories, replacing them with serenity.

I was in Mrs Cracknell's house, I say. *And I convinced the Keil kids to move on, but their parents were going to stop them, so I possessed their mother and the kids were able to go, but then . . . then Sarah took me away and I ended up here.*

Mom's serene smile slips from her face and she stares at me for a long time. Seconds, minutes, hours, days—I can't say how long. Time here has lost all meaning, but eventually she exhales and says, *You didn't die.*

I didn't?

No, she says with a shake of her head. *You were brought here—not by death, but by someone else.*

She frowns. *Like you said, it wasn't your time.*

Although I suspected that, her agreement puts me at a loss for words. Mom picks up on what is running through my head.

You can choose to stay or choose to return.

Stay? Or return? How can I possibly make that choice? It's far too heavy and momentous to make in my current state of mind. Return, and return to all the heartache, pressures, and stresses of life. Stay, and stay in a state of permanent tranquility . . . with my mom.

Look inside, Mom says, pointing at my chest, *and you'll find the answer you seek.*

I nod, close my eyes, and fall into what feels like an instant trance. Above all else—the peace and quiet and warmth and comfort of this place, the In-Between, and what lies beyond, onward—I don't want to leave Mom. She was taken too soon, and this is my opportunity to make up for the life that was stolen from me.

I've made my decision. I'm going to stay.

But then . . . my heart starts to beat. Slow, but powerful. I hadn't even realized it had stopped, but of course it had. What use is a heartbeat here? A pulse, a breath? Those are trappings of the real world, tenuous grips on a mortal life so easily stopped. It's never been so obvious to me just how close to death we are at all times.

Ta-tump.

Ta-tump.

Ta-tump.

My chest heaves with every rhythmic beat.

Ta-tump.

Ta-tump.

Ta-tump.

I feel hands on my chest, pushing down with my heartbeat, then . . . lips on my mouth.

The light fades a little, darkness flickering in and out of my vision. In those flickers I see shadows, people. Standing in a circle around me, looking down in despair. And beside me, Willem. His face pulls back from my face, he places his hands on my chest, and he pushes down in a series of compressions.

Ta-tump.

Ta-tump.

Ta-tump.

He's trying to save my life, trying to bring me back. It's the strongest wake-up call imaginable, like a jolt of adrenaline injected straight into my soul.

I belong back there, with Peter and Dad. They've already lost a mother and wife—they can't lose a sister and daughter so soon, so young. We were starting a life together in Burlington, with Willem, Ash even Triss. Friends. Stability. Happiness.

And Mom, she wasn't taken from me too soon. Like she said, she died precisely when she was meant to, whether I liked it or not. It was her time.

But it's not mine. Not yet.

I need to go back.

Mom's smile returns. *You always were such a clever girl.*

But I don't know how to go back.

It's as simple as waking up, Mom says. *Just let yourself fall into it.*

Suddenly overcome with emotion, I thrust my arms around Mom and hug her tight one final time.

No, not one final time. I'll be back. One day. And then we'll have all the time in the world together.

I love you, Mom.

I love you, Jo.

Ta-tump.

Ta-tump.

Ta-tump.

I let myself fall and am pulled backward, out of Mom's embrace, out of the light, and into the embrace of my own body. Into the dark.

With a choking, sucking, life-affirming breath, I sit bolt upright, blink, and look at everyone around me. Triss and Ash look shocked, Willem looks exhausted, and Peter looks on the verge of a breakdown. But everyone also looks happy and relieved.

Peter practically jumps on me with a hug as tears spring from his eyes. I join him with tears of my own.

"Thank you," I say, my voice sore and hoarse, as if I haven't spoken in a lifetime. In a way, I think I haven't. I look at Willem, Triss, and Ash one by one, and repeat my thanks.

"You scared the shit out of us, Pumpkin Spice," Willem says. "Don't you ever do that again."

I want to laugh, but I'm in too much pain—it feels like I've walked over my *own* grave. Instead of laughing, I manage to smile.

It hurts like hell, but it also feels good to be alive.

Chapter Nineteen

"YOU DON'T *BOTH* NEED to steady the ladder, you know," Dad says, looking down at me and Peter. We're each clutching one side of the ladder he's climbed as if our lives depend upon it.

"We know," I say. "But we feel better doing it, all the same."

"I don't think you should be doing this while your leg is still healing," Peter adds.

"I'm fine, I'm fine," Dad says, waving his hand in the air. For a minute, he loses his balance and quickly grabs the sides of the ladder. Not Mrs. Cracknell's ladder—we took that one straight to the dump—but a brand-new one Dad bought from the hardware store.

"Dad!" I say.

"I said I'm fine." He clears his throat. "That was, um, a joke."

I sigh in defeat, knowing that arguing with him would be a waste of breath. He screws a metal cage around a vent on the side of the house, then climbs carefully down the ladder, favoring the leg he broke in his fall. Peter and I only let go of the ladder once his feet are back on solid ground.

"Well, that's one more small task crossed off the to-do list," Dad says, looking up at his work. "Only about three thousand to go."

I shield my eyes from the sun and look up at the house. *Our* house. It's something most kids my age would take for granted, but I don't think I'll ever get used to it.

"We'll help," Peter says.

"We've got nothing but time," I add with a smile, thinking of—and thankful for—Mrs. Cracknell. Not only did she help force the Keils to move on, but we found out a few days later that she had updated her will shortly before she died, leaving her house—the old girl—to us. As beautiful as it was, made more beautiful by the fact that it had recently become *un*haunted, we decided not to keep it. Not only was it bigger than we'd ever need, but the things we'd seen in it were far too fresh for comfort. The money we made from the sale—after all the thrill-seekers and looky-loos had their fun attending the open house—was more than enough to buy our new home with plenty left over, which Dad put into savings to pay college tuition for me and Peter.

I say our new home, but really, I should say our *old* home.

"Smile," Peter says, taking a picture with his Polaroid camera before giving me a chance to pose.

"What's the occasion?" I ask.

He hands me the gray, developing photograph. "I don't always need one. Life's too short to always worry about money."

I couldn't agree more. "Thank you."

"Hello there, neighbors," a friendly voice calls out from the front porch of the house next door. It's Edith, just sitting down with her husband, Silas, on their swinging bench. It's been a few weeks since we moved in, but I still can't help doing a quick scan every time I see him to ensure Silas isn't holding his shotgun. "Your house is looking better and better every day."

"You know what they say," Dad says. "No rest for the weary, the wicked, or the new homebuyer."

"Especially when the newly purchased home has sat abandoned for thirteen years," Silas says.

"You can say that again," Dad says.

I didn't have the opportunity to ask Mrs. Cracknell why she had a newspaper clipping about my mom's murder, but I suspect it was a coincidence and she hadn't even realized we were the same family when we moved in. We all look completely different from the photograph in the article, and when I returned to her room, I discovered that all the clippings on her bulletin board—and there were many—were about different Burlington murders. I assume living in the most infamous murder house in the city developed in her a morbid fascination. Or maybe misery loves company, and she found some sort of solace in the knowledge that terrible crimes had also been committed in other houses. I don't know, and I guess I never will, unless I see her again when it's my turn to move on. But even if I never find out, I'm fine with that. I've learned that not all of life's questions have answers, and that's okay. I kept the article, mostly for the family photo, and burned the rest in the fireplace. Once they were gone and we found a new home for the insects—the Entomology Research Laboratory at the University of Vermont was thrilled with the donation—the bedroom looked a lot more presentable, but also much emptier, filling me with a pang of sadness.

"Everything going well?" Edith asks, a slight frown signifying that there's a little more behind her question than she's saying. She glances at our house, then back at us. "Everything... calm and peaceful in there?"

"Couldn't be calmer," I say. "Or more peaceful." And it's true. Which is not to say we haven't been haunted. Quite the opposite—we've dealt with our fair share of ghosts here, but none of them have been threatening or violent.

Well, except for one, I think with a shiver.

"Someone just walked over your grave," Dad tells me.

I smile and wrap my arms around myself for warmth. *She's not real*, I tell myself. *Just my imagination.*

"I'm happy to hear everything has been going well," Edith says with a relieved smile.

"That reminds me," I say, crossing the front lawn to Victor. I put the developing picture Peter gave me on the passenger seat and grab Edith's flashlight, then return it to her. "I've been meaning to give this back to you."

She tries to hand it back, saying, "Why don't you hang on to it for a while yet? Or better yet, keep it! I really don't need it."

"I'm okay, thanks," I say, holding up my hands and walking backward off their porch. "There's nothing to fear in the dark of our house. Honest."

Just the occasional nightmare, I think, picturing Sarah's angry, twisted face staring at me in the night. With another shiver, I push the image out of my head and rejoin Peter and Dad. We wave goodbye to Edith and Silas and head inside, falling into our new nightly routine of Dad cooking dinner, me assisting as his sous-chef, and Peter setting the table—after his life-threatening potato peeler accident, it's best he leaves the cooking to us. Before long, we're sitting down and enjoying meatloaf and ketchup, mashed potatoes, and green beans with roasted garlic. I appreciate the conversation, the company, and the plain old normalcy of the evening. It's uneventful, quiet, even a little boring, and absolutely perfect.

Dad clears his throat. "So, uh, I was thinking I might invite a friend from my support group over for dinner sometime. If that would be okay with you both."

Peter and I look at each other and nod.

"Yeah, of course, Dad," I say with a bit of laughter. "You don't have to ask us permission to invite a friend over."

"She's a girlfriend," Dad says quickly, immediately blushing. "I mean, a girl who's a friend. A woman, actually. A woman friend. No, no. What I mean to say is, she's my age. She's . . . really nice." He looks at us almost apologetically, like he's ashamed.

"It's been thirteen years," I say. "We're happy for you and your *woman friend*."

Peter howls so hard that a small piece of meat flies from his teeth and lands on Dad's leftover mashed potatoes. We all laugh together, and Dad clears our plates.

"Thank you," he says.

And then, over bowls of mint chocolate chip ice cream, Peter drops a bomb.

"Hey, Dad?" he says hesitantly.

Picking up on something odd in Peter's tone, Dad lets his spoon fall into his bowl. *Clink!* "Yes?"

"You . . ." Peter pauses, shrugs. "You can call me Petey again. If you want."

Dad smiles and takes another bite of ice cream. "Okay."

The only constant is change, I think with a smile.

After clearing the dishes and putting away the leftovers, we watch a few episodes of TV. Nothing terribly exciting—a couple of game shows and a sitcom—before I excuse myself for the night.

I lay down in bed, play some classical music on my iPod, and read a book I picked up from the library. Twenty minutes later, my eyelids begin to droop, and I drop the book, hitting myself in the face with it. I put the book down on the bedside table, turn off the light, and roll over. As I've done every night since we moved back into our old house, I look at my bedroom floor and softly say, "Good night, Mom."

She doesn't answer, of course, but that's okay. I don't do it for her—she's moved on. I do it for me.

"I'm your mother," a sinuous voice says in the dark.

The voice wakes me with a start. Several hours have passed in the blink of an eye. The long, thin, clawing shadows of moonlit tree branches have shifted from one of my bedroom walls to the other. Floating just below the ceiling, directly above me, is Sarah. Her eyes are dark and penetrating. Her lips are pulled back wide, revealing her teeth.

"Come with me," she says, holding her hands out to me.

My body lifts off the mattress and floats toward her. I struggle, kick, and grasp at the air, but to no avail. My slow ascent toward my mother's—no, *Sarah's* reaching hands continues. She squeezes her hands around my neck—

I wake up once more, again with a start, but this time for real and not just within a dream. It takes a few minutes for my heart to stop pounding and my anxiety to dissipate.

"Just a dream," I whisper to myself in the darkness. "Not the Whisperings. Sarah is gone, and she's not coming back." I close my eyes and focus on taking deep, slow, calming breaths.

Dad and I still hear the Whisperings, still see ghosts. But it's different now, better. We know spirits don't follow us to hurt us—they follow us for help. That's all Alice wanted. A few days ago, I found her father and told him about my abilities, and that Alice was standing beside me. I didn't share how she looked—the split skull, the exposed brain, the blood perpetually running down her face—but he looked at me like I was crazy, all the same. He tried to close his front door, but I held it open with my foot and told him that I knew what movies they had gone to see the night she died: *Rosemary's Baby* and *Night of the Living Dead*. He looked at me differently after that—I think he still thought I was crazy, but his expression was filled with weariness, grief, and above all else, hope. Even if he couldn't see his daughter standing beside me, even if he still didn't fully trust me, he wanted to believe. *Needed* to believe. The mind is a powerful thing, and when it's desperate enough for relief, it can trick itself into thinking and believing just about anything, only in this case, there was no trick. I passed along what Alice wanted to say, told him the accident wasn't his fault, and shared that she couldn't rest until he let go of the guilt he had carried since her death. He broke down and sobbed right there on his front porch, and then thanked me profusely. Alice cried too, but more from happiness and relief than sadness. She thanked me as well, before fading away to the In-Between.

The ghost that had chased Dad across Vermont, from Brattleboro to Montpelier, Rutland City to Manchester, Killington to Canaan, caught up with him at home. He was an old man—and clearly a very determined soul—who had died with a secret of infidelity weighing heavily upon him, chaining his spirit to this world as solidly as if bound by iron shackles. He wanted to make peace with his wife, but couldn't find her in the afterlife, and so Dad got in Victor and the ghost followed him, and they drove twenty minutes east to the Essex Common Burial Ground, where the man led Dad to his wife's tombstone. There, he asked Dad to tell his wife what he had done, that it was the single greatest shame of his life, and that he loved her more than anything. Although he didn't know if the woman's spirit would hear him, Dad was willing to give it a shot if it helped the man atone for what he had done. Once Dad had shared everything asked of him, a cool breeze kicked up, making leaves skitter across the ground, and the man vanished as if he were made of dust. After years of following our family across Vermont, he was finally gone.

There have been others too. Four so far, and I'm sure there will be plenty more. All it takes is a day or two after we've helped one spirit before Dad and I hear the familiar hushed tones of someone lurking in the shadows, and then, when the ghost is ready, they make themselves seen. They talk, we listen, they lead, and we help. This is my life now—*our* life now—but at least we're no longer afraid. We're no longer constantly on the run. And best of all, my dad's mental health has never been better.

I've come to realize that there's not only two ways to react to any stressful situation—fight or flight—but a third option: philanthropy. Helping others makes me feel better than tearing down those who have wronged me, or running away from those I can't overpower.

I know, I know, it's not exactly revolutionary, but it was revolutionary to me. And I had to go through what I've gone through to see it. But now that I have—now that I'm *here*—I'm happier than ever.

THAT'S NOT TO SAY I've lost my edge on the rugby pitch. If there's a time and a place for a fight response, it's there.

I'm not going to lie—my first game since falling off the cliff in Red Rocks Park was rough. Even after a few practices, I was out of shape, a little hesitant, and dropped a couple of easy passes. But it was also fun as hell.

"I'm not going to take it easy on you next practice," Triss says with a friendly, crooked grin as we walk off the pitch after the game, "just because you died a few days ago."

"Shhh," I implore her urgently, eyeing Alicia, Summer, and Laney a few feet away. No one outside of my family, Willem, Ash, and Triss knows anything about what happened with the Keils in Mrs. Cracknell's house, and I want to keep it that way. I don't want to become the girl everyone talks about, and I definitely don't want anyone else to know about the Whisperings. I guide Triss away from the others. "Laney already calls me the Girl Who Fell. I don't want to become the Girl Who Hears Ghosts, as unbelievable as that sounds."

"Tell me about it. I was there, in Mrs. Cracknell's house, and I still have a hard time believing it."

"About her," I say, not wanting to reveal private information that doesn't belong to me, but also wanting to set the record straight and redeem Mrs. Cracknell's name. "I found some pills in her bathroom. Clozapine. I looked it up, and they're for the treatment of schizophrenia. I think that she was probably suffering from dementia or hallucinations that time you rang her bell."

Triss's face falls. "Damn. Well, don't I feel like a world-class asshole?"

"It's not your fault," I say reassuringly. "You didn't know, and you were just a kid. Anyway, you promised not to tell anyone about my abilities, remember?"

Triss laughs, holds up her right hand as if she's being sworn in as a witness in a court case, and says, "I promise, I promise."

Being the friend she's become to me, she holds true to her word—both by keeping my secret, and by not taking it easy on me. During practice the next day, I'm running the ball up the pitch when, out of the blue, the world flips and I land hard on my back. My ears ring and I suck desperately for air, looking at the overcast sky above. Suddenly, Triss appears in my blurred vision.

"Shit, Jo, I didn't mean to hit you *that* hard," she says in a panic.

The rest of the team joins her, looking down at me with concern, before Coach Howerton elbows her way through the ring of people and kneels beside me.

"You okay, Joana?" she says. "Speak to me."

I open my mouth but can't talk. I can barely breathe. I nod at Coach to tell her I'll be okay, then look up at the sky again.

Sarah is floating in the air above me, looking down with the same malice as in my nightmares.

I must be dreaming, I think, but her voice is as loud and real as Coach's.

"Come with me," she says, reaching her hands down to pick me up, to take me with her. "Come with your mother."

You're not my mother, I think desperately, squeezing my eyes shut. *This is a dream, nothing but a dream. I'm going to open my eyes and wake up in bed, and Sarah will be gone, because she's not real, none of this is real, and I'm okay. I'm okay, I'm okay—*

"I'm okay!" I shout, opening my eyes quickly. I'm still lying on the rugby pitch, my teammates and Coach looking down on me. Everyone smiles and sighs in relief.

"Jesus, Jo," Triss says as she releases a pent-up breath. "You scared the shit out of me."

I raise my head and prop myself on my elbows, slowly beginning to feel better. "Guess I have a habit of doing that," I say, thinking of what Willem said after reviving me with CPR.

We smile, then laugh—Triss loudly, me weakly—as Coach looks at us like we're speaking a different language. Triss and Laney help me up and the others give me space to pass. I take a few steps, tell everyone again that I'm okay, and back that up with a thumbs-up. Coach tells me to take a break and sit out the next few drills, and I don't protest. But I can't help stealing the occasional glance at the sky as I sit alone on the sidelines. There's nothing there—*because she's not real*, I remind myself—but every time I look back at the field, I swear I can feel eyes staring down at me.

THE FAMILIAR *DING* RINGS out as I enter Darcy's Diner, and I'm instantly met by the comforting smells of fresh-brewed coffee and thick-cut fries cooking in the deep fryer.

I'm greeted with a "Hiya, Pumpkin Spice," but not from Willem. Meera has taken to calling me by the nickname. I don't hate it. I've never stayed in one place long enough to be called anything other than Joana, Jo, or, *hey, you*.

And Jelly Bean, I think.

"How's it going, Meera?"

"A lot better now that my best employee is here."

"Hey!" Willem says as he passes, carrying a stack of dirty plates and cutlery. "I'm right here."

"I'm just fuckin' joking," Meera says, but as soon as Willem disappears in the back, she looks at me, shakes her head, and mouths, *I'm not.*

Willem re-emerges a moment later with a mug of coffee, which he hands to me. He's made me a pumpkin spice latte at the start of every shift since I returned to work, telling me I'll need caffeine to stay on my feet until closing time. Part of me loves the extra attention, and part of me wants to tell him I can take care of myself, but a bigger part of me just really likes pumpkin spice lattes, so I kindly accept. I blow on the drink, take a long, soothing sip, and sigh in utter bliss.

"All right," I say, setting down the mug and tying my apron around my waist. "These customers aren't going to serve themselves."

The diner is so busy that my shift flies by in a blur of orders and coffee refills and bills to settle and tables to wipe down. Before I know it, Willem and I are counting and splitting the tips we earned—a little less than one hundred bucks each, not bad for a few hours' work after school and rugby practice. I tuck the cash into my pocket and give it a little pat. I've almost saved enough money to buy my own phone—something I never allowed myself to think I'd have one day.

"We still on for tonight?" he asks, placing chairs upside down on tables.

"Yeah, of course," I say. We've gone to a movie one night and dinner on another, and this will be our third date. "What did you have in mind?"

He turns to face me and shrugs. "I thought we'd go for a walk."

"Ooh, la, la. Big spender."

"I have something I want to show you."

"Well, now you've truly piqued my interest."

Willem smiles. "Hey, Meera, can we—?"

She cuts him off with a wave of her hand. "You two lovebirds get out of here. I can lock up on my own."

We leave quickly before she changes her mind. Although most of the stores in the Church Street Marketplace are closed for the night, the light spilling out of the window displays makes the street glow brightly. It's cold enough to keep most people inside, so the streets are largely deserted. I zip up my jacket, lift my scarf over my chin, put my hands in my pockets, and walk closer to Willem. He puts his arm around me, and I instantly forget how cold it is—I feel like I couldn't be warmer even if it was the middle of July.

"So, what did you want to show me?" I ask, looking up at him. "The world's tallest filing cabinet? Because I've already seen it."

"That has put Burlington on the map," he says, pulling a piece of folded paper from his pocket. "But no. I wanted to show you this."

I take the paper, unfold it, and read the title typed at the top.

THE TRUTH BEHIND THE BURLINGTON KILL HOUSE

"You finished it?" I ask.

He nods, but doesn't meet my eyes, which seems a little odd.

As we continue to walk, I read the article he's written. We started it together last week, but I've been so busy with school, work, rugby, and helping Dad fix up our house that it's been impossible to find time to continue, so I'm relieved he managed to complete it on his own. My unfulfilled promise to the Keil kids has been weighing heavily on my soul.

"It's good," I say, once I'm finished. "Really good. So, when do we share it?"

"Yeah," he says, the word drawn out and thin. "I wanted to talk to you about that."

"What about it?"

We're walking side by side, but Willem is leading us somewhere very familiar. He turns onto South Union Street, leaving no doubt where we're going.

"Wait, why are we walking toward Mrs. Cracknell's house?"

"It's not her house anymore," he says.

"You're being really weird and cryptic," I say, coming to a stop.

"I'm sorry, just . . . come with me. I need to show you the house."

I don't move. "I've seen it."

"Not recently." When I don't reply, he takes my hand gently in his and says, "Please. You need to see it now."

His expression is soft and friendly and a little bit broken. I feel my resolve crumbling. With a sigh, I resume walking and say, "Fine."

We reach Mrs. Cracknell's house and stare at it from the sidewalk. A queasy, strangling feeling clenches my gut.

"All right, we're here," I say, wishing I was anywhere else. "Now, would you mind telling me what this is about?"

He takes the article from me, but instead of putting it back in his pocket, he stares at it silently. His eyes are half closed and his upper lip quivers ever so softly. Something's deeply conflicting him, and I suddenly feel sorry—both for him, and for not noticing his distress sooner.

"Willem," I say softly. "What's wrong?"

Finally, he finds his voice. It's quiet, and cracks once as he starts speaking. "We can't share this."

"What?" I say in surprise. "We . . . we have to."

"Why?"

I put a hand to my forehead, genuinely bewildered by what he's suggesting. Is he seriously so dense? "Because I made a promise. A promise to someone on their deathbed."

Mrs. Cracknell's bedroom light turns on and I catch a glimpse of some movement from within.

"Mariah died long ago," he says. "You made a promise to her *ghost*, not to her."

"Close enough," I say, my pulse quickening. "Promising we would share the truth is what helped Mariah and her brothers move on. That's what made Sarah and Abraham move on. And *that's* what saved our lives."

"What about *their* lives?" Willem says, pointing at the bedroom window.

"What?"

"Look."

I look. The new owners have done some redecorating. Mrs. Cracknell's bedroom now appears to belong to a young child, with posters of cartoon characters on the walls and toys and picture books on a shelf. There's a little girl sitting up in bed, speaking with a man seated beside her. They hug tightly, and the man stands up. A second man—this one holding a baby to his chest—bends over and kisses the girl's forehead.

She lies down, out of sight from where I'm standing, and the men turn out the light and leave the room. A moment later, another light turns on in another room. The men lay the baby down in a crib and stand for a moment, arms around one another, looking at the baby, smiling. They kiss, then close the blinds.

"If we share this story," Willem holds up the article, the paper clenched tightly in his hand, "what happens to them?"

"It has nothing to do with them," I say, but I can't keep a note of uncertainty out of my voice.

"No, but if this takes off, will the media care that it has nothing to do with them? Will the fact that the Keils died decades ago stop news vans from lining the streets and stop journalists from knocking on their door? Eventually the media will stop caring about the story, sure, but will the public? Or will curiosity seekers continue driving out here, taking selfies in front of the house to post online, and creeping up to the windows to peer inside, hoping to catch sight of a ghost?"

"People already know the house is haunted. You said kids shared stories—"

"We *thought* it was haunted. Every town has a creepy house or two, and kids love to make up tales. But we didn't know the truth because the truth had been buried by time. We've dug it up, and if we expose it, people are going to come here in hordes, even if we never say a word about it being haunted. They'll *assume* it must be haunted."

"How do you know that?"

"Wouldn't you?"

I look warily at the house and have to admit that if someone told me what had happened in such a large, creepy place . . .

yeah, I'd assume it was haunted. "But I made a promise," I say, sounding defeated.

"To help the Keil kids, and think about it—*didn't* you help them? They moved on. Their souls are no longer tormented nightly by their parents. They're in a better place. If that's not helping them, I don't know what is. And now . . . you saw how happy this new family is. Sharing the Keils' story will jeopardize the peace and happiness they've found here."

"Damn it," I say, running my fingers through my hair and looking up and down the street, hoping to find an answer that will solve everything. But there's only one answer, and I already know it. I spread my arms out to my sides, feeling awful for breaking my promise, but seeing no other path. "Do you think they'll know? Mariah and Isaac?"

Willem has no way of knowing the answer to that, but he shakes his head and holds me. He's warm and smells of coffee, and it feels good to be wrapped tightly in his arms again. "They've moved on to—what did you call it? Onward? They'll no longer know anything that happens here. That's the deal when you die . . . or when you move on, I suppose. We'll be fine. You'll see."

"This is the world's shittiest date," I joke.

He laughs.

I hold onto Willem a little tighter. "Thank you."

"For the shitty date?"

"No, for being here with me, *for* me. For accepting me for who I am."

He looks at me and smiles. "And who are you?"

I look at him deeply, recalling the first time I met him and noticed how perfect his eyes are—hazel with flecks of green. "I'm Pumpkin Spice."

He leans in close, our faces only an inch apart, and hesitates for a heartbeat—*ta-tump*—before pressing his lips against mine. Blood rushes to my head and my feet threaten to lift off the ground. Our first kiss. *My* first kiss.

"Come with me," a voice says from above.

I pull back from Willem suddenly, our lips sticking together for a moment before separating.

"What's wrong?" he asks.

I refuse to look up. I refuse to see her. Because she's not there.

"Nothing," I say. "Just caught a shiver. Will you walk me back to my car?"

"Of course."

We head back toward the marketplace, and this time, I walk a little faster than before.

LONG STRETCHES OF ROAD pass by in the blink of an eye, time skipping ahead. A minute here, two minutes there—gone. I'm distracted. There are too many thoughts on my mind. Too much hanging over my head.

I glance up, fearing what I might find, but she's not there.

Returning my focus to the road, I sigh, rub my face, and tighten my grip on Victor's steering wheel. Home. I just want to get home. I want to see Peter and Dad. I want to say good night to Mom, even if she's not there. And for the first time in ages, I don't want to be with my family for them. I want to be with them for *me*.

It's okay to think of myself first. To use my free time to prioritize rugby, my job, and my relationship with Willem now that Dad has a handle on the Whisperings and there's no threat of being woken in the middle of the night with the order to throw everything in a bag so we can flee town.

Putting my own wants and needs first feels strange. But it also feels good. With time, I'm sure I'll get used to it.

I look at the rearview mirror, and my reflection looks back. My eyes appear tired but happy.

Maybe also a little conflicted.

I shake it off, but a question continues to niggle at the back of my mind, like a small wooden sliver under my fingernail: Did Willem and I make the right decision?

"Shit!" I say, swerving onto the gravel shoulder.

Someone is sitting in the back seat.

As soon as I've steered Victor back onto the road, I look in the mirror again.

There's no one there.

I steal a glance over my shoulder, just to be sure.

Empty.

I'm alone.

Only, I wasn't.

Shut up, Jo, I tell myself.

There was someone there.

I said, shut the fuck up.

A girl.

Don't think about it. Stop thinking altogether. Nothing good can come of it.

Mariah.

Her skin was unnaturally white, pale as frost.

Her eyes were sunken and dark.

Her face was streaked with blood of the deepest red.

And her body . . . her body fell apart, piece by bloody piece, until she was nothing more than a pile of gore.

Jo, I implore myself as tears run down my cheeks. *Stop. Please, please, please, stop.*

But I can't stop thinking about it. I know what I saw. I know what I heard.

Just before her head toppled off her shoulders, Mariah had spoken.

"You broke your promise," she said, blood bubbling over her lips with each word. "So I've come back . . .

"And so has she."

I quickly turn on the radio, hoping that if I can't silence the thoughts in my head, maybe music can. It doesn't work, but I notice something forgotten on the passenger seat. The Polaroid picture Peter took of me standing in front of our house, now fully developed. Only, I'm not alone. Above my head, hovering in front of my second-floor bedroom window, is Sarah. She's staring straight at the camera, as if daring me to look at her, challenging me to accept her existence, forcing me to give up any last shred of hope I had that her return might only be in my imagination. I roll down the window and throw the picture out. If only I could be rid of Sarah as easily.

Oh, boy, the voice in my head thinks. *You've royally messed everything up, haven't you?*

"She wasn't in the picture," I say. "I was alone."

Wasn't she? the voice answers. *Were you?*

I briefly consider turning around and searching for the photo on the side of the road but shake my head. I don't need to do that because I know I imagined Sarah's presence.

I slap the steering wheel a few times, then wipe a tear from my cheek and bite my thumbnail. *I can't risk it*, I think. *I can't do nothing.*

Should I tell Dad so we can go on the run? Or so we can face Sarah head-on, together?

Philanthropy, I think. The third option besides fight or flight. My new path forward. I'll call Willem as soon as I get home. We'll get together tomorrow. And we'll share the Keils' story, just like I said we would.

And if that—*don't think it, Jo!*—messes up things for the family that moved into the house, so be it.

Because I promised to help. And helping is how I need to use my gift—my *curse*. Because if I don't, what are the Whisperings other than voices in my head?

I pull into the driveway—wondering when the next ghost will show up at our doorstep, or in the air above my head—and walk wearily toward our house, telling myself it's not too late. I can still help Mariah. I can make good on my promise.

Not just for her. Not just for my friends. Not even just for my family.

For me.

Author's Note

THE WHISPERINGS IS MY second young adult novel. Both it and my debut, *House of Ash and Bone*, are horror books featuring teen protagonists terrorized by malevolent spirits in Vermont, but that's where the similarities largely end.

I didn't realize this as I wrote the first draft, but a lot of what I was going through at the time shaped the book that *The Whisperings* turned out to be. My mother's health was failing—her balance was off, she lost her hearing, and she began to have difficulty with her short-term memory—and for several years none of the doctors treating her could determine the cause of her ailments. Finally, a diagnosis came, but it wasn't one anyone in the family wanted to hear: she had superficial siderosis, a rare neurologic disease affecting the brain and spinal cord. Persistent and recurring bleeding had been occurring in her brain, resulting in a buildup of iron toxicity. There is no known cure for superficial siderosis, and very few treatments.

My mom passed away on Friday, February 16, 2024. When talking about the hand she'd been dealt, she never complained, not once. Instead, she focused on the positives, saying that she had been blessed with a loving family and a great life. It's been said you can learn a lot about someone by the way they handle a rainy holiday, lost luggage, and tangled Christmas tree lights. To that list—right at the top—I'd add how they face their final days. But we don't just learn a lot about the person by how they face death; we also learn a lot about life in general, and the lesson my mom shared in her final days, without meaning to, will stay with me forever.

I received the first round of edits for *The Whisperings* from my editor on February 26, 2024, ten short days after my mom's passing. I'm sure not everyone would have felt the same, but the file landed in my inbox at the absolute perfect time. I'm the type of person who likes to keep busy when I'm upset, more so when I'm grieving, but I wasn't in the right headspace to write something new. Revisiting the book I had written over the previous two years was both a welcome distraction and as comforting as spending time with an old friend you haven't seen in some time.

And that's when I realized the thing about the book I hadn't before: it was all about my mom. That hadn't been my intention, but I'd written her and the pain I was going through into the story, in a loose, roundabout way. She's not identical to Joana's mom—not by a long shot—but there were plenty of similarities, not to mention that both mothers, the real and the fictitious, were taken from their families far too soon. Despite that, Joanna's mom accepts her fate in life with bravery, stoicism, and, more than anything, the desire to protect her family at all costs. Just like my mom.

The Whisperings, as a result, is the most personal book I've ever written. And I'll be honest, it was tough to work on it at times. But I knew that it was also the type of story that would help readers who have also suffered a devastating loss—what I didn't know was how much it would help *me*. Writing can be free therapy, and *The Whisperings* helped me heal.

Although a little doubt and a touch of darkness linger at the end of *The Whisperings*—it wouldn't be a horror novel written by me if there wasn't—there's more consolation and light in Joana's future. Because that's what truly great horror stories do. They teach us how to defeat the thing hiding under our bed, the monster lurking in our closet, or the voices only we can hear. They give us the tools we need to face our fears. They remind us that we're not alone; when the lights go out, we all get a little scared. But in the morning, the sun always rises.

Acknowledgements

THE TEAM AT TUNDRA BOOKS was by my side through the creation of this book, and the care and support I received from them meant the world to me. I'm so fortunate to work with Peter Philips as my editor, whose enthusiasm for *The Whisperings* buoyed me as we revised the book to reach its highest highs and lowest lows. Jorge Mascarenhas, the cover artist, perfectly captured the sense of loss that permeates the novel. Emma Dolan, the designer, ensured the entire look of the book reflected the story screaming (or should that be whispering?) to leap off the page. Graciela Colin, the publicist, helped *The Whisperings* stand out from the crowd and find as many readers as possible, and for that I will always be grateful. And copy editors and proofreaders are often the unsung heroes of publishing, so let me warm up my voice and sing the praises of Linda Pruessen and Erin Kern for wrangling this book into shape.

I listen to music as I write and typically pick a different band or musician for each new book, but for *The Whisperings*, I mostly listened to a moody, haunting southern gothic playlist

I discovered on Spotify. One song that stood out from the rest and perfectly matched the vibe of the book was "Lay This Body Down" by Sam Lee—if you ever go back and revisit any passages, do yourself a favor and play this song while you read.

And finally, my family. Words can't express how much you mean to me, but I know this: I wouldn't be able to do what I do if it weren't for you. Forever and always, thank you.